Praise for the Writing of Bob Reiss

"Sparkling and fast paced."

—*Washington Post*

"Splendid. Great writing. Great suspense. Great action. Wonderful reading."

—*Los Angeles Times*

"Dead on!"

—*People*

"Makes you think."

—*Good Morning America*

"High-voltage entertainment."

—*Daily News Journal*

"Thrilling, ultra-hip, and completely engrossing."

—*Mademoiselle*

"Gripping...fast paced...riveting."

—*Publishers Weekly*

"Crackerjack!"

—*Kirkus*

THE IMPOSSIBLE DETECTIVE

BOB REISS

A REGALO PRESS BOOK
ISBN: 979-8-89565-196-4
ISBN (eBook): 979-8-89565-197-1

Cover Design by Jim Villaflores

Publishing Team:
Founder and Publisher – Gretchen Young
Managing Editor – Caitlin Burdette
Production Manager – Morgan Simpson
Production Editor – Rachel Paul

As part of the mission of Regalo Press, a donation is being made to the American Cancer Society, as chosen by the author. Find out more about this organization at https://www.cancer.org/.

This book, as well as any other Regalo Press publications, may be purchased in bulk quantities at a special discounted rate. Contact orders@regalopress.com for more information.

Regalo Press
New York • Nashville
regalopress.com

Published in the United States of America
1 2 3 4 5 6 7 8 9 10

For Wendy.

ONE

Artificial intelligence? I'll tell you about artificial intelligence. Look at Congress. Look at the mayor. Look at half the reprobates who show up at my office. There's plenty of artificial intelligence walking around on two legs these days. Who needs a machine to achieve it?

I was being chewed out by the country's third richest man when I spotted the kid again, out on Edgar Allan Poe Street in New York City, across from my brownstone. From three stories up, the figure looked eleven or twelve years old. A blue hoodie hid the face. Pink sneakers. Pink knapsack. Pink fingernail polish, so probably a girl, but you never know. I'd first spotted her at eight this morning, peering over the concrete wall separating my rear garden from the co-op on Eighty-Fifth Street. Then again, two hours later, pacing, caught on the security camera mounted over my front door. *She's scared*, I thought, watching her freeze between two parked cars, looking left, right, left, as if afraid to move. She took a single step forward and yanked her foot back. A car shot past. She dashed across the street.

My business makes me a student of fright. People who show up here tend to be driven by panic. Sometimes they try to hide it. Or they burst into tears. Sometimes they curse or bluster with rage. But it boils down to fright. I think of the leather recliner on the far side of my desk, where the country's third richest man now sat, as the *scare chair*.

The kid was now on my front step, looking up on the security monitor. My client drew my attention back by banging his skinny fist on my blotter, crying "ouch," and pulling it back. The third wealthiest man in the US had a beanpole body, a mop of wild red hair, a MORDOR FUN RUN T-shirt. He sat beneath an old film poster from 1949, *The Falcon Returns*, in which the actor who played my grandfather aimed a pistol at Nazi thugs while cradling an unconscious slinky nightclub singer in his other arm.

Grandfather was the true Falcon in real life—the suave, rich private investigator upon whom those old films were based. And the client sitting across from me now was exactly the kind of person Grandy had taught me to avoid.

"You can't fire me," Bradley Kranepool sputtered, rubbing his thin little hand.

"Actually, I can. You lied to me, Bradley."

"Those were just words, Mr. St. Johns."

"Last time I checked, that's what lies are."

The doorbell rang downstairs. On monitor two, I saw the top of the kid's hoodie. Normally my best friend and partner Oscar Narvaez would answer, but Oscar and his wife Cristina were out co-op hunting, looking to move away from the first-floor apartment where they'd lived for the past ten years. Due to recent tension between us, Cristina was pushing for them to move away.

Distance would fix the problem, I hoped.

Bradley Kranepool was one of those tech geniuses who can't maintain eye contact, grew up without friends, relates to video games more than people, and substitutes, in the popular imagination, for heroes these days, having invented one more way that people need not deal with actual humans anymore. The most asocial people on the planet have designed the principal ways we communicate with each other. No need to go to a real store. Or talk to a real phone operator. Or break up with your lover in person, thanks to Twitter, Facebook, Ghost Me, Emoji, whatever this week's click-it-and-forget-it craze is.

No wonder the world is a mess.

The bell rang again. The pink fingernail kept pressing the buzzer.

Mentally, my client was a giant; emotionally, a twelve-year-old. I explained to Bradley with sympathy—after all, he was probably going to prison for decades—"The contract states that if you misrepresent yourself, we cancel."

"*New York Magazine* said you take on impossible cases."

"Yes, but not ones where the charges are true. You lied to your investors. You funneled their money into a different scheme that failed. I advise you to plead guilty, Bradley. It cuts down on jail time."

"I paid you a quarter million dollars!" he shouted.

"All donated to a victim fund, minus expenses."

"I'll sue you," he sputtered.

"Read the contract."

"My lawyers get me out of contracts every day!"

"And mine will prove every allegation against you. Stuff that even the FBI doesn't know yet."

Bradley's lower lip quivered. "That's not fair!"

The damn buzzer kept ringing. Sighing, I let the kid in. Monitor three showed her in the elevator. Normally, we never let clients in after three, when, rain or shine, I go kayaking and Oscar starts prepping one of his five-star dinners. The bell sounded in the waiting room. A single pink sneaker appeared on the carpet and retreated. The kid must be on the couch, eyeing more Falcon posters. Yep. The sneaker came into view again, swinging back and forth, faster and faster, showing crumpled pink socks on a thin, dark ankle.

Scared.

"You're not listening to me," Bradley said.

My now former client stood up. Bradley's transition from genius to felon would be national news. I warn clients beforehand, I tell them plain out, before we sign papers, *if the story you tell me turns out to be a lie, I'll drop you.* But there's always someone who doesn't listen. They think they're special. They think they're protected. They think once they pay you, they own you. My grandmother taught me this a long time ago.

"I know people," Bradley threatened, "who can hurt you."

"Real ones? Or in a video game?"

"You're so perfect? I saw how you look at your partner's wife."

"Time to go, Bradley."

"I'll *tell my parents*!"

Thirty seconds later, he was gone.

It was an average late-October afternoon in Manhattan, or at least what passes for average lately. Eighty degrees instead of forty. Trees still lushly green in Riverside Park. Joggers and dog walkers out despite the bad-air-quality alert. Beyond them, below, I saw a slit of churning Hudson River.

I checked the time. I had a kayak race scheduled up in Riverdale, but I had a feeling I wouldn't make it.

"Are you The Falcon?" a girl's small voice said from the doorway.

"Yes."

She folded her arms and planted those pink sneakers as if she expected me to kick her out. "No one believes me."

"About what?"

Her jaw thrust forward, quivering.

"The car hit him and backed up and *hit him again*! I saw it! I'm not lying! He was…the man…that man," she sputtered, then shouted, "it killed him!"

"What man?"

"The one in the park!"

"What car?"

The girl began weeping. One pink sneaker toe dug into the other. Her shoulders were heaving. She looked about five now.

"The one with nobody inside!"

TWO

They call me The Falcon, but my grandfather was the original. I inherited the name. "Mark St. Johns was raised by sleuth grandparents," *New York Magazine* wrote of me a year ago. "The former Marine investigator and his partner, Oscar Narvaez, were decorated for uncovering millions in graft during the Afghan War. They were ambushed and almost murdered by fellow Marines."

Reporters never get it right.

It was my firecracker grandmother who raised me in the brownstone. She'd met Grandy, the original Falcon, in Los Angeles in 1951. At the time, Grandy was the suave, Yale-educated, independently wealthy, martini-guzzling sleuth who assisted detectives in post–World War II California. Accurately depicted in film, Grandy had the looks of Cary Grant, the mind of Sherlock Holmes, and the libido of Brigham Young. Women-wise, LA cops nicknamed Grandy "the Divining Rod."

Grandma Eve, on the other hand, was the wisecracking daughter of a Queens trash collector, trying to make it in film and supporting herself as a cigarette girl at the Tarzan Club, where waiters wore pith helmets and waitresses were jammed into fur bikinis rivaling Raquel Welch's in the film *One Million*

Years B.C, attire which, today, would get a woman's head chopped off in Tehran.

In real life, Eve met Grandy at the club and helped him solve the La Brea tar pit dismemberment case depicted in the Columbia Pictures flop, *Silence of the Limbs.* She fell for Grandy and got pregnant by him. She told me, years later, "No way I'd stay with him, Baby F. He was incapable of loyalty to a single woman, although he was dedicated to us as a group. I decided to keep the baby, but I'd had enough of Hollywood. Your grandfather offered to pay the bills, and I said no. I told him I was moving back to New York. I liked private investigating. I asked him to help me get a job in the Big Apple and he did. He was incapable of monogamy but Grandy always kept his word."

The job—the best a woman could come up with in 1952—turned out to be as a receptionist in a Brooklyn firm where operatives were all retired male detectives. They laughed when she asked to be promoted. They complained when Eve—pregnant—got to follow a suspect around after the guys failed. They raged when Eve became a full-time investigator. They quit five years later when she took over the firm and bought the Poe Street brownstone.

Eve used to imitate those guys when I was a teenager. "I ain't workin' for no skirt," she'd say, swinging her arms like King Kong.

Eve built the business into the high-end niche it occupies today. At four foot eight, eighty-three pounds, she was, throughout her life, continually underestimated by targets: the Wall Street mogul who died in Attica prison, the bridge workers' union VP who cheated his members, the DeCesare crime family boss dragged from Federal Court while screaming that Eve would pay.

I'm thirty-five now and still have never figured out how Eve accomplished all she did for us because she'd be coy when asked about it. "How come we don't have to pay taxes on this house?" I asked when I was ten. "How come when we need repairs, guys show up from unions and don't charge you?" "How come the city let us put a driveway out front and have a garage when no one else on the block can do it?"

To these and dozens of similar queries over the years, she'd smile and give one-word answers, usually the name of whomever was Mayor at the time she obtained a special privilege. "Bloomberg," she said, as answer to the driveway question. "Koch," she said, answering the Union question. "Guiliani," was the reply to why Delta Airlines flies us free, first class, when we need to travel. Even today, all I have to do is call a private Atlanta phone number, and next thing I know, other passengers get bumped from flights, seats open up, flight attendants hover, and captains ask if I want to visit the cockpit.

"What did Rudy Guiliani have to do with Delta Airlines?" I asked Eve one time.

"A girl needs a few secrets," she winked.

"You have thousands."

"Hope that someday you do too."

I loved my grandmother and miss her. I came to love Grandy too, even though I didn't meet him until I was twelve. Eve brought him back from California then. He'd turned into a lonely old guy, suffering from cirrhosis of the liver and throat cancer from forty years of smoking cigarettes and drinking lunchtime, dinnertime, and anytime martinis.

By then, Grandy was nothing like the cool PI depicted in films. But Eve still had a soft spot for him. "He can't help who he is," she said. "If he'd never been born, you wouldn't have been either. Get to know him. Give him a chance. You'll learn things from him."

I missed my grandparents, and their photos sat in front of me now, on my desk, reminding me to listen, always listen, especially when I think listening is a waste of time. And over their heads, in the scare chair, sat an undersized, plump-faced kid, twisting her hands in agitation, trying not to cry. In a clear, high voice, she introduced herself as Abani Singh, age twelve.

"The police don't believe me," she said. "Mom says I have too much imagination. I KNOW WHAT I SAW!"

"Tell me the story."

"It's not a STORY, it's what REALLY HAPPENED!"

I sighed. I didn't want the kid to feel worse than she already did. I figured that kayaking was out for the day. "Tell me about the car, the one that ran over the man, the one that nobody was in."

She looked dwarfed in the oversized chair, clutching a math textbook to her chest, its title, *Proportional Reasoning*, representing a talent I find absent from public discourse these days. With the lightweight hood thrown back, Abani had a dusky complexion; her pink-rimmed glasses enlarged upward slanting, striking green eyes. I smelled gum. A glistening spot marked where she'd wiped away a tear. Her wrists were encircled by colorful elastic bands; red, blue, green, yellow, each signaling some cause probably.

Save the whales. Save the rainforest.

Keeping my face straight to avoid further agitating the girl, I thought, w*hatever you think happened, Abani, it's not that.*

"You didn't go to school that day," I prompted.

"It was Dad's birthday. I missed him."

"He wasn't home?"

In a matter-of-fact voice, she said, "He shot himself in the head last year. Mom found him while I was at school. He was a veteran, a Marine. He used to play tennis at those courts when he came home from Syria. I go there sometimes if I feel bad and remember him."

I have no memories of my own parents. They died in a plane crash when I was four. "I'm sorry, Abani," I said.

"Mom says artillery explosions messed up his brain. She said he fired those guns a thousand times and vibrations made him sick. When he came back home, he'd flinch if a car backfired. He'd forget things. He got angry a lot." She corrected herself. "But not at me."

She relayed this matter-of-factly, like other kids I've interviewed after a severe trauma. They try to sound like an adult, but they're screaming with grief inside. *I saw Mom get raped, and both guys got away. My teacher got shot, and the class was hiding under our desks.*

"Abani, tell me about the car."

"There's a parking lot by the tennis courts. Players drive off the West Side highway and pull in. There's a walkway to the courts. Steps."

"I know the spot," I said. It was leafy. The parking lot overlooked oak trees, grass, clay courts, the river. On summer Saturdays, the spot hosts sunset concerts that Falcon Associates sponsors. Jazz. Samba. Chamber music. It's a neighborhood gathering place. People spread blankets. They bring food and wine. I go there sometimes with Oscar and Cristina, or, if I have a date, four of us go. It's not a spot you associate with murder.

"I was sitting against a tree, Mr. Falcon, remembering Dad. He used to wear these ripped up shorts when he played? Mom called them disgusting." She looked up, guilty because she'd said something bad about her dad. “Mom and Dad loved each other. She just hated those pants.”

“Go on.”

“I was remembering Dad when I saw the man. He was on the river path, walking fast. He kept looking behind him.”

“Why did he do that, do you think?”

“Maybe he was afraid.”

“No one was behind him? He wasn’t a jogger?”

“He didn’t wear jogging clothes. Just regular clothes.”

“Then what happened?”

“He came up to the parking lot but didn’t see me. I was sitting against a tree.”

“Did you see anyone else?”

Her eyes grew wider. “No. But suddenly, a car—a parked one—pulled out and hit the man. He flew into the air.”

“The car backed into him, you mean.”

“No! From the front!”

She was breathing faster now.

“I ran to the man. I wanted to help. He was jerking around. His face was bloody, and he made horrible sounds.”

“Did anyone get out of the car?”

“It stayed there, engine running.” Her tears poured out. “I tried to remember from first aid class what to do, like, do I hold his nose? Breathe into his mouth? But I didn’t because there was all this blood. He grabbed me.” Her right hand encircled her left wrist, as the man’s had. “He was trying to talk, but it was hard to hear him because of fire trucks on the West Side Highway.”

“You couldn’t make out anything he said at all?”

“I think he said, ‘My fault.’ And ‘I’m sorry.’”

“Sorry about what?”

“He said, ‘He killed me.’”

"He? You mean, the driver of the car?"

"I DON'T KNOW! I tried to get away, but he held me. Then his eyes got big, and he looked over my shoulder. He pushed me away and said 'run,' and I heard a noise like *eeeeee.* The car was coming again. It hit him again. I saw inside the car, and no one was there!"

I tried to envision it. The girl kneeling. The car coming. The sun, in her eyes, blinding. I asked, "Was the sun shining on the windows?"

"The detective asked me that! No!"

"Were the windows tinted? Dark?"

"My mother asked that. I know what I saw!"

"Was there anything else you noticed about the car? Funny antennae? Camera on it? Anything?"

"No."

"What color was the car?"

"Blue."

"Did you see the license plate?"

"I don't know!" she wailed. "The car sped up. It drove away on the West Side Highway."

"By itself, you mean."

"Why do you keep asking that?"

"Is it possible," I asked gently, "that the driver ran off while you were trying to help and then came back?"

She shook her head.

"Maybe the driver ducked down when you looked?"

When she didn't answer, I asked, gently, "Then how did the car leave, Abani?"

"I don't know! It was like on television, when they show cars without drivers! That's what you need to figure out."

I sighed. *Like on TV.* Her agitation was genuine, but that didn't mean the story was true. The kid had lost her father. She'd been upset that day before the incident occurred. The mind plays tricks even on Marines in battle. It could surely do that to a grieving twelve-year-old.

I asked, "Don't you think, if a car was driving around Manhattan by itself, someone would have reported it?"

"No, because nobody did! *New York Magazine* said you do impossible things. You solve impossible problems!"

I cursed the magazine. Grandy had done impossible things, but only in movies. In real life, he'd grown old. He needed canned oxygen. He died like everyone else. Beating death is impossible.

"You did good, Abani. You tried to help. But cars don't go around by themselves running people over."

"What about self-driving cars on TV?"

"Someone's inside in those clips. Self-driving cars can do a lot of things, but not the ones you said. Not yet at least."

She rocked back and forth, hugging herself. "No one believes me. No one believes me!"

I sighed. Grandy and Eve eyed me from the photo on my desk. Cristina once told me that my grandparents sit on my shoulders all the time: Eve, vibrant and distrustful of authority; Grandy, making jokes, a martini in one hand, a cigarette in the other.

Eve told me now, *Be nice when you turn her down.*

Grandy suggested, *Try the any-other test on her.*

The any-other test is a strategy for dealing with clients spewing fantastic stories. People who imagine or fabricate things tend to tell many crazy tales, not just one. "Ask 'em, Mark, any *other* flying saucer sightings in your past? Any other times people tried to kidnap you? Any other folks on Halloween give your kid poison? When they say yes, odds are you're talking to a nut."

I tried the test. "So many crazy things happen in New York," I said. "I bet you've seen lots."

She dried her eyes. Now she was starting to look mad. I had to give her credit. She was a fighter. "Like what? If I say yes, then I'm a nut?"

From her pink knapsack, the kid extracted a spiral notebook, opened it, and showed me a page filled with numbers, dates and dollar signs, written down in columns, in neat blue girlish loops.

The dates seemed to go on for years, or at least the next page. "I want to hire you," she announced as if the entire conversation up until now had never occurred.

It was time to end this.

"Trust the police. I'm sure they'll figure out what happened. They're good."

"I'm very organized, Mr. Falcon. Mom says so. I can help you. I figured it all out. If I work for you three days a week after school—not on trombone days because I'm in the band, but other days—and if you pay me minimum wage, fifteen dollars an hour, after five years…"

I shouldn't have let this go on so long. Further discussion would only make things worse. I assured the girl that police would eventually provide a logical explanation.

The bottom line, if you eliminated the part about no driver, was that the kid had witnessed a hit-and-run. They happen all the time. Drivers get scared and flee. Abani's problem wasn't a case for Falcon Associates. Besides, since I'd given most of

Bradley Kranepool's advance to his victims, we needed business. I rose to indicate that the interview was over.

"You're not so special. You're like everybody else," she said.

"Honey, understand, what you think you saw isn't possible. How about we call an Uber and get you home?"

My message had finally gotten through. "I can take the subway, thank you." She jerked a thumb at the 1952 poster for *Like Slaughter For Chocolate*, based on Grandy's actual capture of a German war criminal in a Wisconsin candy plant in 1948. She said, walking out, "The movie Falcon wouldn't give up."

But movies aren't real, never mind the *based-on-a-true-story* stuff. Crimes must conform to the laws of physics.

I'd make a discreet call to a friend at the precinct, and ask a couple of questions, make sure the cops were treating the kid well. But I wasn't about to tell Abani that and get her hopes up.

I was curious, that's all.

On monitor two, I watched her exit the brownstone. She turned and looked back up. I couldn't see her expression but had a pretty good idea that it wasn't friendly. I was starting to turn away—maybe I could still get some kayaking in—when a movement across the street caught my eye. A man had just emerged from a sunken alcove fronting another brownstone. The guy, wearing a green baseball hat, fell in behind Abani. Lean guy. Blue jeans. Zip-up lightweight jacket and neat black beard.

The guy turned in Abani's direction.

There's a Juliet balcony outside my office. I unlatched the double door and stepped out. Abani spun around to glare in my direction. The guy turned away, pretending to throw something in a trash can. Abani continued forward and Green Hat started up again, behind her. *What the hell?*

A second figure emerged from an apartment building at the far corner, by West End Avenue, and turned towards the girl. It was a woman. The woman moved toward Abani from one side, the man from the other. They both closed on the girl.

A white van turned onto Eighty-Fourth Street. It was heading toward the girl too.

Now I was the one imagining things.

In Manhattan at that moment, several million people were moving around, including thousands of men wearing green baseball caps, thousands of trim women with short black hair and sunglasses. People were exiting apartment buildings. Cabs were cruising ten thousand streets. Millions were out enjoying freakishly warm weather.

I had a gun safe in the office, beneath a 1950 movie poster for *A Star is Torn: A Falcon Mystery*. My H&K 9mm pistol was in it.

There was no time to get the gun.

I pounded down three flights of stairs. Just in case, I told myself. Just in case.

My fault, Abanai had said the hit-and-run victim had told her before he died. And *He killed me.*

I reached street level.

It will all turn out to be nothing, I told myself.

They were gone.

THREE

Gone.

Edgar Allan Poe Street stretches from leafy Riverside Drive to wide West End Avenue. My block is lined with four- and five-story brownstones and small apartment buildings. Parked cars impede views. Trees bloom in late October. Private gardens lay behind residences and sunken entrances provide concealment for anyone harboring evil intent, despite well displayed Neighborhood Watch signs.

I ran.

It had taken only fifteen seconds to exit my house, but in that time Abani, the man wearing the green ball cap, and the woman in sunglasses had disappeared. So had the white van.

Professionals need only seconds to complete a snatch.

When Edgar Allan Poe wrote the world's first private eye story, New Yorkers rode horses. Cows mooed on Eighty-Fourth Street. There were no auto horns. No ambulance, police, and fire truck sirens, destroying eardrums at the same time. No jackhammers. No pedestrians screaming into iPhones. No pile drivers smashing bedrock up on Broadway, two blocks away.

Maybe I was wrong, I thought. Maybe nothing bad had happened to Abani. Maybe she was ambling toward a subway entrance at that very moment, upset that one more adult had turned down her plea for help.

Ahead, a pack of kids tumbled around the corner at West End Avenue. The elementary school there had just let out. Parents waiting to pick up their children eyed me with alarm as I charged toward them. I spotted a pink knapsack. Not Abani. Just outside the school doors, a group of girls was laughing. Not Abani. Kids ducked into double-parked cars, nannies at the wheel. A pair of uniformed cops pushed themselves off an NYPD cruiser, assigned to protect students. They'd spotted me too.

I slowed, passed the cops, then sped up again.

On Broadway, crowds streamed north and south on both sides of the street. Abani might have gone into a store. There were dozens to choose from. Subway stations lay in both directions, north on Eighty-Sixth and south on Seventy-Ninth, so *which way to go?* She'd said she often visited the tennis courts on Ninety-Sixth Street, so maybe she lived in that direction. If so, she'd probably be on the east side of Broadway, where the station served northbound riders. Charging across four lanes of traffic, I heard horns and curses and dodged a pack of teens doing wheelies on motorbikes. Customers spilled from Five Guys Hamburgers, blocking my way. I pushed past a woman weaving left and right on the sidewalk, shouting into a cell phone. "Hey!" protested a slim Asian guy whose Pitbull, on a ten-foot-long leash, watered a light pole. I spotted a green hat ahead, too far off to see who it belonged to. But there were lots of green hats in the city, and ten thousand guys were wearing jeans and zip up jackets today. The height was right. Was it the same guy?

Half a block ahead, the hat disappeared into the subway. I felt a rumble below, meaning a train was approaching down there, but I was too far away to reach the station before it pulled in. I still had a hundred feet to go to the steps. Abani might be down there. *Sometimes conductors hold a train at a station.*

I sped up, taking the stairs two steps at a time as I charged past a German tourist family staring at their iPhones, trying to locate the Museum of Natural History. At the bottom, beyond the turnstiles, an express train roared past on the middle track, not stopping. That was the rumble I'd heard.

I still had time to find her if she was here.

A crowd packed the platform beyond the turnstile. I fumbled for my wallet and realized I'd left my MetroCard at home. I vaulted the turnstile, earning ugly looks from two transit workers in orange vests and a thumbs-up from a pair of giggling teens who'd probably snuck in too.

A crowd this big meant that no train had stopped here for a while. Maybe she was here. Or maybe the hat I'd glimpsed didn't belong to the man following Abani. Maybe I was the one imagining impossible things today.

NEXT TRAIN TWO MINUTES AWAY, an overhead monitor read.

Mayhem. Peering right and left, I saw a mass of heads turned left, the direction from which the train would emerge from its tunnel. A street musician blasted trumpet music at the south end of the platform, performing an off-key theme from *The Godfather*. Waves of riders surged back and forth. "Train approaching," roared a static-ridden announcement. I'd only have time to check one direction before the train pulled in.

Then, through the mass of bodies, I spotted a green hat.

He was backed against the wall at the north end of the platform. The crowd closed in again, but *there she was*—pink knapsack, pink sneakers, small kid dwarfed by bigger adults. Abani occupied the front line of riders waiting for the train, as Green Hat watched her.

Abani was talking to someone. It was the woman who I'd seen go up to her on my block. Svelte body. Long dark hair. White skin. Sunglasses.

"Move back from the edge," an announcement roared, but no one follows directions in New York. Riders in front of the crowd stepped back but those in back pushed forward. Abani and the woman disappeared, thrust closer to the edge. I fought my way toward them as the noise reached a crescendo., Two express trains passed each other on the middle tracks, one roaring north, one south.

Green Hat, still against the wall, was now eyeing me. Hard.

It's the same guy.

Green Hat thrust himself off the wall with his elbows, trying to reach Abani before I did. His partner had placed her hand on Abani's shoulder. She was laughing, distracting the girl.

The incoming train reached the far end of the station.

Headlights crawled toward us on steel, brightening discarded Styrofoam cups, hamburger wrappers, a soiled T-shirt, a crumpled section of the *Times* that slobs had thrown on the tracks.

I would have beaten the guy to Abani, but at that second, a high-pitched voice in the crowd began screaming. "A rat! Oh my god, a RAT!"

Moscow train stations feature artwork stretching back to the Soviet era. Paris stations offer lovely mosaics on walls. Buenos Aires—I was there once on a case—offers glass displays containing historical artifacts. New York features foot-long rodents that burst from holes in chewed-through supply closet doors.

"Eeeeeeeuwwwwww!"

"What's wrong with its fur? It's sick!"

The rear crowd stampeded, riders shoving other people out of the way. The creature, probably more scared than they were, scampered around feet. Bodies pressed closer to the edge of the platform. Moments earlier, I'd figured no way would Green Hat and Sunglasses harm Abani inside the station. There were cameras here. Witnesses. The snatch crew had intended to get on the train with her.

My arrival here had changed that.

The station was a blur of motion; train rumbling in, crowd heaving, new riders flooding through turnstiles, public service announcement blaring in Spanish and English and probably by next year, five other languages too.

Amid the cacophony, Green Hat, Sunglasses, and I formed three points of a contracting triangle. The woman spotted me and looked startled. *She recognizes me. But how?*

Abani, following the woman's gaze, saw me too. She froze and started toward me, away from the woman. I realized with horror that my presence had just changed a plan. They'd intended to ride along with her before I showed up, but no longer. From the path Green Hat was taking and the look on his face, I now believed he intended to push the girl in front of the train, which was only thirty feet away.

He'd reach her before I would. Riders were distracted by the rat, crowd, train. Later, too much later, camera footage might, only might, suggest intent.

By then, a professional would be far away.

My shout of warning was drowned out by mayhem. Green Hat's hands came up behind the kid.

I'm too late.

But sometimes God steps in at a key moment, sometimes physics does the trick. A heavyset woman in a tent dress knocked Abani one way. The pink knapsack, suspended by one strap, fell the other. I didn't see it hit the platform, but from the way Green Hat jerked forward I realized he'd tripped over it, arms windmilling, cap flying, revealing a bald head and terrified eyes as the guy flailed over the platform edge.

Brakes squealed. People screamed. Abani's face, frozen with horror, resembled an Edvard Munch painting, the one showing a figure on a bridge, mouth open in an eternal shriek.

The train screeched to a halt six inches from the fallen figure, lying on the tracks but amazingly untouched. The woman in sunglasses was gone. Green Hat rose shakily, heaving, looked up at me, looked at the conductor's window, toward the stunned driver whose quick reflexes had just saved his life. Green Hat touched his chest as if to make sure it was still intact. Dizzy, he took a step forward but stumbled. A collective gasp erupted as he fell back, elbows cushioning the fall, right hand flapping down to drop beneath the wooden barrier shielding the electrified third rail.

Instantly, there was a flash of light, and his clothes were on fire. I'd never seen a man combust before. Half-risen, he was a human torch, a stumbling inferno. The station smelled of burning meat. The conductor's face, at her window, was a horrified *O*. The crowd pushed back from the platform edge as if all feared they'd be next. The *Times* pages on the tracks caught fire. An express train thundered past on the center track, faces looking out. Some asshole in a passing window aimed a cell phone, snapping photos.

I fought to reach Abani. She was just standing as if paralyzed, staring.

The kid had lost her father a year ago. I had no doubt now that she'd witnessed a murder last week. Her eyes were huge behind lenses, tilting sideways on her nose. In a delayed reaction, she started screaming. She'd been oblivious to what had almost happened to her, no idea that the cinder-ridden corpse below, reconstituted, would have pushed her to her death. No notion that the man and nice lady on Eighty-Fourth Street had been a professional predator team.

I scooped her up. She buried her face in my neck, crying like a baby. I carried her out of the station and away from Broadway and down quieter Eighty-Fifth Street toward my block.

I'd tell detectives what I'd witnessed later, but at the moment I needed her safe. I phoned Oscar and Cristina, called them back from apartment hunting, told them to get back to Edgar Allan Poe Street, fast.

I had no idea where the woman in black had gone, no idea if she—or others working with her—were still watching.

Grandma Eve used to tell me, *Real falcons are birds of prey, but we're protectors too.*

I'd known without a doubt only an hour ago that Abani's story was impossible.

Now I thought, *Let's see about that.*

FOUR

The morning I turned ten years old, I woke to find Eve standing in my bedroom doorway, dressed to go out on a cold December day. Snowfall in New York was measured vertically then. These days, when meteorologists predict three inches of fall, they mean *in a row.* The blizzard of 25' feet lasted forty-seven seconds.

"Want to go to school on your birthday or watch impossible things?" she said.

"Impossible things!"

"Get dressed. I'll go find a candle for light."

"Why a candle? Did we lose electricity?"

Eve frowned theatrically, having never lost her urge to act. "What," she asked, looking baffled, "is electricity?"

I rolled my eyes. Clearly, she intended a morning of detective lessons to substitute for school, which was better than math class. At nine that day, we stood outside St. Vincent's Hospital on Sixth Avenue, watching an ambulance pull in. "Antibiotics? Pills that kill disease! Impossible!" Eve said.

On Houston Street, passersby yelled into cell phones while Eve scratched her head, acting stunned, an expression I recognized from her performance in the 1949 Hammer Films flop,

The Creature from Central Park Lake. "Look at those crazy people! Talking into a box."

Whirling, she pointed at a chopper heading over the Hudson River toward Newark.

"Every day we see things once thought impossible and don't even think about it, they're so normal now. Heart transplants. Computers. Tell me, Markie," she said two hours later, "what do you see that can't possibly be true?"

We stood in the Museum of Natural History, a Brontosaurus skeleton looming overhead. All around us rose massive bone arrangements pinned together like model airplane kits to suggest prehistoric life the size of commercial jets.

"Dinosaurs?" I asked.

"Evolution? Impossible!" she said. "Let's go to the cafeteria, where they claim to serve vegetables preserved in cans. Ridiculous! It will never work!"

At lunch, as a thousand school kids ate bagged meals or threw food around, Eve pulled a sheaf of papers from her bag. Xeroxed photos. "Tell me who these men are, and you get a birthday present," she said.

"What happens if I'm wrong?"

"You'll get the present anyway."

The first photo showed a gold coin, old, polished, not American, with a man's profile on it; thick curly hair, neatly trimmed beard, powerful jaw, beaky nose.

"Julius Sextus Frontinus," Eve said, "was a Roman engineer at the time of Jesus. He wrote, 'Inventions have reached their limit. New ones are impossible.'"

Next came a black and white lithograph of a distinguished, humorless-looking white guy with a bird's nest beard, like the Smith Brothers on cough drop boxes.

"Baron Kelvin was a British scientist, 1895. 'There's nothing new to be discovered in physics,' he announced."

"I get it," I said, eating my hot dog.

"You get it in your head, but what about in here?" she asked, poking her chest and producing another photo, which looked like it had been clipped from a magazine.

"Guess who this is?"

The guy looked white, old at the time, at least forty, clean shaven and dapper: big bow tie, cow lick, salt and pepper hair, neatly parted on the left. His shirt collar was so tight it looked like it would strangle him.

"He played for the Knicks?"

"Where do you get your wiseass streak?" Eve said.

"From you."

"I'm waiting."

I sighed. "It's not a color shot, so it's old, but not as old as the one you showed me before."

"What else?"

"The bow tie. Was he a sports reporter or a Republican congressman?"

"If you're trying to be funny, you're succeeding."

"Is that a medal he's holding?"

"Are you asking or telling?"

I was enjoying the game by this point, as always happened when Eve held lessons. "Soldiers get medals. But he's not in uniform," I said.

"Soldiers don't wear uniforms every minute. So maybe that's it."

"No. You're trying to trick me. What's that poking out of his hand? The top of a microscope! He's another scientist!"

Eve smiled. "After Robert Millikan won the Nobel Prize in physics in 1923, he told reporters, 'There is no likelihood that man will ever tap the power of the atom.'"

"He won the Nobel Prize and was still wrong?"

"Markie, your whole life, people—important ones, even ones you love—will insist that certain things are impossible. Usually, they'll be right. But only usually. Last night, I told your grandfather I'm considering giving you an assignment, so you can work for me like you've asked for. He said it's impossible a ten-year-old can do surveillance and not get bored."

"It's not impossible! I can do it!"

Eve smiled.

I got a Wilson baseball mitt for my birthday, which was great. I also got my first assignment, which was better.

Eve started calling me "Baby Falcon" after that.

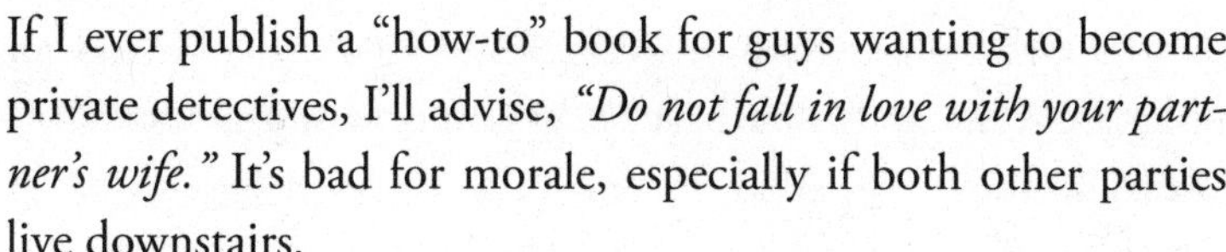

If I ever publish a "how-to" book for guys wanting to become private detectives, I'll advise, *"Do not fall in love with your partner's wife."* It's bad for morale, especially if both other parties live downstairs.

If you fall in love with a partner's wife, I'll write, you'll end up imagining them in bed at night when you hear them laughing and groaning through a ventilator shaft. You'll experience lust and guilt if you're crammed in the elevator with her or get a whiff of her perfume, even when she's not around. Or when you spot her coming back from an urban obstacle course run in cute ripped red running shorts, her ponytail bouncing with each stride of muscular, mud-spattered legs. The way her lips look when uttering, 'Bradley Kranepool's an asshole.' The way the tip of her tongue appears when she throws a 250-pound guy over her shoulder in her Krav Maga school. It will all torment you.

"Your emotions will screw up relationships with other women, even if you never tell Cristina how you feel, because only a traitorous despicable shithead would do that. You'll caress her but only in your head. You'll order yourself to control Big Falcon. Every time you start to like another woman, you'll dream of Cristina and wreck the other relationship. You'll tell yourself over and over to consider her just a valued friend. *Do not let her work on cases with you and Oscar!*

"You'll fail. And having failed, you'll hint that the couple move away, find another place to live, using as an excuse the fact that they told you they're trying to have children. 'This place is small for that,' you'll say. 'We think that too,' Cristina will say, the three of you smiling and telling lies to each other but wanting to stay friends."

Now Cristina stood, back to me, at the corkboard in our second-floor conference room. Having pulled the Bradley Kranepool photos off the wall, she'd tacked up information on the hit-and-run attack that Abani had witnessed, consisting so far of a single article from the *Post*, the neighborhood *West Side Rag* weekly crime report, and social media posts from kids at Abani's school.

I'd calmed Abani down enough for her to fall asleep upstairs. I'd left two messages for her Mom and one at the Twenty-Fourth Precinct detective squad, via a desk officer downstairs because, according to the officer, "They're all out."

The mom message had said, "Your daughter witnessed a terrible accident. I'm a private detective. She's at my house. Please call back or show up. Here's my address."

Mom hadn't responded yet, which was odd.

The police message had said, "I have information pertaining to last week's hit-and-run killing at the tennis courts and today's subway death on Eighty-Sixth Street."

The police had not called back either, which was not odd, considering New York City's law enforcement lag time and the fact that half the personnel from the Twenty-Fourth were probably at the Eighty-Sixth Street subway station right now, interviewing witnesses or working on forensics. I only hoped that when a detective finally showed up, it wouldn't be Brian Benish, who's hated me since fifth grade.

"The hit-and-run victim was Desmond Hodge, age twenty-seven," Cristina announced, reading from the *Post*.

"Is Abani named in the article?"

"It just says a single witness was juvenile."

"Then how did Green Hat find her?"

"Facebook. Instagram. Kinzoo. RealK. Kids posted photos of Abani. They think she made her story up. Cruel little monsters with mobile phones, that's what they are."

Cristina looked tautly muscled beneath a tight-fitting white James Perse T-shirt, her hips strong and round under her jeans, her breasts fuller than I'm generally drawn to in women. Her face was oval rather than angular. She was pale, blonde, and fierce. Her black eyes, flawless skin, and full lips, not beautiful in a traditional sense, were strikingly composed.

She was more curves than sharp lines, the sort of figure that the Dutch Masters liked to paint. "Something to hold onto," Oscar had remarked when we'd first seen her through the plate-glass window of the dojo she owns on Eighty-First Street, dressed in white, kicking some guy in the stomach.

"Your type, Oscarino," I'd said.

"Yeah, not one of those bony runway models you like," Oscar snorted. "*You messed up my hair*! We'll never compete for women, Falcon. Good thing. You'd lose."

Two years later, Oscar and Cristina married, with yours truly as best man. Cristina moved in after that. We were a family. Then, seven years later, out of the blue, I was in their apartment one day and accidentally glimpsed her naked, walking between the shower and bedroom. Just a fraction-of-a-second view, instantly covered up. But the image flicked a switch in my head; the image became a thought and the thought became a cascade. I found myself reliving a hundred impressions I'd absorbed of her over the years—of her candor, vigor, loyalty, and strength. I woke the next morning from the sort of dream better not shared with a friend unless you want to destroy the friendship.

At first, I told myself that the feeling would go away. But it got worse, so much so that even socially clueless Bradley Kranepool had picked up on things earlier today.

They'll move out. We'll stay friends. The feeling will go away. I'll meet a different woman.

Yeah, right.

"Desmond Hodge worked at Inwood Community College," Cristina said now, pulling me back to the present. I envisioned the school. Small campus. Concrete quad. Mostly low-income students, near the A Train stop on 179th Street.

"He was a professor?" I asked.

"Tech Department," she read. "He fixed things. Busted computers. Software installation. Grading systems. Single guy, not married. Lived in Bay Ridge. Police seek witnesses. Anyone with information please call blah blah blah. There's a statement from the school: 'Although Desmond worked here for only eighteen months, he was greatly loved by all.'"

"What did he do before those eighteen months?"

"I'll get on it."

"Anything else about the hit-and-run? Aren't there cameras in that parking lot?"

"Broken, it says."

"Cause of death?"

She turned to face me. Those intense black eyes made my heartbeat pick up. "Massive internal injuries, Falc. He was dead when the ambulance arrived." She spun toward the door. "Well look who's here! Hi, Abani." The kid was standing in the doorway. "Feeling a little better now?" Cristina asked.

"Where's my mother? Why isn't she here yet?"

I tried calling Mom for the third time, and for the third time got a recording. *This is Dr. Singh. If you are experiencing a medical emergency, go to the hospital.*

The girl seemed smaller, frailer, diminished by what she'd seen today, a glass of milk in her hand. I hadn't told her that I believed she'd been targeted in the subway for witnessing a murder, whether a driverless car had been responsible or not. She'd had a narrow escape. Two traumas in a week would make anyone fragile. I wanted Mom around when I revealed to both of them what had actually occurred.

"Tell me more about the lady you met on the street," I said as Abani drained the last of her milk.

"She was nice. Her name was Magda. She was lost and asked for directions. She said she was going the same way I was on the train."

"What a coincidence," I said.

"Magda asked why I was on Eighty-Fourth Street if I don't live here. I said I'd come to see you, but you sent me away."

"He can be mean," Cristina said.

Thanks, I thought.

"I told her about the car I saw, the one that had no driver. She believed me. She said God could make anything happen, that God's hands parted the Red Sea and God could do anything, even make a car go by itself."

"That would be a miracle," I agreed. "But why did she think God made the car run someone over?"

"She said the man it hit probably did something bad, so God punished him. She said people don't always understand that God has a plan. Even for me," she added.

I felt a chill, since the plan had been to kidnap her or worse.

Falcon's Roost, as *New York Magazine* called my home, is quiet, thanks to Pope-mobile thick, bullet proof windows. The master bedroom takes up floor four; living room, guest room, library, kitchen, and pantry on three; office and conference room on two; Oscar and Cristina's 1,200-square-foot apartment on one, with double glass doors leading outside to the deck. Fireplaces warm bedrooms. Intricate 1890s-era original wood carvings adorn walls. High ceilings and multiple windows overlook the garden, where Oscar putters in summers, plants veggies in spring. A lift goes from the one-car garage to a roof deck featuring all weather chairs and sunset views.

Shelves display awards we've won: the New York City mayoral Medal of Valor (for the elephant ivory trafficking case), the

State Liberty Medal for heroic action (for the abortion clinic arson case), the US Association of professional investigators award (stolen Cambodian statues), and the framed shot of me in a kayak, crossing the finish line in Poughkeepsie (the case of the flu I got after capsizing during the Hudson River spectacular).

The house also features special defense measures, thanks to my grandmother. "Why is a military contractor putting steel sheets in the office walls?" I once asked Eve.

"Dinkens," she responded, naming the Mayor at the time.

"Is this related to whatever you did in Abu Dhabi?"

"That trip was just a vacation."

"With five FBI agents in a private jet?"

"Those guys are just friends."

"Then how come they never come here?"

"Eat your dinner, Baby Falcon."

"Was Magda some kind of missionary?" I asked Abani now.

Cristina kicked me under the table. But the question hadn't been a joke. The answer might provide a clue. We get missionaries in Manhattan a lot. "Jesus Saves" folks who buttonhole commuters at the Ninety-Sixth Street subway. Hasidic men in skullcaps who drive around in their truck blaring Chanukah songs at a fighter-jet decibel level. Mormon duos in boxy grey suits and white shirts, exiting the Latter Day Saints headquarters across from Lincoln Center. Hare Krishnas dancing in Union Square Park. And those are the organized types, never mind the solos who forgot to take their Haldol tablets, screaming, "Jesus loves you! You're all going to hell!" on the Q train.

"Did Magda carry religious pamphlets?" I asked.

"No."

"Mention any religion in particular?"

"No."

"Say anything else about God?"

"That good people like me have nothing to worry about."

"Which is usually a sign that you do."

My elevator made a grinding noise, then opened directly into the room. Oscar stepped out, holding a cell phone in one hand and a Ziploc bag in the other. His nod meant that he'd gone door to door to speak to cooperative neighbors and uploaded images from at least one security camera. Hopefully it had captured an image of the man in the green hat and/or the sunglassed woman.

Inside the baggie was residue—gum wad, cigarette butt, McDonald's wrapper—he'd retrieved from across the street, where green hat had been hiding. Perhaps an item in the bag might provide DNA or fingerprints when we got it to the Westchester police lab, where civilians are not allowed to bring samples, unless they bribe a technician, which we do. We'd moved fast to grab the garbage because if we hadn't, it would disappear. Our germophobic neighbor Missy Papoulus—who owns that house—sweeps her front steps every ninety minutes and throws the trash away.

There had been no time to wait for detectives to look for samples over there. As Eve used to say, *First find out the truth, then prove it.*

Oscar eyed the empty table with surprise, frowned at me, and said, "You didn't feed her?" He disappeared into the kitchen and returned with platters of savory leftovers he'd cooked last night: cheese-stuffed arepas, tequeños with spicy pepper sauce, pasticho, Venezuelan lasagna. He put down plates and utensils, and took the seat beside Cristina. She squeezed his hand, which clenched my heart. "Eat," Oscar told Abani.

"I'm not hungry."

"Try one bite."

"Wow, this is good!" she said.

"What else did you talk about with Magda?" I asked her.

"She wanted to know about the man who got run over. She asked what he said to me. And if he gave me anything!" She took another bite of Oscar's tequeños, which can make any murder witness feel better.

"*Did* the man give you anything?" I said. .

"He just grabbed my wrist."

Oscar asked, "Did the woman mention what she thought the man might have given you?"

"No. But she was interested in everything I said, even about you, Mr. Falcon. Like, she asked about your house."

"What *about* my house?" I said, thanking Eve in my head for, years ago, installing bulletproof windows, cameras outside, and fire extinguishers on all floors. "When you work for important people, you piss other important people off," Eve used to say.

"She asked what things look like in here. What floor you sleep on. What floor your office is on. Stuff like that."

"And you told her."

"Yes. She said she lives on a farm. Not in New York."

Oscar's brows went up.

"Did Magda speak with an accent?" I inquired.

"No. I don't think so."

"Did she tell you why she's in New York?"

"Shopping. Oh! She also asked if I saw any takeout food boxes with a restaurant name on them in your house." I resolved not to order takeout meals for a while. We took a break, giving the girl a chance to eat without talking. The arepas were delicious. I excused myself, left the room, and tried to call Abani's mother for the fourth time. No answer.

I tried the Twenty-Fourth Precinct again.

"Everybody's still out due to a subway incident," I was told. "But I left your message for Detective Benish."

It figures. I frowned. *Benish.*

When I got back, Abani was the one asking Oscar questions, which seemed to calm her down.

"The magazine said you and Mr. Falcon met in Afghanistan."

"That's right."

"And saved each other's lives, but not from terrorists. From other Marines. Bad ones. Mom says there's no such thing as bad people, just mixed-up ones, sick ones, but I think she's wrong."

"Me too," I said.

In my mind, the tart smells of Oscar's cooking became a different mix; alkaline-tinged sand, goat shit, wood fires, mountain sage. The village we drove toward occupied a steep valley by a frothing river. Oscar and I were in the Humvee when the flash of light burst and the whole vehicle rose violently up off the ground. Metal ripped. Glass shattered. I was lying behind a boulder with no memory of how I got there. I couldn't hear at all. Then the sound of gunfire burst in.

My heart pounded louder than the sound of bullets ricocheting off our overturned Humvee. Oscar was crawling toward me, his face a mass of red. The attackers were coming at us on foot, moving left and right, wearing US uniforms, *our own uniforms,* our own guys, wielding AK-47s and trying to flank us.

"Those Marines had been assigned to guard cash flown into Kabul each week by the US State Department," I told Abani. "Lots of money. Cash used to bribe Afghan warlords so they would fight on our side."

She frowned. "But weren't they on our side because we were good guys, doing the right thing?"

"Yeah, if we paid them," Oscar said.

Honoring local customs, the Marines had been stealing money instead of guarding it. They'd figured that the Taliban would be blamed for the ambush. I could still hear, in my mind, Oscar screaming with pain and rage as I dragged him toward the boulder, Oscar firing back despite his wounds, turning his M4 on the attacking Marines. Two of those guys live in Leavenworth prison today. They will never get out. The body of the third washed away in the frothing river.

"I came to live with Falc when I got home to the US," Oscar told Abani. "He and Eve saved my life."

Eve had insisted on it. Grandy's old apartment lay furnished and empty. Oscar suffered from "adjustment issues." at the time. . He had no family, no job, no place to go except the VA, where doctors were pushing opioids on him to alleviate his pain. Oscar refused the medication. He preferred living with hurt to enslavement to drugs.

"No one's a better friend than Falc," Oscar said now, and I winced inside, thinking of Cristina. I was a traitor, the best friend who lies in bed at night thinking about a pal's wife.

These days, Oscar was pain-free except for occasional twinges on humid days. His mini farm took up half the backyard, bursting with apple trees, beets, broccoli, figs, and an array of herbs for Sunday dinners. He spent hours out there, planting, weeding, listening to saxophone jazz on his ear buds. Food had pulled him from the doldrums after his injury. Meeting Cristina had brought him fully back to life.

Abani listened to the story raptly, but when it was over, she frowned, turning to me.

"Why were you in the subway station, Mr. Falcon, after you sent me away?"

"I changed my mind about taking your case."

"Why?"

"We'll get into that later." *When your Mom gets here.*

"So you believe me now about the car?"

"I believe it's worth looking into."

She put down her arepa and dabbed a spot of hot sauce off her lip. "Say it. Say you believe the car had no driver!"

What was it with this kid? She didn't give up.

"Remote control!" Cristina broke in. We all turned to her. "Like in Central Park," Cristina nodded. "The kids with those boats! At the pond! Sailing those toy yachts around by joystick! Remote control."

"Drones," Oscar mused, "work by remote control too. Why not a car?"

Abani cried joyously, "You believe me!"

I didn't say what I thought, which was that it's easy to move a ten-pound model around a pond with a joystick or fly a fifteen-pound drone into the air—a device which, by the way, has the whole sky to maneuver in: no moving cars or pedestrians to avoid, no traffic lights, no witnesses at eye level. Hell, if a monkey escaping the Central Park Zoo makes the evening news, imagine the response to a YouTube video of a car driving itself around Manhattan. Twelve million views in the first hour. Five hundred thousand likes. Abani had insisted that no one else had been present on the day of the murder, certainly not anyone operating a remote control. It was impossible for me to believe anyone could move a nine-thousand-pound vehicle remotely, from a distance, with a joystick. That they could thread it through racing traffic, hit a guy and escape, maneuver down side streets, and stop politely at traffic lights as pedestrians gathered, stared, pointed cell phone cameras at it and...*impossible. Not remote control, And New York's not San Francisco, where driverless cars are legal. Everyone would notice it.*

"Interesting idea," I said, trying to avoid further traumatizing the kid. "We'll check it out."

"I'll help!" Abani cried as the door buzzer went off. "It's my Mom!"

Abani rushed into her mother's arms as I opened the door. Wherever the woman had been until now, at least she was safe. Doctor Nageena Singh looked about thirty-five, smashing in a fitted azure blazer, sleeves rolled to soft forearms below a summer-weight white polo. Tight black slacks outlined slender legs. The mules were Italian Nuovas. Her eyes—a cute green in the kid—were darker and striking in her mom. Blue-black hair brushed Nageena's shoulders in a French bob. A thin gold chain rested on her lithe neck. The pulse in her throat ticked slower than the horse sprinting in my chest.

Each time I'd experienced this sort of sensation with a woman, it had ended in disaster because of my feelings for Cristina. But distraction was welcome. In my cramped elevator, where our bodies almost brushed, the smell of Guerlain Shalimar encased us, and when we walked into the living room, Oscar's knowing eyes went from her to me, me to her, sensing the sort of complication that had marred relations with two former clients. Something marred all my relationships with women. That something was Oscar's wife.

Why should clients be different? Hell, some of them are the toughest women on earth; with the looks of Cleopatra, the wealth of Elon Musk, and the morals of Bernie Madoff. They could break the balls off a Rodin statue. What's wrong with sleeping with a client?

"If falcons mate for life," Oscar observed once, "love-wise, you have multiple personality disorder."

"If each one's having a good time, who cares?"

"You do when things don't work out. You act like you don't give a damn but you do, brother Falcon."

Tact was called for now. Sensitivity. I was about to tell Dr. Singh that someone had tried to murder her daughter, to advise a visit to the police, to claim they both might be in danger. This was no time for Big Falcon to pop up.

Clients are off limits, Eve used to tell me.

Limits are off limits, Grandy would counter when she wasn't around, with the casual nasal intonations of a New England patrician, in a voice gone hoarse from the cigarettes that eventually killed him, a lonely but amused man to the end.

FIVE

Kendrick Rainey was preaching to the congregation in the basement rec room when the Lord began vibrating his phone. He was a round-headed, bearded blond man, plain-faced except for dazzling deep blue eyes. His skin was weathered by outdoor work, his left leg thinner than the right, his voice soft even when the Lord commanded him to do harsh things. Before him, in folding chairs by the pool table, sat twelve acolytes; the men, like Kendrick, wearing white button-up shirts and overalls, the women in demure calf-length skirts, clunky lace up shoes, and lime-colored scarves.

"And God said, you will bring my word to the Moabites," Kendrick proclaimed.

The phone in his pocket continued buzzing.

"And God said, you will build an army!"

Kendrick's face swung toward the ceiling. "Is that you, Lord? He has a message for us! Yes, Lord, yes! I will instruct them to pray!"

Instantly, below the neon *Coors* sign, twelve heads bowed.

Kendrick limped upstairs in an agony of anticipation, fearing that something had gone wrong with the devotees he'd sent to abduct the girl. His bad left knee clicked and grated with each step. The only entity he feared in the universe was the Lord. In the bedroom, his laptop had switched on. The screen showed uniformed police moving around a subway station.

"I am displeased with you," God told Kendrick, addressing him through the laptop speaker.

Kendrick dropped to his knees as he used to do in front of his father, when he was nine. *Displeased* back then meant pain. Father had broken his left leg on several occasions. It had healed badly without medical supervision. It always hurt.

On screen now, plain-clothed cops bent over a figure covered by tarp on subway tracks. Coroners and investigators snapped photos. Technicians in body suits dropped evidence into Ziplocs. A train had halted. A cop lifted the tarp.

Kendrick gasped, seeing the blackened lump beneath. It was like observing what happens to souls over and over in hell.

"That's Viktor," God said.

Tears came to Kendrick's eyes. "Did he suffer, Lord?"

"In time, all martyrs will live again."

"And Magda? She's all right?"

"Yes. But you sent two adults to retrieve one child, and the child is still not here. Maybe I'm the one who failed. Is that what you think? That I chose wrong when I made you my prophet?"

"No, Lord. I never thought that.

"And brought you disciples? And told you of miracles to come?"

Kendrick began to tremble. His knees felt as if they were going to explode.

The five-bedroom home overlooked the Belt Parkway, ten miles from JFK airport. Tall shrubs concealed the driveway. Across the road, the view showed an oil tanker in Jamaica Bay. Kendrick had rented the house for two weeks.

"Did I not send my angels to speak to you when you were among the Moabites, Kendrick? Did I not get you out of the hospital?" God asked.

"I am so grateful."

"Did I not bring helpers to your flock?"

Every once in a while, Kendrick thought he recognized God's voice from TV. It sounded like the voice of some important person. A politician. A business leader. A performer.

Who?

"Web security is but a flimsy curtain," God continued. "Cloaking software, digital back doors, self-destructive safeguards, all vanish before the Lord. I smash the firewall. I command all code. My algorithms are a host of righteousness."

"I'll do better. I promise. Where is Abani now?"

The screen changed. Now it showed a brownstone in Manhattan, the private detective's home, which the Lord had revealed to Kendrick that morning. From the speakers came new voices. A woman was talking. Kendrick recognized her voice. God had brought it to him several times over the past few days. The speaker was Abani's mother. God was listening from inside the woman's phone.

"How dare you suggest I delayed coming here! I was with a patient at Riker's Island! They take away our phones there! Abani, get your knapsack. We're going home."

Kendrick breathed easier now. If God was going to punish him, it would have started already. God was giving him another chance. He filled with awe and appreciation. His love for the Lord was a vast desire to improve.

"I don't want to go home, I wanna stay here," Abani's voice pleaded from the laptop.

"Don't argue! And you! Falcon! Whatever you call yourself. What kind of stupid ideas have you put in my daughter's head?"

A man—Falcon—said, "She came here on her own."

"You encouraged her!" the mother snapped.

The girl wailed, "No one believes me!"

"I believe you," another woman's voice said, the tone warm and sympathetic.

"That's Cristina," God said.

"I believe you too," a man's voice said.

"Oscar."

The adults were arguing. Abani's mom sounded enraged. "Police say the subway death was an accident. There's nothing on the news about anyone being pushed. You just want money."

Suddenly the girl started crying. "LOOK WHAT THEY DID ON MY PHONE!" she screamed. "That's not my picture! That's my head on another girl's body. THAT'S NOT ME!"

The Lord told Kendrick, "Social media is so cruel."

"I DON'T HAVE ANY CLOTHES ON IN THAT PICTURE!"

Kendrick envisioned the kid, holding up her phone, hysterical, screaming out the hurtful words she saw on screen. So many venues enabled internet torture.

"I WISH YOU WERE DEAD! JUMP OFF A BUILDING! PUT SPIKES IN YOUR EYES! I DIDN'T SAY IT TO GET ATTENTION!"

Kendrick batted away sympathy. God had explained the truth about Abani. She was not really a child.

God broke into his thoughts, bringing him back to the present. "Send people to her home tonight. Bring them both to me, the girl and her mother."

"Yes, Lord."

"Bring back what she took."

"Lord, may I ask a question?"

"Go ahead."

"The group will be upset about Viktor. It would make them feel better if…if…"

"If I gave you another prophecy? You need more miracles to believe? Haven't I given you enough?"

"It is for them, not me."

"Very well. Sir Edmund Massey, chairman of the Anglo-Empire North Sea Energy Company, will perish when his private plane crashes into the English Channel today. Striking auto workers in South Carolina will start fires in the plant."

"You are awesome, Lord."

"Never mind flattery. Let's go over the blueprints together, especially the rear elevators near the garage."

"The Hands of the Lord proclaim his glory forever."

On screen now, actual movement. Kendrick saw the girl and the mother leaving the Falcon's brownstone, caught on street camera. The mom pulled the small girl toward the corner of West End Avenue. The kid did not want to go.

The Lord remarked, mildly, "Jesus had apostles. I have you."

Kendrick returned to the rec room to catch Sisters Betsy and Gayle whispering with each other. Casual conversation was not permitted during prayer. At Kendrick's command, they stood, ashamed, knowing what was coming. After revealing the Lord's prophecies, Kendrick ordered the group to circle the sisters. There were some original members here, old folks like Jacinta and Roger Ames, from when Kendrick had been a child. And there were more recent arrivals like Cornelius Hammond, retired Navy Seal; Joe Neidlinger, former security guard at the Centers for Disease Control in Atlanta; and Kunio Francis Murakami of Tokyo, wanted by Interpol for terrorist activity—all of whom God had led to the New Hampshire farm where they now lived.

The sisters wept silently, awaiting chastisement. "What will happen now is for your own good," Kendrick told them sadly. He only used physical punishment to teach the flock. It gave him no pleasure.

"Yes, Father," the sisters chorused.

The women bowed their heads. They spread their arms.

At Kendrick's command, the group closed in.

Four hours later, news broadcasts around the world chronicled the death of Sir Edmund Massey, oil executive, when his private jet plunged into the English Channel.

SIX

Picture the environmentally conscious private detective zipping up Broadway on his high-mileage Vespa scooter, dorky helmet on his head, H&K 9mm pistol below his New York Mets windbreaker. "Who cares if you look ridiculous. Do the right thing for the climate," Cristina liked to say.

Abani was in danger and so was Nageena Singh. We'd made their peril worse at the meeting, aggravated things when Oscar challenged Abani's Mom. "If you care so much about your daughter, how come you took two hours to get here?"

Nageena, furious, had hauled the girl home. Riding along now, I kept seeing the face of the man who had tried to attack Abani in the subway. I feared that whoever had sent him and *Magda* after her, if that was even a real name, would try again for the girl.

A clock was ticking as I kept hearing Abani's words in my head. *Magda asked me, "What did that man give you?"*

Oscar was in Inwood at the moment, staking out the apartment building where Abani and Nageena lived. Unknown to them, we'd decided to take turns watching the place tonight.

Cristina was online, backgrounding Desmond Hodge, the victim, and Nageena. "She's impressive, Falc. She testified in the

Chicago bomber trial, the Montgomery, Alabama, mass shooting, and the Guantanamo trials—always for the defense. No such thing as evil, she thinks. He's tougher to find out about. No Facebook presence. No X. No postings, odd for a tech guy."

My role now? In person interviews are the best, Eve used to say. I was heading for the community college where Desmond Hodge used to work, hoping that an answer—or part of one—would be there.

If you need to travel fast in Manhattan, avoid using cars. Grandy and I used to watch his old films when I was a kid and howl with laughter at high-speed chase scenes. High speed travel in Manhattan lasts a block or two at best. Then you end up stuck behind a delivery truck. Fire truck. Garbage truck or double-parked Uber. Add rush hour to the mix and you stop moving altogether. Who named rush hour anyway? Crawl hour is more like it. Curse hour. And even after you get where you're going, what about parking? In Grandy's old films, it was always easy. But in real life, the detective finds himself arguing over spots with some jerk from New Jersey or circling blocks where garages are full. And the garages that aren't full have signs proclaiming "SPECIAL PARKING RATE TODAY. FORTY DOLLARS FOR THIRTY MINUTES!"

Solution? The Vespa.

Inwood Community College occupied a half-acre hilltop campus on Broadway and 135th, across from a Sunoco Station and near the Hispanic Heritage Museum. I locked the scooter to a light pole with a chain thick enough to bind Hercules. A student directed me to the three-story Dinkens building, where a security guard in a Covid mask looked up from his Marvel comic long enough to jerk a thumb at a sign reading "Tech Department Downstairs." On sublevel four, I arrived at a former bomb shelter occupied by two overworked-looking guys at cubicles, laboring away amid tech detritus—laptops, F-drives, manuals, yellow sticky notes. But they'd altered their dungeon digs into a surprisingly warm space. Incense scented the air with vanilla. Strings of tiny Christmas bulbs blinked against the grey of cinderblock walls. Soft sax jazz pumped from mini Bose speakers as a silenced TV on a wall broadcast less happy news, a big fire killing four workers out at a South Carolina auto plant.

"We're closing in five minutes, professor," the heavier, wooly headed, Birkenstocked, wispy-bearded white kid said, mistaking me for faculty. "Mannie," read a plaque on his cluttered desk. His glasses were so smudged that it was a wonder that he even saw my vague outline.

"I'm not a professor. I'm..." I was about to say *private detective* but changed it to "Desmond's cousin."

The guys turned sympathetic. Mannie asked me to sit.

Moe, Black, shorter, acned and skinny, showed off the dead man's former work cubicle turned into a shrine. There were burning candles and potted flowers. On a corkboard, condolence cards were tacked up beside photos of Desmond Hodge walking a beagle, Desmond and a smiling girlfriend on the Staten Island ferry, Desmond and the same girl at a political demonstration. "CLEAN UP OUR OCEANS! "Desmond, beret on and fist up, looked taller than others around him in the photo. His girl was chunky and angry-looking with purple-streaked curly red hair. "SAVE THE TREES!" The UN building rose in the background beyond mounted cops on horseback, holding back the crowd.

Moe explained that "Dezzy," as Detective Brian Benish of the police had told them, had died in a hit-and-run killing, probably an accident where the driver panicked. Police had no leads.

Benish, I thought.

Moe eyed the clock. It was quitting time, he said. I asked if I could buy the boys a beer, and they lit up.

There's a saying that everything changes in life except the avant-garde and college bars, and *The Spot* on Broadway was no exception. Sawdust floor. Chalkboard menu. English majors arguing moral issues beneath football banners, while mid-week half-priced burgers sizzled on an open grill.

"Desmond was a genius. He could fix anything," Mannie said, lifting his bottle of Captain Lawrence Smoked Porter.

"We gave the impossible jobs to him," said Moe, raising his Coney Island Lager. The Falcon was buying, so they'd skipped the Budweiser pitcher, ordering craft beers.

"It's a bird, it's a plane, it's Dezzy Cyberman!" said Mannie with admiration. "I never understood why Columbia University fired him."

"Sequoia is why," Moe said. "She got him involved in all that stupid shit."

"What stupid shit?" I asked.

"Activism," Moe scowled in disdain, placing air quotes around the word. "Throwing paint on the Alma Mater statue."

"Yeah, to protest Columbia accepting donations from fossil fuel companies," said Mannie.

"He didn't throw it. She did," said Moe.

"But he got arrested too," Mannie added.

"That whole house is full of assholes," Moe intoned, draining his bottle, signaling the bartender for another.

"What house?" I asked.

"Out in Bay Ridge. Group House. Earth's Shock Warriors, they call themselves. Ha! Warriors! Buncha jerks."

Moe picked up a peanut, eyed it like it was a Shock Warrior and crushed it between thumb and forefinger. "They're like, let's throw paint on the Picasso at MoMA! Let's throw paint on windshields so cars can't move! Let's throw paint on Wall Street buildings. I bet they work for a paint company." He popped peanuts into his mouth.

On the bar TV, I saw video footage taken over the English Channel. RESCUERS GIVE UP SEARCH FOR MASSEY, PLANE WRECKAGE FOUND, a scrolling banner read.

I prompted, "Dezzy used to work at Columbia, you said."

"Only for a year. After he left that other company."

"What company?"

"The one that folded," Mannie said.

"After it got bought by that billionaire in the news—the crooked one, Bradley Kranepool," Moe said.

I perked up.

"SynchronZE! That was the name!" Mannie said. "Kranepool was gonna build a great new world. Then, oops, sorry! He shuts the whole thing down. Goes broke."

"Total asshole," Moe burped.

"Jerk."

"Scumbag. My Aunt Eliana lost her savings because of him. I hope he goes to jail for a hundred years. And not a country club jail either. A Siberian Gulag."

"How was Kranepool going to change the world?" I asked.

Mannie and Moe began arguing.

"It's impossible!" Moe said.

"Isn't," said Mannie.

"Is!"

"Next evolution of consciousness, my ass!"

"The problem with you is, you don't believe."

"The problem with you is, you don't need proof."

I stood up, quieting them down. "What are you two talking about?"

"Extropians, that's what," said Moe, surprised that I wasn't following their conversation.

"Effective acceleration," added Mannie.

Moe burped. "No guard rails! No gatekeepers! No laws hamstringing progress!" He pumped his fist. "To hell with decels and doomers! Go for it!"

"Which Kranepool did and lost his shirt because it's impossible, or at least five years away at best," argued Mannie.

"Ten!"

"Five!"

"Eight minimum!"

"Earth to Venus," I said.

A slim white girl in the booth behind us exclaimed to her friends, in a disgusted voice, "Shakespeare? Shakespeare was a perverted old white guy!"

The bartender arrived at our booth, setting down a Texas barbeque burger for Manie, a turkey burger, cooked rare for Moe, a Reuben on rye with extra pickles for me. Mannie clearly loved ketchup.

"Explain it like I'm twelve years old," I said.

Mannie plunked the plastic Heinz container on the table. "Doomers and decels," he said, tapping the container as if it was them, "say AI's unsafe. So they want to slow all development work down until we know more about it." He picked up the saltshaker and eyed it more admirably, as if it represented a rival group. "E-acks wanna go for it! No holds barred! Progress! Kranepool was that."

"And extropians?" I asked.

"They come from the planet Extropia," said Mannie, grinning. Moe and I stared at him. Mannie slumped. "Well, I thought it was funny," he said in a small voice. Moe blew out air, and Mannie resumed his lecture. "Extropians believe humans will create a next generation of consciousness," he said, "Hybrid life forms! Nano technology! Life extension! Mind uploading! Enhanced biology! Why stop at artificial hearts? Synchronize humans and tech."

"And the company you mentioned? Where did they come into this?"

"Didn't your cousin Desmond tell you?"

"Uh, he could be secretive," I said.

"SynchronZE was going to pull it all together. Billion-dollar investment. Teams working around the clock."

"Teams? How many people?"

"A lot. If you wanna make AI better, you need all kinds of models, and each one requires a different team. Each model is good for tackling only one specific task. Take face recognition. Just for FR, first you have to design a model. For that, you need to collect and process data. You need to train the model, which is a complex engineering problem. The more sophisticated the operation, the more complex the training. Problems become exponential. The amount of computer resources necessary is enormous. You need money. Different kinds of computers. You need to synchronize between them. You need to figure what hardware you need for each task."

I was getting a headache.

Mannie ticked off points on his ketchup-stained fingers. "Then you need to design the training. You don't just throw an entire mass of data on a computer. You divide it up. This task goes to *this* computer, this other one to a different machine. You slice and dice data again and again. Each phase requires a different skill set. People designing models have different abilities than the people training them. And that's just for facial recognition."

My headache was getting worse.

"And all this happened at SynchronZE?" I asked.

"The point is, it *didn't* happen. Kranepool went bust. He stole from his crypto business to keep SynchronZE running. He failed. Dezzy got fired. Dezzy went to work at Columbia."

I said, considering it, "So he goes from being a top engineer at SynchronZE to tech assistance at Columbia. Isn't that a step down?"

They looked offended. I was talking about their work. "It's not a step down. Dezzy was burned out. Sick of corporate bullshit," said Mannie

"He wanted to help the good guys," added Moe.

"He wanted an easier life and to spend time with his girlfriend," said Mannie.

"Yeah, his girlfriend," Moe said dismally.

"Sequoia," said Manny, staring into his beer.

I needed to get out to Brooklyn, to that group house, to the people calling themselves Earth's Shock Warriors, to Desmond Hodge's grieving girlfriend Sequoia. I got up to head for the door but stopped.

"One last question," I asked Mannie and Moe, "about this extropian stuff you talked about. Could any of those developments result in a car driving itself around Manhattan—now, not in ten years—with nobody on board? And no visible signs on the car that it was self-driving?"

"Impossible," said Moe, raising his glass.

"Impossible," said Manny, putting his down. "And I'll explain why in plain language that a third grader could understand. Even if you could multiply the quantifiable systemic algorithms needed with a spectrum of broader, uploaded, fractional, and angular nano requirements..."

My head started hurting again. I interrupted and thanked him. I put two twenties on the table and left.

SEVEN

My biggest problem with global warming is the way it makes Cristina dress. In late October, sixty-eight degrees out, her thighs fit snugly into lightweight soft Levi's, resting a mere six inches from mine in my car. Her white cotton shirt, compressed by seatbelt, highlighted her breasts. Her toenails shone pearly against cork-heeled shoes when I risked glancing away from the steering wheel. I'd switched the Vespa for the Prius because the R train line to Brooklyn was flooded due to the most recent round of unprecedented rain. I'm sure there will be another next month.

"I'll ask the questions," Cristina said as we hit a bump. "Judging from her posts, Sequoia has trouble with old guys."

"I'm not that old," I said.

Cristina is a toucher. The cool feel of her forefinger on my bicep triggered a boppy triple step in my heart.

"She's twenty-four, Falc. To her, you're biblical."

We exited the Battery Tunnel in a line of cars as thick as an army ant column, moving at similar speed. I smelled Shalimar, my favorite scent. Cristina's wedding ring lay inches away from me. I'd helped Oscar pick out the white sapphire. "What else did you learn about Sequoia online?" I asked to distract myself.

"Her real name is Millicent Wexler, from Westchester."

"Who names a girl Millicent?"

"Parents who want the kid to change the name. She's a grad student in social work. Two arrests for defacing public property. Desmond shows up in her posts starting two years ago. First as a friend, then a Shock Warrior. Lots of shots of them at demonstrations, faces painted green. Gumby and the Grinch. Then there's something called *The Emerald Manifesto.* 'The right finger on the right button can change the world.'"

"Spray paint button?"

"Considering who they're trying to stop, more like delete." In the rearview mirror, I watched as Cristina licked her lips. Reflected also: her soft chin line, the freckle trio on her cheek, the curve of a flared nostril.

"Accident ahead," the GPS warned. "Slow down." I needed that advice for my heart.

"How's the apartment hunt going?" I asked to distract myself.

"We made an offer on a place in Astoria."

"Great!" I said. Nothing was great about it.

"Two-bedroom co-op. Sunny. Top floor. Alcove for a nursery."

"You two will be terrific parents."

"Did you decide what to do with the apartment after we leave?"

I waved my hand as if the issue was no big deal. "Bill Yousef," I said, naming a Deputy Police Commissioner, "is getting divorced and needs a place. Can't hurt to have him downstairs, right?"

We fell silent. She turned away and stared out the window. I-478 dumped us onto the Brooklyn-Queens Expressway, past the billboard of the one-ton tomato. They're really moving away, I thought. She drove me nuts when she was there. When they were gone, I'd miss them.

I realized that she was staring at me, a thoughtful expression on her face. "We both know what's going on, Falc," she said softly. "I mean, *really* going on, about the move. Don't we? Right?"

A clenched feeling gripped my stomach.

"You know what I mean," she said. "Do you want to talk about it?"

I shouldn't have taken her to Brooklyn, I told myself. I should have gone to Bay Ridge by myself. Heat flooded my face. I fought off an urge to push violently down on the accelerator, as if that could propel me from the car. "I have no idea what you're talking about," I said, shrugging. Her finger touched my arm again. This time it lingered. Traffic cleared, and I shot the Prius forward, escaping the road jam but not myself.

She said, "Falc, do you want to say it or should I?"

"Say what?"

"Do you really think anything will be different if we move away?"

I sighed. She wasn't going to let it go. My mouth had gone dry. The moment of truth was here. A years-long friendship was about to blow up. "Does Oscar know too?" I heard myself say in a flat, surrendered voice.

"He thinks everything is great. He wants to keep living on Eighty-Fourth Street, even if we have a baby. He loves it there."

"You can still change your mind and stay," I said, for lack of anything better to say.

"Are you kidding? It's been crazy for me, walking around the house, feeling it. All the time. *You*, Falc."

I felt even worse. *What an idiot I am*, I thought.

We'd reached the turnoff into suburban Bay Ridge, pleasant former seaside home of the Canarsee Indian tribe. At least

Siri sounded normal, directing us down Seventy-Second Street between the Narrows Botanical Gardens and Glory Martial Arts Center. The silence between us grew enormous. The streets here could have graced a small Midwestern town. Grassy lawns. Stately oaks. Large, well-kept Victorian "cottages" with porches, swings, turrets, and widow walks. At dusk, the dog walkers were out.

"I'm waiting," she said softly. "Well?"

"I don't know what you're talking about."

"If you won't say it, I will," she said unable to let the damn thing go.

I pulled over. We weren't at the destination yet, but I needed to stop. I shut the engine but couldn't slow the army of rats chewing up the left upper side of my chest.

"Cristina, what's the point? Nothing will change."

"Maybe not. But at least let's acknowledge it, say it out loud. I hate it, Falc. Hate it. I hate my feelings for you."

It took a moment for her words to sink in. When they did, I was astounded. Her lovely face was inches away, eyes soft, lips parted. I could feel her trembling. Her hands lay on her lap. All I had to do was reach over and *away we'd go*. Her gaze was locked on mine as in a thousand daydreams. Why is it that when you want to kiss a woman, all you can see is her lips?

Dumbfounded, I managed to say, "Your feelings for me?"

"Don't pretend you don't know. I love Oscar. I love you. We're like a family." She slid closer. Her breath felt warm on my cheek. "When you have girlfriends sleep over some nights, when I hear you and those women upstairs, when I saw the way you looked at Abani's mom today, I have to admit I was jealous."

"That's why you asked to come with me? Not to talk to Sequoia? To talk about this?"

No answer. Just that beautiful face.

All I had to do now was reciprocate. Tell her how I felt. Kiss her and set the bomb off. Wreck Oscar. Wreck her. Wreck me. Wreck everything.

Instead, I started the engine.

"I don't know what you're talking about. You're with Oscar," I said.

EIGHT

Cristina and I drove in cold silence for the remaining six minutes it took to reach the Earth's Shock Warriors. They must have exhausted their paint supply throwing it on artwork because none apparently remained to repair their three-story Victorian home, which rose like a derelict Addams Family set on a suburban-type street half a mile from the ocean. Bed sheets covered windows. Bicycle handlebars poked above the porch's wooden railing. Peeling spots on the widows' walk trim resembled pigeon droppings. On the cracked driveway, a skinny bearded guy loading boxes into a Subaru took one look at us, shut the trunk, and beat a double-timed retreat into the house.

Slam.

Only two feet separated Cristina from me as we mounted the stairs, but it felt like a canyon. The temperature outside was seventy degrees but felt like twenty-eight. The buzzer sounded like the submarine dive warning in Eve's 1950 flop, *Mermaids of Atlantis*, a cult favorite. I've seen it at 2 a.m. on Sci-Fi theater. My favorite part is when the giant flipper sinks a French battleship into the Mariana Trench.

"Go away!" cried a man's voice from inside.

A finger moved a ground floor bedsheet curtain aside and let it fall back. I heard whispering behind the oak door. A girl's voice called out, "Nobody's home!"

"Yes, I hear that."

"What do you want?"

"To talk to a person, not a door."

Cristina swatted my hand away when I held it down on the buzzer. No, we weren't reporters, she explained nicely. We represented a witness to the killing of their friend Desmond Hodge. We sought information to help us protect a twelve-year-old girl who had seen the attack and had been threatened, probably by whomever had hurt Desmond.

"Threatened why?"

"That's what we're trying to figure out."

There was a muffled consultation behind the door. "Are you police?"

"Private detectives."

"Are you lying?"

"No."

More murmuring. "Do you have identification?"

"How can you see it if the door stays closed?"

"Back away down the stairs. Hold it up."

Minutes later, we were telling Abani's story to five Shock Warriors in a high-ceilinged living room reeking of lemon-scented vape smoke, furnished in late Salvation Army handoff style. "Redwood," as he'd introduced himself, was the thin guy who'd been loading the car. He sat beside "Teton," a pear-shaped Asian woman, on a cat-shredded, moss-colored Chesterfield couch. "Everglades," a petite blonde who looked fifteen, tucked her bare feet onto the beer-stained, burnt-orange chaise lounge. "Yellowstone," an acne-ridden, mustached older white guy in a leather vest and square-toed boots, slumped his long legs onto a rag rug from a red-lip-shaped Bocca. Sequoia, emotional and strident, clearly lead the group. Tattooed lions and elephants grazed peacefully by a waterhole on her fleshy biceps. The room was hot and smelled of garlic. The artwork was taped-up nature posters: Amazon rainforest, wolves in a meadow, slogans. "THE BEST SOLUTION IS NO POLLUTION!"

The room felt tense. Six suitcases sat in the foyer, as if the entire group was about to leave. I wondered if the flight was connected to Desmond's death.

"I love your names," Cristina told them, looking impressed. She was the best of all Falcon Associates at lying.

"When we take the pledge to become a Shock Warrior, we choose a totem," Sequoia explained as Redwood nudged her and showed her his iPhone screen. Whatever she saw there caused her to brighten. "Just like you did!"

"Me?"

She held up the phone, to that stupid *New York Magazine* piece about me. "Your totem is a Falcon."

"It certainly is," Cristina said. "He always calls it that."

"Do you have a Warrior name too, Cristina?"

"Platypus," Cristina said. "They're cute and in danger from all those South Wales fires."

"Don't they have a poison sting?" Yellowstone asked.

Cristina glanced at me as if I were the target. "Yes."

You break the ice in a thousand ways. Totems had been the way in, and information poured out. Desmond had taken the name "Owl" because, Sequoia explained, he was "wise, stealthy, and dangerous in places where others couldn't see," dark places where owls had "special vision."

"At night, you mean?"

"Owl said in the cyber world it's always night."

"He was a hacker?"

A defiant shrug. "*They* have money. And power. Owl could fly in quietly, screw them up."

"Who is they?"

"Companies. Government. Agencies. The whole combine," he called them. "Working together. Protecting each other. Drilling the earth. Burning down forests. Trashing the seas. Owl said the only way to get to the big guys is as guerrillas. Go in quiet, make an adjustment here, screw a payment, change a delivery date. Owl said paint attacks were the public face of Earth's Shock Warriors, but he was our secret CIA."

"You think that's why he was killed?"

"That cop smirked when we said it!" Sequoia said.

"Detective Brian Benish," Teton sneered.

"That asshole," muttered Yellowstone.

"What else did Benish say?" I asked.

They quieted down, eyed each other, waiting for someone to explain. Sequoia looked disgusted. "Ever since our action at the museum, we've gotten threats. People! They don't understand that the earth is more valuable than a few paintings. Why preserve paintings but wipe out whales?"

"What kind of threats?" I asked.

"Phone calls. Someone broke a window here. Horrible stuff online. *I'm going to kill you.* That's why some of us are leaving. Detective Benish made a list of threats."

"Makes sense," Cristina prompted.

Sequoia grew emotional. "But then he said maybe one of us did it. Maybe I even did it. His questions were awful! He separated us, *interrogated* us. Did anybody hate Desmond? Did we have money problems? Where were we on the day he was killed? Was Dez sleeping around on me? What kind of cars did we drive? He even asked if we all have sex together!"

Do you? I wondered, but instead asked, "What companies or people did Owl target?"

"He would never say which ones, to protect us."

"Did he keep notes?"

"His laptop disappeared in the burglary," Teton said.

"What burglary?"

"This neighborhood looks safe, but there are break ins. We had one the day we threw Owl's ashes in the bay. Owl had no family, just us. We came back from the beach, and the kitchen window was busted. Drawers open. Jewelry gone. Owl's laptop too. We thought it was the hate people who did it, but the police think it was just a burglary."

"Everyone's laptops got taken?"

"Just his. His room got hit the worst," Everglades said.

"What did Detective Benish say about that?"

Yellowstone snorted. "That we should get better locks."

"Did he think the burglary related to Owl's death?"

"He wanted to know if there was porno on Owl's computer. He was *such a pig*!" Sequoia shrieked. Had anything else weird happened here lately, I asked. *No*. Was there any particular company or government agency that Owl had mentioned as a possible target? Any one entity he especially disliked? They all pitched in, answering. Exxon. The FBI. Chase Bank. Wall Street. Republicans and Democrats. A Senator from Kentucky. Apple. Vladimir Putin. Verizon. McDonald's.

"He hacked all of these places? Or tried?"

"I told you. He never told us exactly what he did."

"You just asked who he disliked," said Teton defensively.

"How about Owl himself? His mood? Anything you noticed about him before he died? Anything special?"

All eyes went to Sequoia, whose hands had begun twisting in her lap. "He used to be a happy guy but then turned worried all the time. He wouldn't say why. I'd wake up at night and he'd be staring out the window or working on his computer. He didn't laugh any more. He used to laugh all the time. He started watching the news all day and freaking out at some of the stories."

"Which ones?"

"Different stuff. Unconnected. Like one time it was about Senator Dennis Janovich? The Texas Senator who died from a heart attack? Owl didn't even like that guy. The accident near the Panama Canal last month? Those two ships crashing? Dez had the TV on for hours. Total freak out."

"The Africa thing," prompted Yellowstone.

"The Ebola outbreak! Online every second! I said, 'Owl, it's terrible but doctors have it in check, it won't come here. What are you going crazy about?'"

"What did he say?"

"He made a joke about germophobes and washing hands. He said I was right, but it didn't help."

"What do you think started his mood?"

"I wish I knew." But she'd hesitated before answering.

"Nothing specific triggered it?"

"Maybe when he got fired at Columbia."

I asked, "Do you have any emails or texts from him, anything that might give an idea why he was so upset?"

"I'll forward you stuff. Maybe you'll see something."

I asked the group what Owl's role had been in throwing paint on the Columbia Alma Mater statue. None, they said, but his image had been captured with theirs by university security footage, so he got fired. I asked them what they knew about the company where Owl worked before getting the tech job at Columbia.

"SynchronZE?" Sequoia answered. "They were working on some big AI project that never fanned out, so they disbanded."

"Investors lost millions," added Teton.

"Because of Bradley Kranepool," growled Yellowstone. "My brother got wiped out, thanks to that jerk."

"Owl," added Sequoia, "said that what SynchronZE tried to achieve was impossible. That Kranepool made wild promises to investors and in the end, it was all air."

"What promises?" Cristina asked.

"They'd usher in the next generation of consciousness. Create unthinkable new hybrid life forms! ChatGPT eleven!"

"Leapfrog development!" cried Teton. "Out accelerate the accelerators!"

"Big lies, total dud. They went broke."

Their turn now. They asked more questions about Abani. Was she okay? Had she been hurt?

"It must have been terrible for her, seeing Owl run over," Teton said. "And thinking no one was in the car. Detective Benish explained that part to us. He said the sun was shining on the windshield so she couldn't see inside."

"Thanks for talking to us," I said, rising, hoping that something they'd forward to me—a post, an email, a tweet, a photo—might provide a clue indicating why Desmond had been attacked and Abani had been followed.

Teton's eyes moved between Cristina and I, back and forth, shyly. She'd spotted Cristina's wedding ring. "You two are cute together." she said. "Like, his and her private detectives. I saw an old TV show about people like that once. Are you a couple?"

Cristina smiled back, but not in her usual warm way.

"No," she said.

When we left the house, she told me, "Sequoia was lying in there. Not telling us something."

"I know."

As we got back to the car, my phone started buzzing. Oscar was calling from somewhere close to Abani's apartment building, in Inwood. His voice sounded low and urgent.

It was dark outside now. Night. Temperatures had cooled. Clouds had moved in. The air smelled like rain. Unlocking the car, I saw the first drop hit the windshield.

"I think they found Abani, Falc. A car's cruised past the place twice, like it was looking for parking. But then it drove past a space when one opened up. They're checking out the street. Three people inside."

"Three means more than just surveillance."

"I know. Plus, the Singhs live in a downstairs rear apartment. Ground entry. Private patio garden."

"Barred windows?"

"I can't tell. I'm up on a hill looking down on a rear courtyard shared by a few buildings. The Singh backyard is behind a wooden fence. No doorman in the building.

Visitors have to be buzzed in. So you hit thirty buzzers until one gives you access. Totally vulnerable situation."

"The street? Is it busy?"

"Overlook Drive's pretty deserted at night, plus it's raining here."

I started the Prius. In a best-case scenario, I knew, the drive to Inwood would take forty-five minutes, if traffic was light. Forty-five minutes is a long time.

Oscar's low voice said over my earpiece, "Here they come again, Falc. Hell. They're back."

NINE

Inwood is a middle-class neighborhood occupying the northern tip of Manhattan, close to the George Washington Bridge. The main drag, Broadway, rises steeply past small shops, a C&P supermarket, bodegas, a BP station. Soot-soiled apartment buildings rise off exposed bedrock in places, some atop cantilevered steel terraces like those keeping Los Angeles homes from toppling into canyons below.

Oscar had cut his way through a chain-link fence separating the highest ground from Overlook Drive. A weedy lot there provided a rocky vantage point for us to watch the rear area of Abani's building eighty yards away. The drive from Brooklyn had taken forty-five minutes. At 11 p.m., soaked from rain, Oscar and I shared binoculars, eyeing, beyond parked cars, a common rear courtyard shared by nine- and ten-story apartment buildings.

The car Oscar had spotted earlier had not returned, but he insisted it had been scouting. Temperatures had plunged. Cristina, in the Prius, had found a parking space in front of Abani's building, out of our sight. There, she could observe the front entrance. Oscar carried a .38 caliber browning automatic.

I had my 9mm H&K. Cristina was fortified with tea from the BP station two blocks away.

"Feels like Afghanistan," Oscar remarked, meaning *surveillance*, as rain sluiced down his green rubber poncho. The wise PI always considers weather and diet contingencies when stocking car trunks. Rain gear. Power bars. Water. Army self-heating surplus meals and the all-important empty quart-sized bottle. Products that stock bomb shelters, don't go bad, and enable you to stay in one place for hours.

"Maybe they won't come back," I said.

Below, in the sunken courtyard I saw empty picnic tables, a plastic jungle gym for kids, a propane grill large enough to feed two dozen people, a Bocce court, fallow vegetable garden, half dozen chained up bikes. Inside this larger area was the smaller wooden fence blocking off Abani's back yard. Water flooded Overlook Drive, where access to the courtyard was blocked by a ten-foot-high spiked iron fence. Nothing moved down there, although every twenty minutes, pedestrians emerged from the stone A train station at the end of the block, last stop on the line, which resembled the lair of the cannibal Morlocks in the 1960 film *The Time Machine*, a production that Eve auditioned for but lost out to Yvette Mimieux.

"I don't get it, Falc," Oscar said. "If they want the kid, they could have snatched her off the street today."

"They tried, remember?"

"Why not wait 'til tomorrow, when she goes out?"

"Time factor. Once she came to see us, maybe that freaked them out."

Oscar shielded his phone screen so only we could see the glow. Googling Abani's address for information about the building, he'd found a real estate ad for apartment 1A from two years ago, when Dr. Singh had purchased the place.

"Bars on windows and the back door," Oscar observed.

The ad provided a break-in guide for would be intruders. "PRIVATE GARDEN. QUIET VIEWS." Interior photos showed a chef's kitchen, food island, living/dining area overlooking the garden, and shots of three rooms that "can be your new study, bedroom, or guestroom," said the ad. Four rooms looked out on the private patio. Dr. Singh and Abani probably slept one glass pane away from attack. If they could see out, intruders could see in from the backyard.

I studied the glass rear door, photographed from inside the apartment. Black vertical bars crossed the door, a defense against intruders. But the spaces between the bars were wide enough for a hand to pass through. A hand that can make contact with glass can break it, reach in, and unlock a door. Abani and her mom were safe from idiots but not pros.

"Subzero fridge," admired Oscar. Lately, looking for new apartments, he'd adopted New York's principal preoccupation: real estate. "But look at the asking price!"

At one am, the rain fell in sheets. The temperature finally had dropped to normal October levels, cold enough to appeal to global warming deniers. Oscar stiffened. The car that had appeared below was tan, cruising slowly down deserted Overlook Drive. It stopped by the black fence, idling.

Breath frosting, Oscar said, "That's them."

No one got out of the car, which started up and rounded the corner, entering Cristina's field of vision on 189th Street. My phone buzzed. "They're pulling in front of the hydrant. I make out three people inside," Cristina said.

Oscar pulled out his pistol. I did too.

"Driver stays," Cristina said. "Two guys get out, dressed in black, wearing balaclavas. They're going around to your side."

"Call 911," I said. Cristina hung up.

Two figures came around the rain-slick corner, fast-moving shadows, slipping through wan streetlight and into a dark area at the iron picket fence. They were over it in seconds. We slid down the wet slope and ducked through the hole in the chain link fence. Crossing the street at a crouch, using parked cars for cover, we reached the iron picket fence.

I could not see the attackers below in the dark, but from down there, all they needed to do was turn around to spot us above, at street level.

Close up, the fence was higher than it had looked from across the street. Peering down into the courtyard, I saw abandoned toys, plastic monkey bars, and a vegetable garden, but no humans. Where had they gone? Had they entered a building? Had they, in the twenty seconds it had taken Oscar and I to reach the fence, already penetrated the wooden one shielding Abani's backyard?

"Those guys moved like pros," Oscar whispered.

He cupped his hands and boosted me up over the fence. I dropped, reached back, and hoisted him over. I heard the growl of a truck on Broadway, two blocks away, as we descended toward the courtyard on a long concrete wheelchair ramp. Above us were at least ninety apartments in five buildings, but only two windows were lit, which didn't mean anyone was looking out. The buildings were like hulking gapers peering down at a traffic accident.

Where were the two attackers?

Crossing the courtyard toward the flimsy-looking wooden fence around Abani's backyard, I eyed the planter containing the vegetable garden, high enough to shield two adults if they crouched behind. No one was there.

Where the hell are they and how are they armed?

My breathing sounded louder to me than the rain. We reached the wooden slat fence shielding the Singh property. The door had a wrought iron handle.

The door was ajar.

Cristina must have called 911 by now.

Oscar and I crouched by the wooden gate, one on each side. Our eyes met. I pushed the door open slightly with a foot. Now we had an inch-wide view.

There they were.

Two men crouched by the glass back door to the Singh apartment, which remained dark. One figure had placed a rubber suction cup on the glass. The second man handed him a glass cutter.

The hinges on the wooden gate, swinging open another half inch, creaked.

With blinding speed, the men spun. Diving left, I saw flashes of suppressed gunfire, but in the rain, heard only *pfffft*s, silenced bullets hissing past and splitting wooden slats. My shoulder hit the concrete patio. I rolled left. Wood splintered above us. If the attackers were professionals, they'd come at us now, charge us or try to flank us. Otherwise, they'd be trapped in the yard.

From the damage and sound, I believed the attackers were armed with high-caliber handguns. I fired three echoing shots into the vegetable planter, to let the attackers know we were armed, to keep them back. I couldn't risk firing into the air because the courtyard was surrounded by windows, potential gapers. I couldn't fire into Abani's backyard without risking a bullet going through glass, hitting the girl or her mother, especially if, hearing shots, they were looking out.

All firing paused suddenly, meaning the attackers were reloading or seeking shelter, maybe overturning a picnic table, maybe coming at us silently from both sides, on the other side of the fence.

"Police! Come out, hands up," I tried.

Another round of splintering wood was the answer, the bullet hole pattern crisscrossing right to left.

Oscar and I scrambled behind the planter. A pumpkin exploded, sending moist vegetation bits into my face.

Lights went on above us now, in surrounding buildings. I had a momentary glimpse of a white face pressed to a seventh story window.

Only seconds had passed. I held up my phone. Oscar nodded, rose slightly, and aimed at the patio door. We needed to keep the Singhs away from their windows. I punched in Abani's mom's number. She answered on the first ring, sounding frantic, clearly linking the phone call to the shooting she was hearing outside.

"It's Mark St. Johns. I'm outside. Stay back from windows. People are trying to get into your apartment."

A pause. I felt her astonishment come over the line. "It's *you* out there?" she said.

"Stay away from the windows," I hissed.

"What are you doing here?"

"I'll explain later. People are here for—"

"People? What people? Who do you think you are?" she demanded.

I clicked off as a fresh round of shots tore through the fence. I heard distant sirens, then another sound from behind the slats; metallic scraping, like lawn furniture being dragged on concrete or overturned. The sirens were getting closer. The attackers would be hearing them too.

They needed to get out at once. Or into the apartment.

Oscar and I made eye contact. We wriggled out from behind the planter, heading back toward the fence. More lights were going on in apartments above us. More faces appeared up there. I heard more sirens. *There's no way the shooters will wait for police to get here.*

Oscar went in on the right, me, the left.

Floodlights were on all over the Singh patio.

The attackers were gone.

No, not gone. A wrought iron lawn chair had been dragged to the fence at a far corner of Abani's patio. One attacker must have already gone over. The second was at the top of the fence, ready to drop. All three of us—Oscar, me, and the attacker—fired at the same time as the guy leapt off the fence. I aimed toward the spot where he must have landed.

Whamwhamwham.

Lights were now on in the Singh apartment, but thankfully no one was in sight, just a living room—bookshelves, a mounted TV, sculpture artwork, a potted palm. Abani and Nageena were safe at least. The attackers were gone, fled back toward 189th Street.

But then, "Cristina's out there!" Oscar cried, racing for the fence.

The attackers would be headed toward their car, trying to get away before police got here. They would have determined escape routes before coming. They'd know a back way—an alley maybe, a building, a construction zone—*some route that Oscar and I did not know about.* They were headed for the front of Abani's building, where their car waited, *and Cristina too.* There had to be a way to reach that spot from the fence, or they wouldn't have gone over.

Oscar jumped the fence as I banged on the glass door of Abani's apartment. The fastest way to reach the front of the building would be for Dr. Singh to let me in. No one appeared. I shouted for her to open up, that I needed access, that there was no time to reach Abani's attackers by leaving the same way we'd come in.

I tried phoning Dr. Singh. She did not pick up.

I cursed Dr. Singh as I ran for the fence, followed Oscar's route over the top. Lights glowed in windows overlooking the patio. Probably lots of Abani's neighbors were calling 911, giving them my description. *I see a man down there with a gun!* Running down the alley, I envisioned blue and whites racing up Broadway, turning onto 189thStreet, where the attackers would materialize out of the rain, in front of Cristina. *Please, please don't let anything happen to her.* Ahead, I saw a partially open steel door to a different building. The attackers must have gone that way. I ran into a basement corridor where, on the floor, I spotted wet tracks left by the two intruders and one from Oscar's running shoes. I saw drops of fresh blood, floor spatter, growing in size.

Not from Oscar, I hoped.

I slowed at a corner, peeked around the wall. No one there, but more blood, now in a streak. Another door at the far end of the corridor led me into a big storage room smelling of mold and piled with bulging garbage and recycling bags. *no one hiding behind them.* I charged up three stairs on the far side of the room and pushed the bar lock on a steel door. It led to the street, a service exit through which building workers must routinely bring trash out for collection. I emerged into sheets of driving rain, lit by police headlights and dome lights. Squad cars blocked both ends of 189th street. More sirens were on the way.

"Droptheweapondroptheweapon!"

The shouted commands sounded like one long word over the roar of the downpour. Oscar, handcuffed, was being pushed by a cop into a squad car. Guns were pointed in my direction from over the roof of a second car.

"Down on the ground now!"

Cristina's voice cried, out of the glare, "He's with us!"

Thank God she's all right!

One of the attackers lay in the street, clad in black, unmoving. I saw a white face, tangled legs, a ragdoll immobility that told me the man was dead. His blood pooled with rainwater rushing toward the curb.

I lay on the wet ground, cheek pressed to asphalt, hands cuffed behind my back. A cop shielded my head from bumping the squad car roof as she eased me into the back. An ambulance had arrived. Through slashing windshield wipers, I observed Cristina arguing with cops, hands on her hips. White clad EMS attendants bent over the body and, even at 2 a.m., in a storm, a small crowd of gapers watched or photographed the drama unfolding on their street.

The squad car I sat in lurched into motion.

The second attacker was gone. So was the car they had arrived in.

Abani and Doctor Singh were not part of the crowd.

As we headed off, I tried to tell the cops that someone needed to check on the Singhs, see if they were unharmed. They told me to calm down. They told me to wait until we got to the station. They turned on the siren, in a rush. But we were going, I kept trying to tell them, the wrong way.

TEN

The sun was rising as I stepped out of Inwood's Thirty-Fourth Precinct. I'd been answering questions for hours, but detectives had refused to respond to mine. The storm was over. Orange light bathed George Washington Bridge–bound traffic on 183rd Street. Angled at the curb were squad or private cars belonging to officers on duty. Exhausted, I spotted the Prius double parked by a towed-in, smashed up Lexus, one more metallic victim of Manhattan's ugly moods. Oscar must have been released earlier because, approaching the car, I observed him and Cristina asleep in back, in each other's arms. Oscar's mouth gaped open.

Cristina's face tilted back, soft in repose. I'd nearly kissed that mouth a few hours ago.

Quiet city. Dangerous city. After two attacks on Abani, her story, however unlikely, needed reconsideration. The angled-in cars facing me seemed malevolent, front grills like metallic teeth. Oscar and Cristina snored lightly as I slid in and started the engine. A shift must be changing because as I pulled out, so did a half dozen other cars. A Ford SUV, a four-wheel drive Hyundai, a vintage Miata, and a silver, late-model Honda Accord.

The Accord stayed behind us as I drove west and, along with traffic exiting the bridge, onto a southbound ramp to the West Side Highway. Two cars back in the mirror, the Honda matched my speed. Probably a cop heading home.

But I kept tabs on it as my thoughts went back to the precinct interrogation room, which at least had smelled of fresh paint, not the usual foul odors marking such a place.

"Let's go over things again," Detective Ronald Ingbar had said.

"No, let's decide to let me sleep," I'd responded. Ingbar had seemed like a decent guy; heavyset, cigarette breath, wooly headed, neat brown jacket and green tie. Cops who've heard of me tend to display one of three attitudes. They're extra respectful because they know that Falcon Associates sometimes hires moonlighting shields. They're antagonistic, resenting rich PIs—or, actually, any PIs. Ingbar occupied the third category, normal treatment, but his grilling had still pissed me off.

"You admit you fired first," he'd said.

"Not first and in self-defense."

"You have a thing for twelve-year-old girls?"

"No. Do you?"

"If there's something you need to tell me, Mr. St. Johns, better to say it now."

"I know. I have to go to the bathroom."

"Oscar told us a different story than yours."

"We both know that isn't true."

In the end, my version was verified by a witness who'd observed the fight from nine stories up. The woman had been indulging in a late-night telescope habit, staring not at distant stars but into other bedrooms facing the courtyard. It can pay to have a pervert around. *Two men were trying to break in. I saw flashes when they fired first,* she'd said.

Quiet city. Dangerous city. Traffic remained light as I detoured off the highway at Ninety-Sixth Street to visit the parking area where Abani had witnessed the murder of Desmond Hodge. To the west, sunlight reflected off the Hudson. A tug was hauling an oil barge north. A line of early morning tennis fanatics was forming before the chain link fence shielding the padlocked courts below. Everything in New York starts with a line. Airports. Theaters. Bus stops. Cemeteries. But in the lot, most spaces remained empty at this hour. Perhaps the cameras here, broken during the attack, were functioning again. But even if they were, it wouldn't help me figure out what had happened in the past.

In the rearview mirror, Oscar snored softly. Cristina's hand rested on his lap. A sunbeam lit the diamond on her wedding ring as, continuing south on the West Side Highway, I found myself scanning autos around me as if to make certain that actual humans were inside.

What does a driverless car look like anyway? Can you tell from the outward appearance that nobody's at the wheel? Is there apparatus on the roof? Cameras? Sensors? That's the way the self-driving cars look when cruising in San Francisco.

Oscar and Cristina woke minutes later at the sound of my garage door opening. Famished, we showered and changed into dry clothes and walked to Broadway's Parthenon Diner, open twenty-four hours a day, where we occupied the back booth, beneath the plaque that owner Demetrios Kostos had nailed up—RESERVED FOR FALCONS—after we helped him beat off a protection racket three years ago.

We needed to talk about last night, but first, coffee. Cristina ordered fruit and granola. For Oscar, the Mexican frittata and hash browns. For me, the lumberjack: pancakes, scrambled eggs, sausages, and syrup. The good stuff Demitrios brought back from Vermont.

"The detective who interviewed me tried to phone Benish at the Twenty-Fourth. He never answered," said Oscar, forking frittata into his mouth. "What's with that guy?"

I picked up a bacon strip and bit off the end, reliving the speed with which Abani's assailants had carried out their attack. "All together so far, two attackers in the subway. Two last night. Driver makes five."

Cristina shuddered. "When they ran into the street and saw me…if Oscar hadn't shown up at that second…" Trailing off, she took her husband's hand.

Any earlier talk of feelings between us was, for the moment, forgotten. Oscar and Cristina were wedged into the booth hip to hip. A news show broadcasting above the lunch counter showed a banner: BRITISH OIL EXECUTIVE PRESUMED DEAD. Wreckage floated in the English Channel.

BREAKING NEWS: SABOTAGE IN SOUTH CAROLINA AUTO FACTORY. On screen, smoke billowed. Flames leapt.

"Five attackers means someone has money," I said.

Outside the plate glass window, an Entenmann's delivery truck went by. A girl on a scooter went by, long hair flying. A late-model silver Honda went by. There are probably thousands of them in New York.

"We have no idea who they are," Oscar said morosely, finishing the last bit of frittata. "But we can bet by now they know about us. Let's go over Abani's story again."

And again.

"The woman asked Abani if Desmond gave her anything," Cristina said. "But what? What could he have to start with? He was a tech repair guy at a little community college?"

"And before that, the same job at Columbia," I mused. "What do tech guys do? Everyone comes to them with computer problems. Professors. Administration. Students. They access passwords. They keep computers overnight. A crooked tech guy could get into half the systems on campus."

"And do what with it?" Oscar said, chewing on a cherry Danish.

I envisioned the campus of the Ivy League behemoth a mile north, straddling huge swaths of Upper West Side real estate. Columbia constituted a billion-dollar brain trust empire. I'd taught an adjunct course there a few years back to law students titled "The Private Detective's View of Justice." Now I provided a detective's view of the school.

"Think of it as an entry point to money and power. The school has a huge endowment. Professors partner with medical and tech companies. They do cutting-edge research. They consult for the Pentagon, White House, State Department. They travel to China and Russia. They correspond with world leaders and independence movements. The school enrolls students from every country."

"So if a bent tech guy gets into the systems..." Oscar mused.

"There's a lot he'd learn. But for who?"

"You think Desmond was spying?"

"That would account for a professional hit."

"Why would he give anything to Abani?"

"She was the only one present when he was attacked."

"What if this whole thing has nothing to do with Columbia?" said Cristina, signaling for a coffee refill. "Maybe it's about the vandalized art. Maybe someone's pissed at Earth's Shock Warriors. Or maybe it's about Desmond's job *before* Columbia. At that tech start up. SynchronZE."

"We need to talk to Bradley Kranepool," I groaned.

"We need to convince Dr. Nageena Singh that she and Abani need protection," Cristina said.

"Good luck with that," Oscar remarked.

Demetrios, at the cash register, ripped up my check as usual. And as usual, I put down cash for payment anyway and added a hefty tip.

The morning sun had dimmed, and grey clouds had returned.

Commuters streamed past a donut stand and Halal food truck, heading down into the subway station where Abani had been attacked. I scanned traffic for a silver Honda, trying to recall whether the car had any distinguishing features. Busted headlight, maybe. *My kid was valedictorian* bumper sticker.

No distinguishing features came to mind.

Back at the brownstone, Oscar and Cristina disappeared into their own apartment. I set our home alarms and fell into bed, instantly unconscious.

The dream that came transported me into a Humvee with Oscar, back in Anwar Province, bouncing toward the village where, in real life, we'd fought for our lives. Instead of combat armor, we wore New York clothes, jacket and tie for me, Oscar in a guayabera and sandals. Instead of M-16s, we holstered pistols. Suddenly, Cristina was in the back seat with Oscar, kissing him. We crested a hill, and the Afghan village turned into the courtyard behind Abani's home. My stomach contracted. Cristina was gone. I knew what was about to happen, but was powerless to stop it.

Faces in lit windows above—Eve, Grandy, Brian Benish, and Nageena Singh—peered down at us as gunfire erupted on both sides, as the ambush began. The Humvee overturned. I dragged Oscar toward the fence shielding Abani's backyard. *If we can get inside, we'll be safe.* But the bullets stitching across the concrete courtyard would reach us in seconds. I was moving too slowly. Oscar seemed to weigh a thousand pounds. From out on Broadway, I heard the whine of incoming artillery.

No, it's not a mortar, I realized. *It's the door buzzer to my home.*

I shot awake.

On the monitor, Abani stood on the front step with her mother. The girl wore her beloved pink—pink knapsack, pink sneakers, pink jacket, and white blouse. Nageena looked smashing in high-waisted, fitted, black ankle-length pants, black cashmere sleeveless turtleneck, and black cashmere cardigan over her shoulders. Blue-black hair framed the face of the most photogenic shrink I'd ever met.

Red digits on the clock read 2 p.m. I'd been asleep for hours.

I groaned. Being chewed out again by Nageena was the last thing I needed. At least the Singhs were, for the moment, safe, and I had a new chance to try to convince the mother of the danger. I pulled on jeans and a Columbia U sweatshirt. I opened the front door expecting another argument, but I got a surprise. The passion lighting Dr. Nageena Singh's green eyes turned out not to be rage but fear, protectiveness, urgency, and regret.

"Detective Ingbar told me what happened. I'm sorry for the way I treated you," she said, clutching her daughter's hand. The sharpness in her voice was gone. She glanced over her shoulder at the street as if expecting attackers to materialize there any second. "You saved Abani's life, Mr. St. Johns. The police have no idea who's after her. You tried to warn me, and I didn't listen. Please forgive me. We need your help."

ELEVEN

Kendrick Rainey led the group in song during the drive to the shooting range. They sang "Light Is but His Shadow Dim" and "No Master but God." George Washington Bridge traffic was light this early afternoon. The R&P Gun Range, a windowless, wood-sided building surrounded by a grey gravel parking area, lay eleven miles from the city. The lot was empty other than a Ford Ranger in back, where Frank left the van.

Kendrick knocked. The door opened to reveal a big-bellied, bearded guy in baggy jeans and a leather vest, his flabby biceps inked with dragon tattoos. He looked surprised to see twelve identically dressed people, all smiling.

"I'll give you one hour in here, then whoever threatened me on the phone will never call again, right?"

"I promise," Kendrick said.

"And no one will tell the police about me?"

"Our secret," said Kendrick. God had told him about the man, the things he'd done. "You turned off any cameras in here?"

"Hell yeah, dude, we're supposed to be closed until tonight."

Inside were displays of trophies, gun-club sign-up lists, ammo for sale, a chemical air-wick smell. Kendrick saw a gag hand grenade on a shelf and sign beside it reading, *To reach the complaint department, pull this pin.*

"What are all you guys, a family?" the attendant asked.

"That's exactly who we are."

"Which targets do you want me to put up?"

"Evil people," Kendrick said. *Like you*, he thought.

Joe Neidlinger and Cornelius Hammond were excellent shots. Kendrick had trained with firearms while a boy. His movements were fluid and accurate. Betsy and Gayle were hopeless, giggling. Kendrick showed them the high-ready position, how to aim their pistols with both hands.

Murakami was better with chemicals than marksmanship, but it was essential that everyone in the group had fundamental knowledge of self-defense, in case the main plan failed.

When the hour was up, the group removed their noise suppressors. The range smelled of smoke. Kendrick asked the tattooed man for a final favor. "Can you go to the front and run across the range, left to right, please?"

The guy frowned. "What?"

"It's easy to hit a target straight on, harder if it's moving. My friends need practice with a live person."

The guy laughed nervously. "Very funny," he said.

"No, I mean it." Kendrick smiled.

The fat guy's eyes widened. Sweat popped on his head, beneath plastered-down hair. "The voice on the phone said one hour. I gave you the hour. It's late. You have to go."

The group kept smiling. Joe blocked the door. All the guns came up at Kendrick's signal. The attendant looked from person to person. Gulping, he began to cry.

"Are you the parents? You're the parents, aren't you? I didn't touch those kids."

Kendrick stared flatly at the man.

"I only watched," the man said. "Please!"

Kendrick put his arm around the man, who smelled of sweat and dirty leather. "Tell you what. It's a test. If you make it across the room, we'll leave you alone," he lied.

The guy blubbered, terrified, "Twelve shooters!"

Cornelius pressed his pistol to the attendant's head.

The man began crying. Snot ran down his face. He dropped to his knees like a church congregant, rocking side to side.

"I won't do it again! *Never again!* I promise!"

"Five…four…three…"

The man stumbled to the front of the range. At first, he hugged the wall, refusing to move. Kendrick fired over his head to get him started. His crying grew louder. He ran forward suddenly, across the range, as gunfire erupted.

The attendant ripped a target in half when he fell.

On the way back to Manhattan, Kendrick led a rendition of "God Hides Some Souls Away!"

They'd brought bagged, fresh food from the farm. Pickled vegetables, free-range chicken, homemade breads. Betsy and Gayle weren't allowed to eat because they'd broken discipline at the range by laughing. Bridge traffic remained light. The group ate in the van.

Kendrick was starting to get nervous, though. God had not contacted him since the attack on Abani's apartment failed. Another member had perished last night. It was the second time that the detective had caused a member's death.

God is angry at me, Kendrick feared. *Because of that detective.*

God, please call.

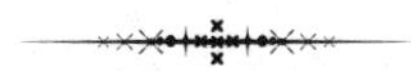

God's Hands' rules: No cell phones allowed unless Kendrick provided one. No computer access for anyone except him. All private monies donated to the farm. Work assignments from dawn to dusk. Children remain back in New Hampshire. Sexual relations forbidden until after the changeover, which would happen days from now. At that point, Kendrick had told the group, sex would be allowed, and all resulting pregnancies would produce baby angels.

Kendrick had eliminated the worst of his father's old rules, the whippings and "touch me" sessions with kids, and the punishment closet. Father had slept with all women in the group. Kendrick preached otherwise, that abstinence now would lead to heaven later.

I'm kinder than my father was, he thought.

He needed to scout police precinct houses serving neighborhoods around the target, so the van cruised past the Twenty-Sixth near Columbia University, the Thirtieth on 151st by Hamilton Heights, the Thirty-Third on Amsterdam Avenue. Kendrick pointed out street corners from where Betsy, Gayle, and Jacinta would call 911 three nights from now and report bogus crimes in progress.

"You'll draw police away from 168th street."

Next stop, Columbia Presbyterian Medical Center near Riverside Park. A sprawling mini-city along Washington Street; a warren of hospitals, research centers, physical therapy centers, dorms, the school of public health, the school of nursing, the Millstein Heart Center…more diseases floating around one square mile than God had unleashed in Egypt two thousand years back.

"You've studied maps of this area, but we want to know hiding places in case things go wrong. Dumpsters. Alleys. Twenty-four-hour markets. Anything that catches your eye."

To the sisters, "Find the street cameras."

To Murakami, "Identify one-way streets and which way they go. Everyone back in thirty minutes."

They went off and, alone, Kendrick finally permitted himself to feel the full impact of fear that had been building since last night's failure. He took out his phone.

"Call, Lord." But nothing happened.

"Give me another chance. Please."

Silence. It was over, he knew. God, disgusted, had moved on, found a better prophet. God was through wasting time on Kendrick. Kendrick wasn't *worth the effort,* as he used to hear when he was seven, eight, nine, a frightened kid locked in a closet, hearing rats in the walls, hearing his father through the door. "You're worthless. You're pathetic. Your mother left because she couldn't stand you."

Of course God was mad. Out of billions of people on earth, God had made Kendrick his messenger. "Spread my word," God had said. God had raised him up and told him things that were going to happen, not vague predictions of a distant future, but day-to-day ones that *always came true!*

All God wanted in return was competence.

It was useless. The phone might as well be dead: The dark screen. The silvery housing, inert. A stupid machine.

Kendrick clenched his teeth in distress. The girl was still alive and the item she took still missing.

He shook off worry. *I'll concentrate on the job, and God will see how hard I work and give me another chance.* He walked away from the medical complex, one block north, to a large plaza fronting the sixteen-story Gertrude Ames Medical Research Center, which was not part of the hospital complex. Kendrick squared his shoulders, crossed the plaza, passed a bronze statue of "Dr. Edward Jenner, who defeated smallpox," and pushed through a revolving door into a large sun-drenched atrium.

God had told him what happened upstairs in this place.

Kendrick knew he was being recorded by security cameras, but God had assured him that all footage would be erased. Hopefully his group would never actually have to enter this lobby, but he needed to scout security arrangements in case they had to fight their way in, or out, three days from now.

No one noticed him. A long, granite check-in counter was manned by two uniformed guards. Visitors had to pass through electronic barriers to reach banks of elevators. Unlike older New York buildings, no list of occupants was displayed. *At 2 a.m., this place should be empty,* he thought.

Suddenly, a voice behind him cried out, "Kendrick! Kendrick Rainey, my old friend! Is that really you?"

Shocked, Kendrick turned to see a rotund, balding Black man in a medical jacket striding toward him, Dunkin' Donuts bag in hand, wide grin on his face. Red stitching on the medical jacket read "Doctor Ben Elgin."

The last time he'd seen this face, he'd regarded it from a laboratory floor. He'd been handcuffed.

"I thought that was you!" the man said loudly, drawing glances, coming up to Kendrick. A scene came back to Kendrick from years ago—a college research lab, a dozen medical students peering into microscopes at granite-topped lab tables. Kendrick had been paired up with Ben that day.

The guy looked heavier now, face rounder, and there was a big paunch. "You left Boston, Kendrick? Are you working here now? It's good to see you," Elgin proclaimed as a security guard turned to look.

"Yes, I work here now," Kendrick lied.

"Which company?"

"Fourth floor."

"I'm on six. Bridgestein Pharma."

The grin faltered, and Kendrick cringed inside, knowing what was coming. Even back then, years ago, Ben had been socially awkward, blurting out uncomfortable things.

"I always felt terrible about that day, Kendrick."

Kendrick's knees had gone weak. He heard himself say, "Don't worry about it. It was a long time ago. I was ill."

"When you turned to me and asked me to look into your microscope...when you asked me, *Do you hear them?* You really freaked me out!"

"I don't believe that stuff anymore," Kendrick said. His left leg had started trembling.

"Man, you were out of it, fighting and screaming when the cops pulled you out of there. I wanted to say something to them. I felt awful, especially after Dean Bachman came to the lab and told us about how you grew up! I mean, in a cult! I'm babbling, right? Jan says I have no mental filter—thoughts come into my head and shoot right out of my mouth."

Kendrick squeezed the man's shoulder sympathetically. "That's all in the past. I'm on medication now, Ben."

"And you finished your studies! You graduated! That's great!"

"Yep! Good to go!" Kendrick said. "I got your get-well cards in the hospital. I should have replied, but I was out of it those days, you know, all drugged up."

What Kendrick wanted to do now was shove his hand into that mouth, stop the guy's words, stop the images.

Ben dug into his back pocket and produced a business card. "Jan will be thrilled to see you again. Will you come for dinner? I can't believe we both ended up working here! Wait 'til I tell Jan!"

The phone began vibrating in Kendrick's pocket. He checked the screen. God was on the line.

"I have to take this call, Ben. Sure, I'll come to dinner. Maybe next month."

His breathing finally slowed down when he got outside to the plaza, where he could talk to God without anyone overhearing him.

Half the people in this building will be dead by next month, he thought.

Kendrick wanted to weep with relief. God was back, commanding yet soothing, not angry at all. A sympathetic voice. A loving voice. A voice of pure compassion, coming just when Kendrick had been reminded of the most horrible afternoon in his life.

"It's not your fault the detective showed up last night, Kendrick. Your people who perished will return. Their death is only temporary."

"May I ask a question, Lord?"

"Of course, my friend."

"It's about the detective. Mark St. Johns."

"He's not a real detective. He serves the dark one. He looks like a man, but he's not."

Kendrick felt a happy swelling in his chest. The Lord was confiding in him again.

"I have a plan for him," God told Kendrick. "Don't worry."

The day seemed brighter, much brighter, finally.

Kendrick basked in the pleasure of the Lord.

TWELVE

Green is the rarest of eye colors, a genetic mutation affecting two percent of people on earth, characterized by low levels of melanin which, in Dr. Singh's irises, produced high levels of excitement in me. The eyes fixed on mine from three feet away were yellow-green, slanted upwards, almost feline in intensity against her smooth, dusky skin.

"When Detective Ingbar told me what happened last night, I almost died," she said. "I didn't believe my own daughter. Then I didn't believe you. If you hadn't shown up," she shuddered, "if they'd gotten into our apartment..." Her eyes shut as if to block out images. Glass smashing. Her daughter screaming.

The eyes opened. *BOOM* went my heart.

Abani was downstairs in the kitchen with Oscar, helping him prepare dinner. Croatian *ćevapi*, grilled and minced meat fingers, cheesy *štrukli*, *sarma*, and a veggie pie called *soparnik*, my favorite.

Cristina was in the office, reading up on self-driving cars. I'd brought Dr. Singh into my living room, where we faced each other amid deep-cushioned seating. Potted palms flanked tall windows. Artwork had been accumulated over decades, much of it from travel jobs overseas. There was South African bead work. A hand-carved limestone chess set from Kenya. A vintage Soviet ski vacation poster, where men and women glided cross-country, none of them smiling. "ATHLETICS MAKE SOVIET WORKERS STRONG!"

Speaking of strong, I imagined taut muscles moving beneath Dr. Singh's clothing. I had to tell myself to pay attention to what she was saying.

"Did Detective Benish keep Abani's jacket as evidence?" I asked.

"No. He said he already had blood samples from the body. He didn't need the jacket," she said.

"Do you still have it?"

"I threw it out. It was soaked with blood and ripped. Her father bought her that jacket. She loved it. But it was time for it to go." She frowned. "Why are you asking about this? Is it important?"

I imagined Abani at the Ninety-Sixth Street tennis courts, kneeling beside a dying man as an idling car faced her like a predatory animal, exhaust rising like breath. The man grabbed Abani's wrist. She never saw his other hand go into her pocket, drop something in there. *It could have happened that way, but that doesn't mean it did,* I thought. And even if it did, how would anyone see it if no one was in the car?

I answered my own question.

Self-driving cars use cameras to navigate.

"Dr. Singh, did you find anything in the jacket pockets before you threw it out?"

"Gum wrappers. Tissues. Why? And please, call me Nageena."

"Old jackets have holes in the pockets. Did you feel around inside the lining to see if anything dropped in?"

Her frown deepened. "Should I have?"

"I'm just asking. Don't worry about it."

Her eyes searched my face. No wedding ring, I thought. No engagement ring. Soft light highlighted her moist lips and thick hair. Fluid sensuality marked the crossing of a leg, the perfect posture. Her back was a petite, taut bow.

"I can't believe I told you to go away," she said.

"Forget about that."

"Or that I called 911 to complain about you."

"Everybody does."

She tried a smile and failed. "Those men will come back, won't they?"

"They believe she saw something. Or took something. I don't think you should return to your apartment. No school for Abani the next few days. Do you have a safe place to stay? Country house? Friend's apartment? Grandparent somewhere far away, like Antarctica?" But even as I said it, I knew that sending them off by themselves was ridiculous. No way would I allow the Singhs to go into the world alone.

"Can you help us?" she said, squeezing her thigh in agitation. Squeeze. Relax. Squeeze. Relax. I wondered what her hand would feel like on me. *Pig.*

"I'll pay anything to protect my daughter," she said.

"Right now, we're running a two for one protection special. First month free," I said. "Get your coat."

"Where are we going?"

"To see Detective Benish. To get you help."

"That guy?" She bit her lip. "He hates you."

"That's because I got him arrested when we were kids," I said as we headed downstairs. But before I could explain further, Cristina appeared below, frowning up from the landing. At first, I thought it was because I was with Nageena. *Is she jealous?* But it turned out the problem wasn't personal, it was business.

"Something's happened, Falc. You better take a look at this," she said, gesturing us into the office. "There's something weird going on."

The first email allegedly came from someone named Wolfe Crane-Owsley, head of security for the Abu Dhabi–based Ralston-Rayes Shipping Conglomerate. I knew the company name. I'd seen it on shipping containers in New York harbor. Ralston transports cargoes globally. Singapore. Buenos Aires. Shanghai. San Francisco.

"Dear Mr. St Johns," the message read. "In light of recent increased piracy activity in the Red Sea, we're conducting a security audit at our home office."

Translation: *We're concerned that one of our employees is telling Somali pirates about our cargoes.*

"You've been recommended as an excellent choice for the job. Our attached offer lays out generous terms for a two-week visit, plus expenses. How quickly can you come to Abu Dhabi to handle a most sensitive, important job? Call my private number at any time if you have questions."

"What's weird about this?" I asked Cristina. We get jobs overseas all the time.

"Nothing, until you look at this next email from Norway."

"Dear Mr. St. Johns. We are an Oslo-based energy company with assets in the North Sea. We are conducting a security audit and wish to employ your well-recommended agency to assist in a most sensitive and important job. First-class travel.

First-class accommodations. Double your usual fee. How soon can you come?"

The email had been sent by someone named Jens-Eirik Width. An attachment labeled "Arc-Energy" probably provided, for those who opened it, a write-up of services that the corporation performed. There was an Oslo phone number. Cristina poked the screen. "Most sensitive and important job. Same exact same wording. The messages arrived within four minutes of each other."

"What does that mean?" Nageena asked.

I frowned. "Maybe nothing. Maybe if we open an attachment, we're infected. Maybe someone wants us out of New York."

"You think both emails came from the same place?"

"That's the question."

"Can you track the messages back?"

"I'll try," said Cristina, taking a seat.

"Are you always this cynical?"

At the same time, Cristina and I said, "Yes."

"But if you leave New York," Nageena said, blood draining from her face, "then Abani and I..."

I lay a reassuring hand on her shoulder, felt heat emanating from beneath her blouse. "No one's leaving New York," I assured her. "We have a client here. You."

I did not add what I was thinking, which was that if both emails had come from the same people, ones who could hire muscle, fly us overseas, and instantly wire us thousands of dollars, the importance of their goal was growing. I didn't want to frighten Dr. Singh further, so stayed mum on a next thought too: That Abani had stumbled on the tip of an iceberg. That the murder in the parking lot was small compared to some larger scheme. Consequences were spreading, jeopardy growing.

Falcons fly high and spot rivals at great distances. But I didn't feel like a Falcon at the moment. I was grasping.

I felt blind.

The time difference between New York and Abu Dhabi is nine hours, which made it 3 a.m. overseas. I pulled out my phone. I punched in Wolfe Crane-Owsley's private number. When people say *call me anytime,* they don't generally mean *3 a.m.* But the voice that answered on the third ring sounded hearty and alert. The accent could have been South African.

He confirmed the offer. The money could be wired to me within hours. A flight would be arranged. The situation overseas was "urgent." The company would pay for three weeks, whether or not I stayed the entire time. First-class travel. First-class hotel. Wolfe's father, he added, had worked with my grandmother. He'd heard wonderful stories about Eve. He looked forward to renewing the relationship.

"Old friends are the best kind," he said.

"I'll get back to you," I said, and hung up, frowning.

How had he known about Eve? I'd never learned what she'd done in Abu Dhabi, years back. Perhaps the email had been genuine. Perhaps identical wording in two emails arriving four minutes apart had been coincidence.

Either way, no one from Falcon Associates was heading overseas. "Anything big happening in New York during the next two weeks?" I asked Cristina and Dr. Singh. But in New York, everything is big, every day. Rush hour is big. The UN is big. Stadiums. Wall Street. Deals. Protests. The only small things are restaurant portions, but the bills for the meals remain oversized.

"The president is scheduled to visit," said Cristina.

"New York Marathon," said Dr. Singh. "Halloween."

"We're guessing," said Cristina.

"Are we still going to see Detective Benish?" asked Nageena.

"Unfortunately," I said, leading her downstairs, toward the garage, "Yes."

She touched my elbow. I felt the pressure of slim fingers beneath my shirt. "If what you say is true, Mr. St. Johns, if someone is trying to lure you out of the country, you could be targets too," she said.

The city looked dark when the garage door opened. The streetlight outside our building must have broken since last night. A man—big guy, stranger, bald head averted, leather flight jacket—stood leashed to a small dog by a hydrant as I pulled into the street. In the rearview mirror, the dog watched the Prius head away. The guy smoked a cigarette.

The subway was out as a mode of transportation tonight, as was a cab, Uber, or transport on foot. My grandmother had installed Pope-mobile thick windows in the brownstone, but the windows separating Nageena and I from the world at the moment were only quarter-inch glass.

Benish's precinct house lay a mile and a half away on 100th Street. As we passed West End Avenue, headlights fell in behind us. Yellow left beam. White right beam.

I rounded a corner. So did the headlights.

"You said before that you got Brian Benish arrested when you were kids. What happened?" Nageena asked me.

"Actually, I got us both arrested," I began.

THIRTEEN

The most humiliating day of my life began on my sixteenth birthday with a present: two new one-hundred-dollar bills from Grandy and Eve.

"I wanted to impress a girl in my class, so I took a bunch of friends for treats after school," I told Nageena, making a left turn off Eighty-Fourth Street onto Broadway.

Yellow headlight and white beam kept pace behind.

"We were private school kids, mostly wealthy. Brian was a scholarship student. His mom worked in the cafeteria. His dad was in prison on drug charges. Brian liked the same girl I did, Laticia Hayes. He was always hanging around her. The only reason he came along that day was because she was there. I chose the most expensive after-school place I knew. Zabar's. I announced, *Hey everybody! Grab whatever you want, and I'll pay!*"

I passed through a yellow light on Eighty-Ninth Street. The mismatched headlights behind me ran the red as I remembered the scene on the day of the arrests. Busy Zabar's, the outdoor tables, the specialty foods, and me acting like royalty, paying for all the pecan-raisin biscotti, prosciutto paninis, iced lattes, and Dove bars my friends could eat.

I made a couple of quick turns to see if yellow headlight and white beam would stick behind us. In the rearview mirror, they idled two cars back at a red light.

"Brian's father went to prison, and he still became a cop?" observed Nageena. "Interesting."

The Twenty-Fourth Precinct sits between Amsterdam and Columbus Avenues on One Hundredth Street. As I rounded Ninety-Ninth, the car behind us peeled off. A white van took its place. *Probably nothing to worry about, but keep watching.* In my mind, I was sixteen, king of my group, eating ice cream with Laticia Hayes, cracking jokes, snickering with the other kids when a red Mercedes pulled up on Broadway and double-parked. Short, fat State Senator Ray Rambone got out and waltzed into Zabar's to stock up on bagels and lox for his weekly drive to Albany. The guy was a jerk. He was always hounding Eve for campaign donations.

"I realized that he'd dropped his car key on the sidewalk, and the Mercedes was blocking an old lady from getting out. That's when I had the idea. 'Let's take his car,' I announced. Not steal it. Just move it around the block. Laticia loved it. I told everyone, 'It'll be hilarious, Rambone will come out and his car will be gone. He'll freak out!'"

"Brian got involved?"

"He saw if he didn't go, he'd lose points with Laticia. He followed me into Rambone's car."

I remembered slipping into the Mercedes, filled with hilarity as I put the car in drive. Brian had gone white. With his dad in prison, he knew exactly what the consequences would be if things went wrong. But I felt great. I was the big hero, instigator, leader.

"I pulled the car around the corner and double-parked eighty yards away from where we started, grinning like a fool."

"Let me guess. The cops showed up," Nageena said.

All these years later, I still felt shame burning in my chest at the memory of the siren sounding. "The squad car was just sitting there. Grandy and Eve bailed me out and insisted on doing the same for Brian. They paid his legal bills too. They were furious. My defense to them, 'We just took the car for a minute,' fell on deaf ears."

"Bad luck," Nageena said. "Kids do dumb things."

"Bad decision. Rambone went on TV to address 'a plague of car theft' in Manhattan. Eve called every politician she knew for help, but none of her magic worked. Rambone loved that car. He made the theft a campaign issue. Our lawyer said we were going down for grand larceny, no way out."

I remembered the morning of the trial, my shame and fear exploding at the sight of Manhattan's Criminal Courthouse. Eve had taken me there as a spectator previously. But on that day, I was the criminal walking up those long steps, with my grandparents, past Rambone, who was addressing reporters, calling Brian and I thugs. I didn't know whether the law-and-order judge assigned to our case had been arranged by the Senator or was one more piece of bad luck.

"Our lawyer told me, in the hallway outside the courtroom, 'The only question is how bad it will be.' I could see Rambone down the hall with more reporters. The *Post* had called him dumb for double parking and losing his key, which didn't help. I heard my lawyer hiss 'stop' as I walked toward the Senator. But I had an idea. I was remembering that Rambone was a decorated Marine vet from Vietnam."

"You spoke to him?" Nageena asked.

"I said, 'Sir, what if I volunteer to join the Marines? I'm sixteen now, but I promise to join up when I graduate.' I told him, 'I was wrong to take your car. I want to make amends. At least let Brian go. It wasn't his idea.'"

Even now, my gut clenched as I remembered Rambone growing thoughtful as I begged, inside, *Go for it.* He eyed the journalists, deciding whether my offer would satisfy them. I told Rambone, 'If I go back on my word, prosecute me later. You're right about discipline, sir. I'll get it in the Marines.'"

Nageena and I had arrived at the Twenty-Fourth Precinct, a brick two-story building across from a library and next to a fire house. Blue-and-white squad cars, officers' private vehicles, and towed-in wrecks lined both sides of the block.

"Rambone asked me if Brian would join up too. He wanted a two-man package. If he got that, he'd go along."

"Did Brian do it?"

"He started crying when I told him. He didn't want to be a Marine. He finally offered to enlist in the navy."

"The charges were dropped?"

"Yes. But Brian hated everything about it—taking the car, Eve's help, the Navy, all of it. Even his father, in prison, called Brian a fool. His parents were ashamed."

"Did you hate being in the Marines?"

"They straightened me out, and I met Oscar there."

"What happened to the girl you and Brian fought over?"

"She's a judge now in juvenile court. Funny, huh?" I said as we walked into the station. I saw headlights rounding the corner. One looked yellow. One looked white.

"What happened to Senator Rambone?" Nageena asked me.

"He died in a car crash on the New York Thruway, two years later, a bagel in his mouth."

FOURTEEN

At first, Brian Benish could not have been more cordial. He escorted us to the detective squad room on the second floor. He seated us at a corner desk, away from other cops, so we could more easily talk. He brought us coffee. He apologized for not getting back to us earlier when we tried to reach him on the phone.

"I was on Long Island, Dr. Singh. My mother's in a rest home there. I took a day off."

Maybe this time he'd leave his animus toward me out of it, I hoped. Maybe we could help each other, for a change.

"I'm glad you came away unhurt, Dr. Singh," he said.

Brian was a former high school linebacker; broad-shouldered, soccer ball stomach, weightlifter thighs, bristle mustache, oddly small feet. Off duty, he coached his daughter's soccer team, volunteered at church fundraisers, and, at Christmas, was a driver for Meals on Wheels. He was a civic-minded, by-the-book detective, but not a creative thinker.

"I've been in close contact with Detective Ingbar at the Thirty-Fourth," Brian told Nageena. "We're doing everything we can to help. I feel for your daughter. I'm a dad myself."

Unlike Falcon, his tone implied. His corkboard showed photos of Brian spending off-hours with his three young children. Ingbar's report on last night's shooting lay on the desk as Nageena told her story. When she reached the gunfire part, he began tapping the eraser end of a pencil on his desk. Tapping is a Brian tell.

Uh oh, I thought.

"Have you considered alternative theories, Dr. Singh?"

"Like what?"

Reaching into his desk, Brian produced a hardback copy of *See No Evil* by Dr. Nageena Singh. I knew she'd written the book, but I hadn't seen it yet. The pencil tapped a photo on the back cover: Nageena sitting in a club chair in a private library, wearing a fitted black suit, stylish glasses on, posture terrific, slender hands in her lap.

"What if Abani's not the target? What if it's you?" Brian asked.

She paled. "What?"

"You've defended some pretty bad people, Dr. Singh."

She sat up straighter, clearly familiar with this line of reasoning. "I don't *defend* them," she replied stiffly. "I work to get them institutionalized."

"Some people think that's the same thing," he said.

I had a feeling that *some people* included Brian. Truth was, me too. Brian addressed us both now, listing possibilities. "A client who holds a grudge. A victim's family member. A wacko who blames you."

I picked up the book. The author bio described Nageena as "one of the country's foremost forensic psychologists, who has testified in high profile cases, including the Hannah Haverford kidnapping and Guantanamo terrorism trials. Her controversial work has been hailed by mental health advocates and condemned by those who favor stricter law enforcement."

Dr. Singh looked horrified at Benish's suggestion. "If I'm the target, why go after my daughter?"

"To make you suffer," Brian said, at least not adding, *like they did.*

I turned to the author's introduction in the book and began skimming. "When I was nine years old in India, I watched a mob hack my parents to death because we were Sikhs. An uncle in New Jersey raised me and my older brother, Hari. Hari was my hero. He comforted me when I cried and defended me at school from bullies. But when Hari reached his twenties, he changed, suddenly filled with hate. He speech grew rambling. He attacked a man on a bus. He was hospitalized with schizophrenia, and I realized that what the public calls evil can be an imbalance in the brain. I've dedicated my life to stopping this misconception and helping people like Hari."

Jesus, I thought, eyeing the composed woman sitting two feet away, envisioning a screaming mob in some far-off village, swords waving, dust swirling. *She watched her parents murdered. She lost her husband to suicide. Now someone is trying to kill her kid.*

Nageena was saying, "But if it's about me, what about the murder Abani saw? Why kill Desmond Hodge?"

"The simplest explanation is usually the best," Brian replied. "Abani didn't see a driver because she was watching Hodge. The driver knows that your daughter goes to the tennis courts. He parks and waits, intending to run her over or kidnap her. Hodge shows up by accident. Hodge gets hit instead. The driver backs up and retries for Abani."

"And misses twice?" I asked with skepticism. But I was thinking, is it possible?

Nageena's breathing came in short, agitated bursts. "I get emails sometimes. Ugly things. Threats. But no one's ever actually tried to hurt us."

Benish sat back and nodded, as if to say, now they have.

Brian asked her to provide copies of the hate messages she'd received. He assured her that he and Detective Ingbar would do all they could to protect both Singhs. He explained that there were still "several other possibilities" that they were following up on.

"Be patient. I know it's tough. Tips and whispers, can't chase 'em all," he added.

Brian turned to me like a teacher explaining a problem to a slow student. "I'm glad you were there to help her, Bird."

Bird.

"Speaking of that, Brian, they need protection."

"Of course! I'll arrange for a car to be posted outside your apartment tonight, Dr. Singh."

"But Abani and I are staying with Mr. St. Johns."

The only change in Brian was a slight tightening of his nostrils, a slowdown in breathing, the barest nod.

"So you already have protection," he said.

"She needs more," I urged.

"Let me talk to Captain Lavernius. We're overextended at the moment, but I'll do my best. Bird, I don't need to say it, but I'd appreciate you staying out of our way."

"We're not going to get police protection, are we, Mark?"

I'd told her it was unsafe to return to her apartment, but she'd insisted that Abani needed textbooks for school and that she needed patient files for Zoom sessions. A neighbor had texted her that police were still outside. " It will be safe. I'll be quick," she'd said. I didn't like it.

Outside her bedroom window, crime scene tape outlined a body shape on her patio. Floodlights illuminated the lone forensics tech poking about in a row of shrubs. I shut the blinds. Nageena was throwing items into the suitcase on her unmade bed: red cashmere sweater, lacy bra, Reeboks with bunion holes, rolled-up athletic socks, stuff that on a guy would look worn but somehow, for her, seemed cute.

"No, Nageena, you won't get police protection unless you stay here."

"We're staying with you if the offer is still open. Do you think the target is me, Mark, like Benish said?"

I liked the way she said my name. "It's possible," I said. "But if I had a grudge against you, I'd go straight for you, not your daughter."

"The emails I told Benish about? One came from someone who lost a son in the Wyoming shooting. 'I hope you lose your child too,' it said."

There was little I could say to make her feel better. Brian had been right when he'd said, *tips, can't chase 'em all.* I tried to soothe her. "Look, in any investigation, work gets split up. Brian works one angle. We try another. In a way, we're all a team, Nageena, whether he thinks so or not."

"He didn't talk like we're a team."

"He doesn't get to decide."

She neatly folded away Abani's black leggings, a raglan T-shirt with a "just chill out" logo, jade hoodie, kids' blue jeans, solid colored stuff for mom, patterned pinks for the kid. Orchids. Doggies. Tie-dyed pajamas.

"Hacked to death," I whispered. "Christ."

Nageena crossed the room and padded close, looking smaller without shoes on. One strand of white hair showed in the left eyebrow. A tiny scar showed beneath her lower lip. Her green eyes seemed softer now but no less arresting.

"You're a good person, Mark."

"Fooled you."

"No," she said. "You didn't fool me."

"The ten minutes are up. We have to leave now."

Outside, we pulled away with the suitcases and her laptop. The block looked darker. Streetlights were on. The squad car that had been stationed here when we'd arrived had gone.

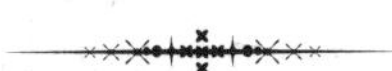

Oscar and Abani's dinner tasted fantastic, the *štruckli* gooey and succulent, the *ćevapi* a hot sweet mix, the apple pie deep and sugary. Oscar announced at the table, "Abani is a future five-star chef."

She giggled. It was good to hear her laugh.

No business talk allowed during eating, but while Nageena and I had been gone, Oscar and Cristina had locked the house into defense mode. An email alert had gone out to a half dozen neighborhood teens who we call "the Poe Street Irregulars." For ten dollars an hour, they observe anything out of the ordinary in the area—that is, when they're not on their phones.

Weapons in the gun closet were loaded. Floodlights out back would be on all night. Roof cameras were recording a forty-eight-hour loop. Nageena and Abani now knew the seven-digit combination to the safe room, but not the safe.

Nageena had phoned Abani's teacher for homework assignments. After dinner, Cristina showed Abani self-defense moves. Oscar gave Abani the film poster tour, grinning when she asked questions about background items depicted, like the rotary phone in *Dial Me A Murder* (What are those holes for?), or the typewriter in *Hitler's Correspondent* (Where's the printer for it?).

By ten, she was asleep. By eleven, my partners were downstairs in their apartment. By 11:30, I'd put fresh sheets on my Milo sleeper for Nageena as Abani slumbered in the next room. Soft jazz, Earl Klugh's version of "Living Inside Your Love," played on Spotify. It turned out Nageena was a Klugh fan too.

"What's your plan for tomorrow, Mark?" She'd changed into cotton pajamas with a moose logo and wore one of my robes.

"I need to ask Bradley Kranepool about Desmond Hodge."

"He'll talk to you even after you fired him?"

"Nobody can resist my charm."

My terrycloth robe looked large on her. Her small hands poked from the sleeves like a monk's. She was propped on a pillow on my couch, bare feet up on a cushion.

"Your partners are nice, Mark. Oscar's a great cook."

"So is your daughter."

"Is Cristina really a black belt?"

I sighed. "I wouldn't make her mad if I were you."

She regarded me intently. Was she giving me a shrink look? Wondering about my feelings for Cristina? Psychologists! She was analyzing me! *Stop looking at me like that!* I thought.

"You believe Abani now? That the car drove itself?"

"Well, I'm the impossible detective, right? So, let's leave the obvious theories to Brian for the moment and be open to all ideas. Your turn. Can I ask you something?"

"You want to know why I wrote that there's no such thing as evil."

"Yes."

"You want to know if I still believe that after what happened to Abani."

I shrugged.

She ran her fingers through her hair, scattering loose strands across her forehead. Only a few feet separated us on the couch.

"Mark, I was nine the day my parents died. We went to the market to buy fresh spices. We were going to make a birthday dinner for my Mom. But that day was also the anniversary of Indira Gandhi's assassination by two of her Sikh guards."

"The mob came because of that?"

"I heard them before I saw them. There was a sense of the air thickening. A vibration. A holy man had set them off. I was terrified."

"You hid."

"Kids crawl under a table and think they're invisible. But it worked at first. When the door broke in, I thought the people attacking us would be strangers. But they weren't. They were people I'd known for years. My parents were passed around, in the air, screaming. I saw a sword. A neighbor pulled me out from under the table. I thought she was going to hurt me, but she hid me. The faces…I thought I knew them…but they were different, ugly. Everyone was screaming."

"The others never saw you?"

"Someone must have. But they left. I heard them outside, getting farther away." Her voice was a whisper. "My parents had been," she said, shuddering, "torn apart."

"And that convinced you there's no evil?"

"Of course not," she snapped. "Only later, in the US, when Hari got sick and changed from my sweet brother into one of those people, the hating ones, only then did I understand that I had a choice. It would determine the rest of my life."

"What choice?"

"Something horrible had transformed the people who killed my parents. It was inside my brother now. Was it the true nature of humans? If I decided evil was the real face of people, that would make the rest of my life ugly. I chose not to go forward filled with hate. Hate never gives up. It's always trying to get into you. It waits for an opening. It finds ways."

"Sometimes you need hate."

She stood and began rearranging bedding. The sense of intimacy between us was gone. The face regarding me now was her professional one, unreadable.

"I don't know, Mark. I'm tired."

At 2 a.m., a text dinged on my phone, coming from a Poe Street Irregular. *There's a red car on the block!!! Oh, sorry, it's an Uber. It picked up Mister Jackson and it's driving away.* At 3 a.m., unable to sleep, I was googling self-driving cars. At 3:30, alarms went off and the backyard floodlights went on, and everyone was up. The raccoon must have come from Riverside Park. It eyed me from Oscar's vegetable garden, then slipped over the fence as quickly as the attackers at Nageena's apartment last night.

There are 2.2 million registered cars in New York City, Google informed me, but it failed to mention how many came with self-driving features. The state ran an "autonomous vehicle testing unit," I learned, through which corporate or scientific applicants could apply for permission to test AVs, which were otherwise illegal in New York unless a human being sat at the wheel.

This was useless. *I need to speak to a person.* With dawn approaching, I stood at the window, bleary, eyeing parked cars on Eighty-Fourth Street as if they were aware. I thought, *Rocket ships lift into space and come back to land in a designated spot without humans inside. Why not a car?*

A lone cyclist, a late night or early morning fitness addict, shot past.

I nodded off and in two hours awoke, excited, from a dream of Cristina and Nageena, but could not remember what had happened in it—not what I'd done, not what choices I'd made, not what consequences I'd faced in the steamy cauldron of unconsciousness.

It was time to find Bradley Kranepool.

Time to see if the impossible could be true.

FIFTEEN

Bradley Kranepool lived in a penthouse atop one of the needle-thin high-rises lining Central Park South, where football stars and Chinese oligarchs own apartments. Upper floors sway in winds like cruise ships in typhoons, doormen dress like Czarist generals, and an hour's fee in the parking garage equals round trip airfare to Miami.

"I think Cristina's interested in another guy," Oscar said, pausing on the sidewalk outside the revolving door.

The morning had started badly all around. Everyone at Falcon's Nest had been pissed off since breakfast, a delayed reaction to yesterday's attack and to some new defensive restrictions in place.

Why can't I have my phone? Why can't I see my friends? That had come from Abani. Spared the knowledge that she'd been targeted by killers, she believed she'd witnessed a hit-and-run killing, subway accident, and bungled robbery. "She doesn't need to know the truth as long as we keep her safe," I'd told Nageena. Oscar had burned the pancakes. Cristina had snapped at him when he mentioned that they had to decide soon whether to make an offer on a new apartment. Feeling a foot touch mine under the table, hopefully by accident, I'd jerked away. The foot had not returned, but now Oscar, on the street, made a fist as if squeezing another guy's throat—the guy he had a feeling Cristina was seeing.

"Cristina? Fooling around? Impossible," I said.

"You're the one who always says nothing is impossible."

"She's committed to you, Oscar. She'd never even look at another guy."

"You're the one who always says trust your feelings."

"She's nervous about the move, I bet. Buying an apartment's a big deal."

Oscar grunted. "First, she wants to move away. Then she doesn't. I wake up, she's staring out the window. 'What are you thinking?' I ask her. '*Nothing!*' We're making love and her lips are moving. I think maybe it's a guy's name."

The only happy voice at the moment came from a radio blaring from a pedicab on Fifty-Seventh Street. "Fifty thousand runners and a quarter million spectators are expected in town for the New York Marathon this coming Sunday! Biggest field in years!"

Flying at 230 miles an hour, a real falcon can reach a ninety-sixth penthouse floor from earth in seven seconds. I required the elevator blocked by a doorman whose name tag read Mauricio and who called Bradley up on the house phone. *Could Mark St. Johns come up?* The stream of invective that poured from the receiver lasted forty-five seconds.

"He said no," Mauricio said, hanging up.

Brian Benish would have produced a badge and gone up anyway. Oscar and I—subject to trespassing charges—offered a fifty-dollar bill instead.

"Are you kidding? I'd lose my job," Mauricio said.

"We'll just wait for him in the lobby," Oscar said.

"Sometimes he stays up there for days."

Mauricio smiled, working the revolving door to allow a resident and her pet corgi to enter, both wearing rain hoodies even though the sun was shining outside. The dog looked sad to leave the street. It looked like it felt stupid in the hoodie.

"This is a life and death situation," I told Mauricio.

"So's my job."

"How about taking a bathroom break for thirty seconds."

"Nope."

"A twelve-year-old child's life is at stake."

"Uh huh."

"Someone tried to kill her."

"Then how come real police aren't here? Why you?"

I held up my phone to show him *Daily News* headlines. "Gun battle in Inwood." I jabbed the photo in his face. "One attacker killed."

Mauricio sighed. At least he was thinking it over. "Inflation just topped six percent," he said.

"A hundred and you'll let us up?"

"No, but I'll tell you where he goes Thursday nights."

I held up two fifties. Mauricio the magician went into action. Viola! Cash disappeared!

"He leaves at ten usually. His driver told me they go to a warehouse in Brooklyn, near water."

"What's there and what's the address?"

"How do I know?"

"That's the best you can do? You know how big Brooklyn is? It's practically surrounded by water."

"You're the detective, not me." Mauricio snorted. "What do you want? I should do your job?"

* * *

"Cristina says she can talk to you," Oscar said, when we got back in the car, starting up again about his love life. "Have you picked up anything weird in her lately?"

"No."

"Are you sure?"

"Let's see what we can learn at Columbia."

* * *

Columbia University is called an Ivy League school, but the term *concrete league* would be more accurate. No grassy quads. Lots of plazas and terraces. Statues, not trees. My adjunct faculty card got us past a guard into Chandler Hall, home of the robotics club. This morning, a half dozen students poked at laptops, drank coffee, and rubbed red eyes due to whatever they'd smoked or imbibed last night. No *Star Wars* type robots lurched around in the basement room. "TRY THE NASA BIG IDEA CHALLENGE," read a poster on a corkboard. "Help us design lunar infrastructure to enhance prospecting on the moon!"

I love students. They're interested in things. They answer questions openly. They're eager about what they do.

"Does anyone here work on self-driving cars?" I asked.

"I do," one kid said, introducing himself as Ralph, a sophomore. Tall, Asian, handsome, he wore an oversized Columbia hoodie, black jeans, and white Reeboks.

"Do you test self-driving cars on the street?"

"Are you crazy? We don't work on real cars. It's all virtual."

"Is anyone in the city using real autonomous cars?"

"It's illegal, dude. Dangerous. They'd risk jail."

"Maybe a corporation," I suggested, pointing to a half dozen corkboard notices advertising robotics competitions sponsored by top automobile, aviation, and investment firms.

"Nothing involving actual driving. There's a bill in the state senate to allow it in a couple years. Not now," Ralph said.

"We're more interested in right now. Which cars out on the street come with driverless options?"

"Tesla's the main one, but Audi, Ford, Mercedes, and BMW also contain features."

"Features like full self-driving? The works? I'm talking about the ability to go out for a few hours…no apparatus visible on the roof, like Waymo cars in San Francisco. No way from the outside, if you're not close up, to tell if the thing is moving by itself, without a driver."

"There's nothing like what you're saying. Teslas are the most advanced, but you have to pay extra for the top features. And you can't tell from outside a Tesla whether it has the capability or not. And even then, the cars can't do the things you're talking about. The best you get is level three. Level five is a couple years away. That would be full automatic, no human control. Sit back. Sleep. Read *War and Peace*. Whatever."

"Are you sure you haven't heard about a test model out there somewhere, pushing the envelope?"

Ralph looked from Oscar to me, shrewdly. "Why are you asking these questions?" he said.

Hearing I was a private detective perked them all up. When I said we represented a twelve-year-old who'd witnessed a hit-and-run murder, their eyes widened. When I added that the kid insisted that an autonomous car did it, three of three students lost interest.

"Can't happen," said Ambrose, a chubby white kid wearing a US Open pullover, a rising phoenix tattoo on his wrist.

"Not possible," said Vanessa, a short, pimpled girl with straight black hair, torn jeans and a university hoodie. "That's movie stuff, not real. Not yet at least."

Ralph disagreed. "What if a Tesla got hacked?"

I perked up as Ralph crossed the room to rummage in a desk, top drawer, nope, side drawer, nope, lower left drawer, *aha*! He pulled out a glossy brochure. Tesla!

"Elon calls Teslas 'laptops on wheels.' Laptops can be hacked."

Elon. Like they were on a first name basis.

"David Colombo found a way to use remote control in '22," Ralph continued, waving the brochure. "He won Elon's hackathon."

"Hackathon?" I asked.

"Elon sponsors annual contests to see if people can break into his systems. Elon pays you to find flaws."

Vanessa snorted. "Hacking is one thing. Full control is another. Even if someone did manage to hack it, to get it to do what you're talking about, they'd have to change the whole mission plan of the vehicle."

"And override instructions not to hit a person," Ken, a soft-looking white kid in a yarmulke added, nodding.

"How would the hacker get in? Theoretically?" I asked.

They started arguing about spoofing attacks, whatever those were, then jamming attacks and something called *meaconing* attacks, which I gathered involve intercepting GPS signals.

Replay attacks could fool a GPS receiver into misconstruing its position or time, Ralph explained.

"*Synacktiv* cracked Teslas and won $350,000," Ralph insisted, standing his ground.

"They drove the car around full automatic?" I asked him.

"No. But they got into the infotainment network."

"You're telling me if someone hacked into a car…"

"Big if," Vanessa said, shaking her head.

"If," I continued, envisioning the streets along the Upper West Side and dozens of Teslas parked there. And not just Teslas. Audi A8s had some autonomous ability, the kids had said. Mercedes S Class sedans too. Ten minutes ago, they'd all been doubtful. Now they were considering possibilities at least.

Like I said, I love talking to students.

"So, bottom line, *if*. It's conceivable?" Oscar asked.

"Malicious alteration of programming code," Ralph summed up, "is not probable, but conceivable. Every month, there are new advances. Everyone thinks we're three years away from stuff, but," he added, "people always say five years, three years, ten years. It's just guesses. One day, out of the blue, whaddaya know, it's here."

I called Brian Benish as soon as we left the building. For once, he picked up, even on the second ring. He sounded friendly, which could only mean he believed himself to be making progress on his "alternative theory." I asked him whether he could check theft reports on neighborhood Teslas and other cars with autonomous features on the day Abani witnessed the hit-and-run attack.

"You're still talking about the car?" He sounded relieved that I wasn't considering his theory.

"Humor me."

"I tried that in high school. Look what happened."

"Get over it," I said.

"I'll check with stolen vehicles, Bird."

Bird.

"I'll get back to you."

Yeah, right, I thought, clicking off.

I called Detective Ingbar at the Thirty-Fourth and asked the s ame favor.

"I'll get right on it," he said.

Oscar double-parked on Broadway while I ran into Virgil's BBQ to pick up our lunch order for the house and for the Poe Street Irregulars: trash ribs and train wreck fries and beer-battered onion rings. Cheddar cheese grits for me. Crispy fried chicken sandwich for Cristina. We had seven hours to go before trying to find Bradley Kranepool in Brooklyn. At least we were making progress. My better mood evaporated when I got into the car.

"I'm going to talk to Cristina about it," Oscar said. "I'll say, we're always honest with each other. Whatever's bothering you, I want to know."

"Maybe," I suggested, appetite fading, "she's working a problem out for herself. Give her time."

"You don't know what it's like, knowing there's something she's not telling me."

Yes, I do, I thought.

The spicy smells emanating from the Virgil's bag had deteriorated from appetizing to nauseating. The phone rang. CRISTINA, the screen read. All I needed was the truth coming out in the car. Riverside Drive hosts a parade of memorials to New York dead. Grant's tomb. Veteran's Monument. Fallen firefighter monument.

I wondered what my memorial would look like when Oscar finished with me.

"Falc! Oscar!"

Cristina sounded frantic. I heard Nageena in the background, on another phone, her tone high and strident, but too far away to make out words. Whatever was happening, it was going to be bad.

"Abani's gone!" Cristina cried.

SIXTEEN

Autumn light was waning at 3 p.m. Shadows disappeared as the sky went grey. Neighbors on Edgar Allan Poe Street were setting up for Halloween, two days from now—laying out plastic skeletons and red-eyed ghouls on stoop steps. At Falcon Associates, we usually display a full-sized Styrofoam Eve created by the Hammer Film publicity department for 1952's *Vampire of Sunset Boulevard.*

Putting up decorations would have to wait.

"Gone! She's gone!"

Nageena and Cristina had checked every room in the house. The girl had been acting sullen all morning, they reported. *Why can't I see my friends? Why can't I use my phone? Stop watching me every second!*

"We should have told her the truth last night! She still doesn't know she was the target." That from Oscar.

"I shouldn't have taken her phone away!" Nageena said. But the phone—the bullying on it—had traumatized the kid.

In my office, I ran the afternoon's security footage and *there she was,* pink zip-up jacket and pink sneakers on, quietly closing the front door, turning toward the park angrily, hands thrust in pockets, a walking mass of grief and confusion.

Nageena turned on Cristina. "Why weren't you watching her? I told you I had a Zoom session with a patient."

Cristina shot back, "Why didn't you cancel your precious session for your daughter's sake?"

They weren't angry at each other, just themselves. On screen, a blue van cruised past, its occupants invisible. Everything out there looked suspicious now. On screen, a stranger—male, heavy, white—hurried west in the direction Abani had gone fifteen seconds before.

"Maybe she went to visit a friend."

Brian Benish was speaking, on the phone with Nageena.

"None of her friends have heard from her," Nageena replied.

"Is there a special place Abani likes to go?"

Brian explained with sympathy that he could not yet call an Amber Alert—a national warning to locate missing children. "She walked off by herself, Dr. Singh. No witnesses saw an abduction. Rules are clear. Alerts get delayed until a search eliminates other possibilities."

"You won't help us?"

"I'll get officers out there but," he sighed, "we're shorthanded. There's a situation on Amsterdam Avenue. Big fire. It would be helpful if you provided details. What was she wearing? Any identifying features? Height? Weight? That red knapsack?"

"Pink."

Over the phone, I heard the scratching of a pencil. "Abani is four foot six," Nageena said. "Straight black hair. Pink band on the smart watch."

Brian asked if the girl had a tattoo. These days, so many people have tattoos that "no tattoos" counts as an identifying mark.

"What about birthmarks, Dr. Singh?"

Nageena winced. To envision a birth mark, a parent imagines a child at the beach, in a bathtub, donning pajamas at bedtime, a tiny life at a vulnerable time.

"Oh God," muttered Nageena.

Brian asked, "Can you speak a little louder, please?"

"Freckles. A circle of freckles on her left hip."

Nageena was tearing up. "When she was little, I would touch them when I bathed her. Stars, I called them. Here's your nose star. Your ear star. This one is your little finger."

"Stars," Brian repeated.

"Abani constellations."

Benish spoke soothingly, but you can't soothe truth away. "Can you send me photos of her, please, Dr. Singh?"

"You'll find her, right?"

"We'll do our best."

I sent an email blast to the Poe Street Irregulars, including a photo of Abani. *Check the stores. Check the subway stations. Call if you see her. Get out there now.*

Cristina had her arm around Nageena. We'd spread a map of Riverside Park over my desk, showing the thin green strip stretched along the river, four miles north to south. Forested areas. Piers. Playgrounds. Public bathrooms. Boat basin and bike paths and dog runs.

"She's probably blowing off steam, walking around, honey," Cristina told Nageena.

"We're great at finding people," Oscar added. "Mark is more bloodhound than falcon."

"Oscar and I will head south," Cristina said. "You," she told Nageena, "go with Mark."

We headed toward the tennis courts on the Vespa. The park whizzed by at street level, where its rock wall boundary ran along Riverside Drive. But below that were multiple levels, including a busy promenade and river walk, both invisible to us. I could only imagine what scenes Nageena was fighting off in her head. Hundreds of people were out.

School was over for the day, so lots of kids passed. Frisbee players. Roller skaters. Nannies walked baby carriages. Nageena clutched my chest so hard I could feel her heartbeat through my jacket. *Abani likes to go to the tennis courts. She goes when she's upset. She's upset now, so she'll go there*, I told myself.

Ahead, I glimpsed a pink jacket. Abani! No, not Abani.

Same jacket. Different girl.

SEVENTEEN

Where the hell is Doctor Zisk? thought Kendrick Rainey.

Kendrick sat nervously on a bench in J. Hood Wright Park, by the Hudson River, seven blocks from Columbia Presbyterian Medical Center. The small grassy recreation area was mostly deserted. He could see the span of the George Washington Bridge to the west, and the mini "Little bridge by the big bridge" playground fifty yards away. With relief, he fixed on a tall, slim white man walking toward him, shoulders back, stride long. Even from a distance, the man seemed annoyed.

The man sat down on the same bench, as far as possible from Kendrick. Close up, he was collegiate looking, in his early forties. Lavender knit shirt beneath white V-neck sweater. Khaki painter's pants. Ivy League haircut, short on the sides, longer on top. "Are you really from a pharmaceutical company?" he demanded with a high pinched voice.

"Of course, Dr. Zisk." Kendrick smiled.

"Then you must know what we're dealing with," Zisk snapped. "H7N9 is more lethal than Covid, especially in a modified state. If it ever escaped a lab…"

Kendrick patted the man's bony shoulder. "It won't. We want to create a vaccine. To help people, not hurt them."

"I still don't understand how you found out I was working on it to start with."

You have no secrets from the Lord, Kendrick thought.

Kendrick pulled a stapled copy of a printed report from his rear pocket. "Federal Select Agent Program Suspension of Registration," he read out loud. "You're the one who cut corners, endangered things, skirted safety rules. The feds shut you down, but you kept going anyway, started your work up elsewhere."

"Where did you get that? That's an internal government document. You're not supposed to have that!"

Kendrick flipped pages. "Dangerous errors in the operating system. Lack of properly trained talent. Two escaped animals reported."

Zisk looked as if he had eaten something unpleasant. "Nobody got sick," he insisted. "Any vulnerabilities were corrected."

"Faulty gasket on a safety room door."

"It was replaced."

"Manipulation of a select agent outside a biological safety cabinet, Dr. Zisk."

"Bureaucrats!" the man hissed. "All they know how to do is tell other people what to do."

"Well, *we* use the strictest precautions at our lab," Kendrick assured Zisk confidently. "Masks and proper air flow. Security scanners for access. Mandatory protocols. We've never had an accident. The virus will be safe once you hand it over. We want to help people, like you do. To do good."

"But I made it, not you," Zisk hissed.

"You took the money. You paid your debts. Now you owe us." Kendrick said, more harshly. Up until now he'd been civil with this man. *That just ended*, he thought.

Sweat collected at Zisk's scalp. Twenty feet off, two women pushing baby carriages walked toward them, caught up in conversation, laughing. Zisk's nasal, upper-class New England accent came out so low it was almost a whisper.

"How did you even find out about me?" Zisk demanded.

"A higher power."

"Well, I changed my mind. I won't do it," Zisk said, like a petulant six-year-old. "I don't know why I ever agreed to help you."

"You should have thought of that before making that twenty thousand dollar bet on the Mets."

Kendrick felt the phone buzz in his left pocket, God was calling, probably listening to this. Kendrick fought off a wave of dizziness. He needed to make the problem go away and not come back.

Kendrick sighed, reached into his pocket and, one by one, laid out photographs on his lap. The first showed a smiling teenage girl, in a one piece bathing suit, at an outdoor swimming pool. The next showed Zisk and a woman who resembled the girl in an airport. The third showed the girl in a high school graduation gown, smiling, proudly holding a rolled diploma.

God had provided the photos.

Zisk buried his face in his hands.

Kendrick made his voice more reasonable. "Look, one quick trip down the elevator, doctor. Fifteen minutes, all done. I know you're upset, but in the end, does it make a difference who gets credit if the result is a cure? Some of your samples got compromised, you'll say. You threw them out. Experiments fail all the time."

Zisk's resistance collapsed. "You'll leave me alone after this? And my family?"

"I promise."

Kendrick watched the arrogant asshole walk back toward the medical center, taking shorter steps now, and looking hunched over.

Kendrick did not trust Zisk but at least could now report progress to the Lord. His phone was vibrating again. Kendrick pulled the unit out and clicked accept. Sure enough, God demanded, "Where were you?"

Kendrick started to explain that he'd been calming the scientist. But the Lord didn't seem to care about Zisk at the moment. The Lord had more important things on his mind.

"The girl is in Riverside Park," the Lord told Kendrick. "Get your people over there and bring her to me, now!"

EIGHTEEN

Dusk.

Abruptly, park lamps switched on. Wan globes of light glowed atop iron poles situated every twenty yards along the riverfront, replicas of models that, back in 1911, illuminated women wearing wide-brimmed hats and ankle-length dresses, men in trousers featuring the first machine-made pleats.

Have you seen the girl in this photo?

In New York, even disappearances constitute a form of competition. Worried about a missing loved one? Join the line. Posters taped to poles in the park begged passers-by for help. *My Mom wandered off. Our lost cat Edmund is gone.*

The Poe Street Irregulars had not located Abani. Neither had police cruising the Upper West Side. Nageena and I zipped along the river walk on the Vespa, its headlight picking out a last random jogger. But two people weren't enough to carry out a real search. We might pass right by Abani if she was one level up, wandering on the promenade, or on a bench, or gazing disconsolately down at the soccer fields.

We buttonholed the few people still in the park. *Have you seen my daughter?*

Call us at this number if you do.

A siren whooped behind the Vespa. I slowed, feeling Nageena's fingers dig into my chest. Bathed in headlights, two officers ambled toward us, the shorter one female and Black; the taller, lean one white and mustached, his shirtsleeves rolled to show muscled biceps. I looked for the form of a twelve year old girl in the car behind them but saw nothing. The officers weren't smiling.

This is going to be bad, I thought.

"You're not supposed riding that thing in the park," white cop told me, jerking his thumb at the Vespa.

"What?"

"A scooter's illegal here. Can I see your license, sir?"

It was a traffic stop? I swallowed a scream. A real detective would have produced a badge and gotten cooperation. I pulled out a wallet instead. Nageena, furious, was begging the cops to help us search for Abani instead of issuing a ticket.

Benish, you asshole, I thought. *These two have no idea about Abani. Did you even call an alert at all?*

The male cop strolled off with my ID, going back to their car, taking his time.

The license check wasted seven minutes, then the officer handed back my ID with sympathy. Whomever he'd called had verified that Abani was missing. He was letting us go without giving us a ticket, he said. But we needed to move the Vespa out of the park.

"We don't want anyone to get hurt," he explained.

Hope was fading. The park looked almost empty now. A lone cyclist passed. I chained the Vespa to a light pole up on Riverside Drive. We'd give the area one last check on foot. But I was feeling sick, imagining all the places that no one had searched yet—clumps of bushes, dark areas behind benches, playground bathrooms—a hundred locations, a thousand shadows where a body could be found. *Tomorrow, cops will be all over, looking for the girl.* As we reached an entrance in the rock wall, a young woman emerged from a wooded area, dragging a powerful looking brindled pit bull by a chest leash. The dog, like us, did not want to leave the park.

"Sorry," the woman told us sympathetically, eyeing Abani's photo. "I haven't seen her. I just told her grandparents the same thing."

Nageena froze. "Grandparents?"

The woman nodded in a northerly direction along Riverside Drive, where she'd met Abani's "grandparents" ten minutes ago, she said.

"You must be Nageena," she said.

"They knew my name?"

The woman frowned, because of course grandparents would know a mother's name. "They told me Abani didn't come home from school today. They said her brothers are crazy with worry."

I broke in before Nageena could say anything else and scare the woman away. "Did they say how to contact them?"

"They gave me their phone number. But don't you have it?" The woman's frown deepened as she realized she was alone in the dark with strangers. The dog cocked its massive head, picking up on its master's mood.

"Abani doesn't have any brothers," Nageena snapped.

Mistake. Now the woman was scared. The pit bull issued a low, soft growl. I reached for Nageena's hand and squeezed it, meaning, *be quiet.* But she pulled away, crazy with fear.

"*TELL ME WHAT THEY SAID!* What else did they say?!"

The woman retreated a foot, understanding now that either we or the "grandparents" were lying. She did not want to get involved. She muttered, "I'm sorry but I don't remember anything more. I really hope you find her, but I have to go. My boyfriend will be worried. Attila, snap to it!"

Attila. It figures.

"Can you give us that phone number?" I asked, trying to keep the urgency from my voice.

Attila did not want her to give us anything. The dog's ears were up, chest huffing in and out with low sound like a tank engine. The jaws looked strong enough to chomp a falcon in two.

Pit bull owners insist that their pets are sweet and child friendly. Goebbels claimed the same about Hitler.

The woman let one hand drop from the leash. Only one hand now restrained the dog. "I don't want to get in the middle of a family fight," she said.

Nageena hissed, "Give us the number."

I held out both palms in a plea for peace, noting that Attila was thinking about peace also. A piece of me.

"Call the Twenty-Fourth Precinct," I urged. "Ask for Detective Brian Benish. He'll confirm what we're saying. Please! Help us find a child. Of course her mother is upset. Of course you don't know who to believe. Let us work it out among ourselves."

The woman eyed the far side of Riverside Drive with yearning, like it was the border of Switzerland.

"I know you're confused," I coaxed. "We don't know who those other people are, so we need to talk to them. If you don't want to come closer, just put the paper on the ground and walk off."

That did it. Her hand came out of her jacket pocket. I grabbed the paper off the sidewalk before a breeze could whip it away. I saw a number, a 603 area code, scrawled in neat, looping letters. *Six oh three means New Hampshire.*

Attila led a retreat across Riverside Drive, moving them as fast as marathon runners crossing a finish line I punched in the "grandparents" number.

"Hello?" a sixty-ish sounding male voice said.

"We've found your granddaughter, sir."

"Oh, thank you! Thank you! Jacinta, they found Abani!"

He was a good actor. He sounded truly concerned. I held the phone away from my face and spoke louder, pretending to sound puzzled. "What's that you say, Abani? They're not?"

I pressed the phone back to my mouth. "I'm confused. "She says you're not her grandparents," I said.

In response, a pause. A nervous chuckle. "Oh, that girl," the guy said. "Crazy imagination. We had an argument earlier today and she must still be mad at us. Tell me where you are. We'll come fetch her right now."

I hesitated. *Make him sweat.* I was thinking that first, a couple had followed Abani into the subway. Then two professionals had tried to break into Nageena's apartment. Now two more. *How many people are we dealing with here?*

"Where are you?" Abani's phony grandpa repeated, this time more urgently. They'd be rushing now, concerned that we believed Abani. "Of course we're her grandparents. You're where? Good, you're close! Her Oma and I are only two blocks away! We'll be there in a minute!"

"Go back to the house and wait, Nageena."

"No."

"This may be dangerous."

"Then you'll need help."

I moved my H&K from my waistband to my jacket pocket. I speed dialed Oscar and Cristina, but they were too far north to help. I punched in Brian's number as Nageena eyed a pile of severed branches by the curb, left by tree cutters for removal. She pulled a long, knobby stick from the pile. *That ought to help against guns*, I thought.

"Nageena, I really wish you'd go." My call to Benish went to voicemail. *Figures.*

Nageena hissed. "There they are!"

Two figures had appeared up the block in the lamplight, hurrying toward us. My throat had gone dry, a pulse roared in my head. I told Nageena, "Stand beside me so they think Abani is behind us. Look, the good part is, if they're looking for her, it means they don't have her yet."

She was breathing like a horse and trembling as we eyed the approaching couple: a tall, thin white guy wearing a dark ball cap and running shoes, and a petite, grey-haired woman in an ankle-length dress. I was surprised. *They're old.* After the previous attacks, I'd expected professionals, but the man looked frail. The woman, bowlegged, moved like she needed arch support. The pair looked more suitable for a Florida beach than a kidnapping.

I watched their hands to make sure they remained visible. I put my hand into my pocket, felt my gun.

The woman's voice floated out of the darkness, warm and loving, like a grandmother's. "Abani? Dear? Come out! We've been worried about you!"

They were slowing, realizing Abani wasn't with us. "She ran into the park," I called out to them to keep them moving as we headed toward them too.

The woman hesitated, but the guy kept coming. The four of us converged in a circle of lamplight. Traffic hissed past on Riverside Drive. Somewhere in the park, a drunk began singing. The old guy froze, staring into my face.

"You," he said, backing a step.

I didn't know him, but he'd surely recognized me. The woman's hand thrust into a pocket but did not come out. Something dangerous is in there, I thought.

"Do I know you?" I asked.

Only a few seconds had passed; only a few feet separated us. Nageena's self-control collapsed. "Who are you? Who are you people? She's twelve years old! Leave her alone!" she cried.

Mace, I thought, as the canister came out of the old woman's pocket.

Taser, I thought, seeing the four-inch-long electronic box now in the man's shaking hand. The wired prongs shot out but missed me. The guy lurched forward, aiming to press the Taser's metal prongs into my side. If the couple hadn't looked so frail, I would have grabbed my gun earlier.

I avoided the Taser thrust, but safety-wise, this still turned out to be a step too late.

Maybe if Nageena hadn't been shouting, I would have heard the car roll up behind us. Maybe I would have heard a door open or running footsteps in time to turn around. The woman's gaze had moved over my shoulder. I started to turn, but a guided missile crashed into my back, driving me into a parked car. I bounced off. A second blow hammered into my side. I looked up from the ground. Three men were coming at me. The old guy had the Taser. A Japanese guy had a baseball bat. A big bald-headed guy had hands the size of a pro quarterback's. He was smiling and in the lead. He's the one who had hit me. The beating began.

NINETEEN

White car, I thought, rolling left on the sidewalk to avoid a kick. *It's not the silver Honda that followed us before. New Hampshire plate,* I saw, glimpsing Nageena's stick going up, ten feet away, and a stream of mace missing her face, flying over her shoulder.

My pistol had fallen under a car.

The big guy hissed, "Moabite!" Whatever that was.

Still on the ground, I pushed off with my feet to get back, give me room. The three guys were all jostling to get at me, instead of acting as a team. They were a mob, not professionals. I kicked out and made contact between two legs. The big guy doubled over, clutching himself, enabling me to push further back into the narrow space separating two parked cars and force the attackers to come at me one at a time.

Go for the windpipe, neck, nuts, or knees.

Thanks to neighborhood slobs, the street provided former Marines with a variety of weapons. I thrust the broken lip of a discarded vodka bottle at the old guy. I heard retching from the big guy as he stumbled around. The overhead light caught a baseball bat swishing toward my head. I ducked just in time. The Asian guy was small, but the bat was big, and he lifted it high instead of jamming the barrel toward me as a pro would have done. I charged, maneuvering inside the swing, locked his wrists in the crook of my elbows and yanked. He screamed.

"Grandma" was wrestling with Nageena on the sidewalk.

Who the hell are they?

I pulled the old woman off Nageena.

Then the Taser hit.

In Grandy's old films, he'd fight off four attackers at the same time using karate, bazookas, flamethrowers—even a sword once in the duel scene with a mob boss, shot in the medieval armor exhibit at the Metropolitan Museum of Art. In the film, unhurt, he went off after the fight and drank martinis.

Tasers did not exist then.

I was back on the sidewalk, shaking like a holy roller, teeth clanging with more force than a Con Ed drill. An M5 bus rolled past, its riders oblivious. The bat was going up again. This time the guy wouldn't miss. One shoe was off, my left eye ballooning, and there was something sharp and cracked in my mouth. Tasers work by something called "neuromuscular incapacitation," which is tech language for *ten thousand wasp stings.*

"Hit him again, Orsen!" someone cried.

"Father said to bring him, Murakami!"

Thin, high pitched, over the mayhem, I heard a siren.

French sommeliers are experts in identifying wine variations, but they're not as good as New Yorkers when it comes to sirens. There's your ten million decibel Mount Sinai Hospital siren, the Hebrew volunteer ambulance siren loud enough to summon worshippers from Riyadh to Tel Aviv, the fire command vehicle siren, the asshole-on-Seventy-Fifth-Street's vintage Dodge Challenger siren.

What I heard now was a police siren.

I'd been wrong about the bus. A good Samaritan inside it must have called 911. Our attackers poured into their car, screeching off as red pulsing lights materialized two blocks away. Nageena was vomiting on the sidewalk. Traffic on Riverside Drive pulled to the curb, allowing the incoming cops to pass. The squad car shot through a red light and reached us.

It continued past, racing toward a different emergency, and not even in the direction that our attackers had fled, up Seventy-Eighth Street.

Why do I stay in this town?

"What's a Moabite, Nageena?"

"Sounds like something in the Bible."

Nageena and I held onto each other as we limped toward Edgar Allan Poe Street. Taser recovery is almost instantaneous. I'd retrieved my pistol. Blood welled from a rip in her pants. My tongue felt torn, my vision was blurry in one eye, and I heard clicking in my right ankle with each step. My body was a mass of throbbing pain, but I'd suffered less than the amount of damage professionals would have done.

We rounded the corner of Eighty-Fourth Street to be greeted by cheerfully macabre Halloween decorations. A jack-o'-lantern glowed in a window. A bloody mummy, wrapped in bandages, looked the way I felt. I spotted shadow figures on my step, live ones, not displays; a taller, heavy adult and a shorter dwarf type. But Falcon Associates had not erected our holiday scene yet, and our decorations did not include a Hobbit-sized figure.

I heard Nageena gasp, "Abani!"

The hobbit ran down the steps toward us, safe, utterly safe, pink jacket, pink sneakers. The only danger threatening her at the moment was a flopping shoelace.

"Mommy!"

Brian Benish sauntered down the steps more slowly behind her, grinning. *Ta-da!* Smiling like a hero.

"Can you believe it? I found her just sitting on a bench!" announced Brian. "She said she was at a friend's apartment all afternoon. Holy shit, Bird Man! What happened to you?"

TWENTY

"I was angry at you," Abani said. "I'm sorry I freaked everybody out. I told my friend Samantha to say she hadn't seen me when you called."

Falcon Associates, the Singhs, and Benish were debriefing at my dining room table. Brian had arranged for a squad car to sit outside tonight. I'd provided him with the partial license plate number of the attacking car. Our phones kept ringing with neighbors and Irregulars, asking if Abani was unharmed, congratulating us for finding her. A *Daily News* reporter's number flashed on screen. Forget it.

"After I left Samantha's, I just walked around, Mommy."

Mommy.

How can you be angry at a child you've lied to, whether you did it to shield her from danger or not? My body was a mass of bruises beneath bandages Cristina had wrapped after applying hydrogen peroxide and shoving three Tylenols in my mouth. The only one eating Oscar's comfort food was Brian, who was wolfing down last night's leftover arepas.

Abani's sneakers barely reached the floor. From now on, we'd allow her to hear all our talk. Brian produced a handful of mug shots from his brown stretch blazer and spread them out on the table.

"Recognize anyone, Dr. Singh?"

Nageena reached for the photos with hope and put them down with disappointment. "No. Who are they?"

"Bird? Anyone look familiar?"

The faces I observed shared many features, as if they were related; wide-apart eyes, high, thinning hairlines, large ears, small chins. Benish recited names. "We tracked those emails you got, Dr. Singh. You're looking at Harvey Lee Humphrey, Loretta Humphrey, and Nikki, Barney, and Donald Stamaty, cousins, all pissed off that you're defending Ian Ross in Indiana."

He explained to the rest of us, "Ross was the Elkhart, Indiana, shooter. Seven dead. Two of them were named Humphrey."

"I'm not *defending* Ross," Nageena said.

"That's not their opinion."

"Ian Ross is sick and should be institutionalized."

"The Humphrey family seems to think *you* should be dead. The Elkhart police checked on their whereabouts. None are in Elkhart. They're gone," Brian announced. "Maybe they're here."

Abani looked stricken. Maybe it had been a bad idea to let her listen in. Despite all that had happened, Benish was clinging to his alternative theory, that the target all along was Dr. Singh.

I re-examined the photos, one by one. "None of the people who attacked us are in this group, Brian."

Brian shrugged. "Lotta cousins. Big family."

"Brian, the attackers called each other by name. Murakami. Orsen. Any of those on your relative list?"

"They could be friends. You said something about them mentioning a *father.* Father means family."

Abani piped up in a thin voice. "Or a priest, right?"

Maybe letting her stay was a good idea, I thought.

Brian grunted and changed tack. "'Father says get him,' you said he said. Or did he say, *said*? Which exact word did he use?"

"Says. Said. Who cares?" Nageena said.

"*Says* means he's right there with you," Brian theorized. "*Said* means he wasn't. See? Like he'd given them orders before they left."

"Or maybe he called them on a phone after they left," Abani piped up.

I suppressed a smile. The kid had promise. I told her, "Abani, if I'm The Falcon, you know who *you* are now?"

"Who?"

"The Sparrow!"

She beamed. Cristina and Oscar smiled. We had a new member.

"I'm the Sparrow!"

My head hurt. My shoulders hurt. My mouth hurt. I needed sleep, but we were far from finished. "How did they know Abani was missing in the first place?" I mused.

"I alerted a lot of places," Nageena said. "Police. Facebook. X. Classmates. I sent it out a million ways."

"I wasn't missing," Abani insisted. "I knew where I was every minute."

This time, when we ordered her to stay in the house, she bowed her head yes, grudgingly going along. I sweetened the pot. I told her that I'd reconsidered her offer to work for me. From now on, she was on the payroll. But as an employee, she had to follow orders.

"I promise," she grinned.

Brian was starting to lose his pleased look as Abani's gratefulness switched targets from him to me. Was Abani sure, he asked, that she didn't remember anything useful about the hit-and-run car? *Yes*. Really sure? *Yes*. Because sometimes people think they're sure and a memory pops up later and suddenly they…

"I'm *sure*!" Sparrow insisted, reaching for the food.

Cristina looked up *Moabite* on Google. "The term is from the Bible. Moabites were cursed by God after their king put a curse on the Israelites," she told me.

Oscar was trying to track the car that our attackers had used by contacting homeowners who owned security cameras along the street they'd fled down. Maybe he'd spot a license number.

I needed sleep. Lots of sleep. On the way upstairs, I checked my phone, but the only message that looked interesting had come from the handsome student, Ralph, at the Columbia University Robotics club, who'd taken my business card earlier that day. Making one last call couldn't hurt. Ralph answered on the first ring, despite the hour, 11 p.m.

"You said to call if I thought of something, sir."

"Yes?"

"About the cars? Autonomous cars? You know who you should talk to about it? Who really might have answers?"

My hope rose. "Who?"

"Elon."

Elon again. Like I could ever reach the guy. I sighed. "I'll see what I can do."

"If not him, then Bradley. You know, Bradley Kranepool?"

"Yeah. Well, Bradley can be difficult to find."

"Not on a Thursday night."

I remembered Kranepool's doorman's words this morning, which felt like a week ago now. Wearily, I repeated what I'd been told. "He's somewhere in Brooklyn, near water."

"Oh, everyone knows where he goes."

I perked up. My bed suddenly seemed further away.

"Lots of e-ack people go there," Ralph continued. "It's right by the Gowanus Canal. He's there every Thursday by midnight. Want the address?"

No, I thought, *I want to sleep*.

"Yes," I said.

TWENTY-ONE

Travel writers call Venice's Grand Canal earth's loveliest man-made waterway. Others prefer Amsterdam's Reguliersgracht with its bridge of sighs, or the palm-shaded canals of Alleppey, India. St. Petersburg, Russia, offers the Griboyedov Canal. Stockholm boasts the Göta.

New York has the Gowanus, toxic dump ground, rodent mecca, two-mile long cleanup site and graveyard for mobsters and old Maytags.

The cobblestone dead-end street bumped Oscar and I past parked Lexus, Mercedes, BMWs, even a Lamborghini. A line of partygoers streamed beneath streetlights like ants marching from the L Street subway stop four blocks away to a canal-side warehouse, admittance blocked by private security guards.

BOOM...BOOM...BOOM...BOOM...

Inside, a crowd danced to Grimes, singing "Oblivion." The red, green, and blue-colored strobe lights would have produced seizures in epileptics. An enormous banner proclaiming "ACCELERATE OR DIE!" pictured a python restrained by whirling atoms. Smaller posters dangled from a metal ceiling: "NO GATEKEEPERS!" "NO REGULATION!"

"There's Kranepool," Oscar said, pointing at a corner.

Through the mass of gyrating bodies, half of them dancing alone, and mostly men, I glimpsed our former client sitting at a red, scallop-shaped banquette. Whoever hosted events here must have stripped an old wedding hall of Naugahyde seating. Bradley—wearing matching charcoal-colored Loro Piana shirt and slacks, trying to look casual—sat shoulder to shoulder with a plain-faced white woman with orange-streaked braided brown hair. Two guys who looked like Spetsnaz defectors—Italian suits, black turtlenecks—blocked access to the disgraced billionaire at a stanchion barrier. The crew cut topping Tweedledumski jutted forward like an aircraft carrier runway. Tweedledeeski's bowling-ball head featured a tiny goatee.

"No pass you!" said Spetsnaz One, an articulate fellow.

Spetsnaz Two lumbered back from consulting Bradley. "Must to go away!" he said.

The Tweedleski brothers stiffened when I reached into my pocket, and relaxed when I waved a tiny F-drive stick at Bradley from behind the rope, mouthing "evidence."

That did it. His girlfriend didn't look happy, heading out alone toward the bar. When I sat down, Bradley reached for the stick like an infant grabbing for a bottle. *Talk first.* Oscar and the Tweedles were locked in a staring contest. I waved the F-drive back and forth like a hypnotist dangles a pen.

BOOM...BOOM...BOOM...BOOM...

"My file on you, Bradley. Your secret set of books for your crypto business. The DA doesn't have it yet, but once a jury sees it, sees proof of how you tricked investors, you're dead. Two sets of books, Bradley."

"Why should I believe you?"

"Because I know about it. I need your help. I'm trying to save a little girl whose life is in danger."

"What about my life?" he whined, eyeing his bodyguards speculatively. Then the stick. "I can make them take it," he said.

"In front of witnesses? Oscar will record it! Also, it's not the only copy."

"You'll keep quiet about it if I talk to you?"

I wagged the stick.

He blew out air, reluctant to give in to pressure. The act lasted nine seconds. "What do you want?"

"To discuss a former employee of yours."

"I had a lot of those. I don't remember them all."

"How about Desmond Hodge?"

He rocketed to his feet, spilling his drink. The transformation to rage was astounding. "Hodge? HODGE? All my troubles started with him!" he yelled.

The rave going on around us had drawn the kind of crowd that Mannie and Moe had told me about at Inwood Community College. Judging from the posters, I was surrounded by Effective Accelerationists, proponents of the most rapid, unregulated development of artificial intelligence possible, a no-holds race to a future enhanced by the engineers, investors, hackers, and podcasters around us, now trading stories, schemes, and theories—or dancing to Taryn Southern's "Red Lights."

"Desmond promised me his team was close!" Bradley said.

"Close to what?"

"Breaking the last barrier. The holy grail! Then suddenly, 'We're wrong. We didn't figure it right,' Desmond tells me. I had to shut it down after pouring in all that money."

Other people's money, I thought.

"What holy grail," I asked, "were they aiming at?"

"An AI that builds other AIs by itself." His antagonism had disappeared. The dream still made his eyes wispy. My whole body hurt from this afternoon's beating as I concentrated on his words. "The core breakthrough," he breathed. "An AI that writes its own code. Every morning, it wakes up and thinks *what do I need today to make my job easier*? And it goes out into the cyber world and pokes around and does it. It can link to other systems. It can hack. Smarter crypto! New defense! Cancer research! It thinks faster than all the humans put together who filed patents for blockchain technology. It can access all knowledge on the net. It can identify a problem without relying on lesser intelligence to solve it."

Lesser intelligence. I guess that meant us. "What's blockchain technology, Bradley?"

He waved an impatient hand. "Separate links between pieces, without any central ledger or control. But when Desmond told me his team was days away from success, he lied."

"Would this new AI system improve driverless cars?"

"Why stop there? Why stop anywhere? We had the most advanced algorithms. Plus," his eyes gleamed, "we had the one and only Zeus!"

"And Zeus was…?"

"Our supercomputer! Think nine exaflops, ten to the nineteenth power of operations every second."

"Is that more than five?"

Bradley eyed the banners dangling above us. The bar in the corner served a crowd nine deep. At 2 a.m., new arrivals were still coming.

"Imagine reaching ChatGPT nine, even eleven!" Bradley said. "If Desmond hadn't insisted that he was close, I wouldn't have kept investing. It's his fault I'm in this mess. Not mine!"

"Hodge is dead," I said. "He got run over."

"Good!"

I watched Kranepool carefully but saw no tell. Selfishness lit his face but not guilt. His talents so far did not remotely include acting. I did not think he'd been involved in Hodge's killing, at least not yet.

But now another idea was forming, and I liked it even less than the last one. "What if," I said, "Hodge *did* find it, Bradley? Your Chat GBT eleven or whatever it is."

"What?"

"What if he sold it? Or tried to?"

Bradley Kranepool had gone still. "He did?"

"How much would that be worth?"

Bradley laughed wildly. "What would it be worth? It could do things you and I can't imagine. It would accelerate human knowledge to the trillionth degree. It could apply itself to any problem, any damn problem at all. What do you think that would be *worth*?"

"No human supervision, ever?"

"Blockchain means no central authority."

"It could hack into other systems, you said?"

"If it needed something, why not? Every day, something new."

"But wouldn't existing security programs detect it trying to probe into other systems?"

Bradley shrugged. "Security is a cat-and-mouse game. Always a question of which system is the cat. It could write itself a code saying, 'Help me evade security.' Chinese hackers got into Defense Department files for years before being found out. Nothing is impregnable. You're naive."

"You talk like AI is God."

"What did God ever do for me?"

I looked at his clothes, his guards, the bottle of Veuve Clicquot Brut on his table. "Seems like a lot."

"You said you'd give me the file if I answered your questions. Or did you lie about that too?" He smirked. "What happened to your face anyway? Another pissed off client come around, beat you up?"

He was a sad, spoiled boy sitting alone in a corner. He would be going to prison whether I helped the DA or not.

The F-drive I handed him contained all records of his malfeasance that Falcon Associates had dug up. The celebrants around me would probably have called the act of giving away valuable information *ineffective deceleration*.

But I'd been programmed by Eve and Grandy, not blockchain technology. I called what I'd done keeping a promise, telling the truth.

"You think Hodge sold the research?"

That from Oscar, who was driving.

"You think he lied to billionaire boy to make a fortune on his own, Falc?"

I couldn't tell whether my head hurt more from thinking or today's beating. On the way home, the Battery Tunnel's overhead lights flashed like strobes. What I needed was sleep, not reasoning. I shook my head to try to clear it.

"If he sold it and was rich, why work at a community college? Why live at that crappy house in Brooklyn? Everything there looked twenty years old."

"Maybe he stole the research but hadn't sold it yet. He could have been auctioning it. One of the bidders—a company, a government, whoever—tried to take it instead."

"Bidders would be professionals. The attackers at Abani's apartment were that, but the ones in the park today...an old couple, a baseball bat, mace, amateurs!"

"Two groups! Fighting over it!"

"And where does Abani come into this?"

"They think Hodge gave her something."

The trip to Brooklyn had been planned to get answers, but all it had produced were more questions.

"We need to talk to Hodge's girlfriend again," I said. "Everyone in that house was scared, and not of me."

"Sequoia. That was her name, right?"

"She said someone broke into the house, stole his laptop. And what about Hodge? After running research for Kranepool, he could have gotten a great job anywhere. Instead, he fixes computers at a little community college. Why?"

"Sick of the rat race?"

"Maybe. Or maybe we're missing something? And what about that whole Moabite business? The Bible?"

Oscar pulled into the garage. The door slid down behind us, and the dome light came on. "That place," Oscar said, meaning the rave, "scared the shit out of me. What they were celebrating, Falc? What they *want*? No humans at the wheel. Ever. 'Trust everything to a perfect machine. Life will be wonderful!' They're like partying passengers on the Titanic."

"You and me, we're cave men, Oscar. Soon to be extinct."

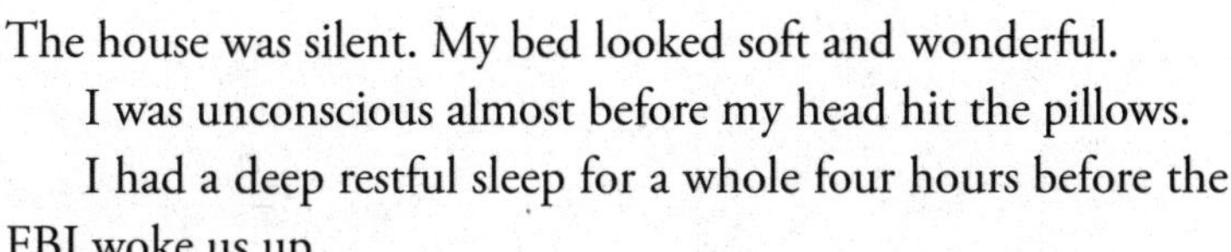

The house was silent. My bed looked soft and wonderful.

I was unconscious almost before my head hit the pillows.

I had a deep restful sleep for a whole four hours before the FBI woke us up.

TWENTY-TWO

Kendrick was handing out burner phones and Halloween masks to the Hands when his snatch squad arrived back at the house from Riverside Park without Abani. The group stood frozen in shame, battered and bruised, against a wall.

Everyone else could sit. They were all waiting to see how Kendrick would punish the failures.

"On judgment day, all humanity will pass before the Lord for reckoning. *You* will become Angels," Kendrick said.

Kendrick hid his rage as he handed Kathy Phillips a Barbie mask, beneath the basement rec-room Coors sign.

"Make your 911 call when you get my signal," he told her.

"I'll report shots fired on 159th Street."

Former hippie Gina Mostriello got a Sinbad mask with big eye holes, a plastic turban, a swirl pattern on top. "Gas leak. I smell gas on 130th, I'll say."

"Robbery in progress. The baseball field," Gail said.

From the FedEx box, Kendrick distributed a beagle mask, Darth Vader mask, gorilla mask.

"The masks are precautions," Kendrick said. "Those of you making calls, we don't want your faces showing up on street cameras. Those at the medical center, same thing. On Halloween, plenty of adults will be out in costumes, going to parties, visiting patients, walking with trick-or-treaters. You'll blend in."

The disgraced attackers had not moved. Roger's face was purple with bruises. Jacinta winced, putting weight on her left ankle. Orsen, a national guard cook before his dishonorable discharge, looked miserable. Kunio's face was as placid as always, but he would be hiding fury.

The main group turned festive, posing and preening with their masks.

"Boo!" This from the ghost mask, laughing.

All smiles died as Kendrick turned to the disgraced *Hands*, his silence constituting a demand for their report. Roger, the former college music professor, explained what had gone wrong during the snatch. "We heard sirens. We had to leave."

Kendrick eyed Roger mildly. "You drove away?"

"The siren was coming closer, Father."

Kendrick's voice rose a bit. "Closer."

Jacinta sensed Kendrick's rising fury, and reached for her husband to quiet him, but the elderly man shook her off.

"We had to leave," Roger insisted.

"Did the police car stop, Roger?"

Roger halted, confused. "What?"

Kendrick screamed, "Did they stop?"

"I...I don't know. We were gone by then."

"You were gone by then." As Kendrick stepped closer, Roger drew back. Kendrick saw a drop of his spittle run down Roger's cheek. "Roger, the Lord sent the police past you. The Lord made you invisible. You should have finished what you started."

Roger's blue eyes squeezed shut, his breathing grew audible. Yet astoundingly, he did not back down. "How do you know that's what happened?" the old man asked.

Kendrick lifted a barstool and threw it over the counter. It smashed into a row of bottles. The sound of dripping liquid filled the room. God had shown Kendrick the incident on his computer screen, that's how he knew.

Kendrick thrust his face within inch of Roger's. "The Lord trusted you to smite an enemy and you failed!"

"Then why didn't the Lord smite the enemy himself?"

Kendrick stepped back, barely believing what he was hearing. No one ever questioned him except during Bible study, and this was not that. Stubborn light glowed in Roger's eyes. He was protecting his wife. Emboldened, Roger raised his voice, appealing to the others. God would be watching this rebellion among Kendrick's flock.

"Viktor, dead! Alan, dead! You blame us, but if the Lord can do miracles, why does he need us at all?" Roger said.

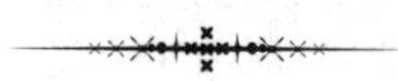

Pain started up in Kendrick's head, as blunt and rhythmic as a piston striking steel. His ears burned. His hands formed into fists. He wanted to ram them into that stupid face and hit and hit and not stop. Roger, an original member of God's Hands, frail Roger, *of all of them, he should be the last to rebel.* Kendrick saw unshaven patches on the cheeks. The yellowed flesh was disgusting.

Kendrick observed something moving beneath Roger's skin, like worms, larvae wriggling inside his cheek. Suddenly, Kendrick understood what he was seeing. Roger was not controlling his words. Something evil was under there.

Of course the devil would try to stop us.

"I'm just asking," Roger said.

That was it! The devil, wanting Kendrick weak, was playing tricks to undermine the Lord! Kendrick detected, behind his back, a hint of a nod back there, the Sinbad mask moving up and down, as if Gina agreed with Roger.

I am stronger than you, Kendrick thought. *Now that I recognize you, I know how to fight you.*

Surprising everyone, Kendrick smiled and calmed his voice.

"You're saying your failure is my fault, Roger?"

"No, Father."

"God's fault then."

He was not only addressing Roger, he knew. The group, only days ago, had been awed when God prophesized the death of the British oil company executive. Yet still, like Israelites worshipping a golden calf even after God parted the Red Sea for them, Kendrick's flock had doubts.

I will crush those doubts.

"Roger, remember your Bible? The prophet Jeremiah warned the Israelites of danger, but they scorned him and stoned him to death. Do you believe this story?"

A frown. "Of course, Father."

"But why did the Lord need Jeremiah? Why didn't the Lord solve the issue himself? Why need a prophet at all?"

Roger's frown lines grew deeper, became furrows.

"And Jonah! Ordered to the wicked city of Nineveh, to urge people to repent. Why did the Lord need Jonah? Why didn't the Lord send his great voice from the sky, to warn the sinners himself?" Kendrick's voice was rising. He couldn't help it.

Roger slumped. "I-I don't know," he said.

Kendrick whirled to face the others. "Roger doesn't think God needs prophets. He thinks I'm no prophet. Roger, how many miracles do we need before you believe in the Lord?"

Roger looked around the room. No one else appeared sympathetic to him anymore. Even Jacinta had stepped away from him. "I didn't mean it like that," Roger said.

Kendrick shouted, "And the Lord of their fathers sent warnings through messengers! But people mocked the messengers of God, despised his words and scoffed at the prophets until there was no remedy!"

Roger dropped to his knees.

Kendrick shouted, "And the Lord said, if there is a prophet among you, I make myself known to him in dream!"

Kendrick felt a great truth coursing through him, down and down and through his entire body, just as powerful hands might press upon Roger's shoulders, flattening opposition, crushing it.

Roger whispered, ashen, "It was just a question."

Kendrick left Roger alone, kneeling in a corner, contemplating his faults. He allowed Jacinta, Orsen, and Murakami to join the group. Jacinta got a witch mask. Orsen got Batman.

"Murakami! You're up," Kendrick announced.

Murakami opened a Lil' Oscar cooler and distributed small glass vials to the group, the sort that often holds cocaine. Each vial was filled with harmless tap water, Murakami explained as he divided the group into threes. "It's for practice today."

The first trio stepped forward, vials in their pockets. "Now!" The vials came out but remained hidden inside fists.

"Caps off!" Murakami barked.

Each person used a thumb to wedge a plastic cap loose. The caps, attached by rubber strips to the vials, did not fall. The vials remained invisible, hidden by fingers.

"Unload!"

Drops sprinkled the floor, then the vials disappeared back into pockets. Murakami watched, frowning.

"In Tokyo, we moved faster! Do it again!"

Anita Bridger was deft at it. You never saw her vial. Henry Wallace's hand shook slightly, but he did the job.

Lincoln Goethal dropped his vial.

Everyone stopped moving. Linc stared down at his vial in horror, picked it up, and pulled a crumpled tissue from his trousers. Kneeling, he began wiping up spilled drops.

Murakami shook his head at Kendrick, over the humiliated man's bowed head. "He's clumsy. Switch him for someone else," the former chemist observed.

Kendrick considered what to do. Linc, forty-two, a new member, had shown up at the farm months ago after seeing one of their flyers at a bus station. *Have you wondered about the afterlife? Do you want to improve your relationship with God?* Linc had stayed for dinner and never left. His wife had deserted him, he'd announced at confession. He'd lost his job. "I did drugs." He never questioned Kendrick. His face had shown nothing but obedience during Roger's outburst today.

"Try it again," Kendrick said kindly.

Linc shook out the liquid perfectly this time.

"Roger, what shall I do with you?"

The others had gone upstairs. A puddle of urine spread around the kneeling man. Roger stared straight ahead, his breaths coming in short, quick bursts. His face had regained its normal appearance. The little larvae things were gone. Nothing moved under the skin.

A wave of sympathy washed over Kendrick. His earliest memories of Roger stretched back to when he was a boy. Kendrick remembered the punishment closet on the farm, the door swinging open one night, the flashlights blinding him, the terrifying strangers looming. *It's all right boy, you're safe.* He saw his father in handcuffs. He saw state police cars. He saw Roger, a younger Roger, arguing with the woman from the state child services department. "Let him stay with us. We love him. We will care for him."

Roger had tried to look out for Kendrick that day.

Now Kendrick gently placed a hand upon Roger's shoulder. *The merciful man doeth good to his own soul,* he thought.

"Feel better now, Roger? Like a fever is gone?"

"Yes, Father."

Kendrick helped the man up and gave him a moment to feel the blood flowing in his legs. Hugging Roger, he smelled wet wool, old man. Kendrick felt a great wave of love pour from him, down and down and into Roger.

"I'm sorry I got angry before, Roger. That was wrong of me. You were always good to me when I was a boy."

Roger said nothing, crying quietly.

"You were one of the few who stayed on the farm until the Lord returned me there from the land of Moabites. I know that you were not yourself today. I know who was speaking through you."

Kendrick wrapped the weeping man in his arms. The tall, thin body felt frail. Kendrick could feel Rogers' bones.

"The Lord has one last job for you, Roger."

Roger's eyes glistened with gratefulness.

"You will go to the detective's house tomorrow. You will carry out the most important distraction of all. If you really believe in me, as I know you do, it should be easy. Painless."

Roger's tears wet Kendrick's hands. Kendrick felt a great wave of affection for Roger. It was just bad luck that Roger's group in Riverside Park today—sent to find Abani—had included none of the warriors.

"Shall we pray together? You and I?" Kendrick said.

TWENTY-THREE

FBI Special Agent Billye Grassley was pencil thin as a model, tall, with bobbed red hair and pale skin, lightly freckled. Her two-button navy-blue jacket was padded at the shoulders, the grey slacks creased as sharply as the look in her doe-brown eyes.

"The Honda that followed us was *you*?" I said.

She smiled, not in a friendly way. "Surprise!"

"Why not identify yourself?"

"How'd that work out last time the FBI asked Falcon Associates for help?"

"That was different. I was protecting a client."

"This time you're not?"

"This time, protection means cooperation."

"Good. Cooperate. Recognize this man?"

The dark-skinned forty-ish stranger in the photo gazed back with intelligent black eyes, magnified by aviator style wire rimmed glasses. Oval head. White hair. Yellow button up shirt and polka-dotted bowtie beneath the white lab coat.

"No."

In the next shot, the same man slumped in a swivel chair, wearing a blood-drenched terrycloth robe, glasses hanging off one ear by a stem, eyes vacant, mouth gaping. Grassley tapped the face. "Dr. Raymond Ballogian."

"I said no."

"When's the last time you were in Boston?"

Surprised, I said, "Boston? Never."

"Red Sox game? Faneuil Hall? Harvard? Boston College?"

"Oh, *that* Boston? No."

"How about tropical diseases? Any interest in those?"

The rest of the Falcon team was downstairs, probably trying to figure out why the agents had shown up. Grassley's partner, Special Agent Regina Kwan moved around my office quietly, eyeing the film posters, bookshelves, awards. Shorter and rounder, she wore a grey pin-striped pants suit and flats. Her open, engaging face contrasted with Grassley's frown.

"Your grandmother," Kwan said, poking a tiny Eve on the *Son of Kong* poster, "was a big hero at the Bureau."

"She was?"

"What she did for us back in the Mideast was *amazing*."

"You mean the trip to Abu Dhabi?"

Both agents froze. "She told you about that?"

"Of course," I lied, hoping to finally learn what Eve had done there. Grassley snorted. Kwan pulled a book from my shelf and joined her partner at my desk with the volume—*Emerging Pathogens in the Twenty-First Century.*

"Got a special interest in diseases, Mark?"

I felt a tic in my throat become a throb. "What kind of doctor was Raymond Ballogian?" I asked.

"The research kind. And speaking of research, look at this."

Kwan produced from her Tumi bag, a file stamped *Westchester Police*. It contained a lab analysis of the evidence samples—hair strand, gum wad, cigarette butt—that Oscar had recovered across the street from my home on the day Abani first showed up here. We'd hoped one of those items might identify the man who had died in the subway. Grassley had obtained the report before we did. *Hair sample* was circled in the report, starred in red ink.

"How did you get this?" I asked.

"Legally, not like you."

"Who'd you match the sample with?" I asked.

No answer, of course. That would have been too much to hope for. The throb in my throat became a pulse. The test results must have triggered an automatic alert at the Bureau. Our Westchester lab technician—well, maybe not actually *ours*, since we bribed him—was in trouble. He wasn't supposed to help civilians.

"Why are you asking about diseases?" I asked. But it wasn't hard to guess the answer.

"Why do you think? There's a credible threat."

I told them the story.

There was no point delaying. Cooperation could only help Abani, and, if a credible threat loomed, other people too. Out came the tale: Abani's claims, the driverless car, the subway, apartment, and park attacks, which, I gleaned from nods, matched some of what the agents knew already, probably from Brian Benish.

I said, "Detectives took DNA samples too, from the subway attacker. Did our sample match theirs?"

Grassley's frown deepened. "They didn't put a rush on their sample, and they don't bribe technicians. Their stuff is still at their lab."

"Then how about putting in a good word for my guy in Westchester, since he helped you out."

"By screwing up the chain of evidence?"

"What chain? Cops never took samples here. If you don't want the results, give me back the report. I paid for it. Not you," I said.

Kwan suppressed a smile. I was getting pissed off. "If you would have come to me two days ago," I said, "I would have helped you. You want to play games? I have a Monopoly set in the closet. You want cooperation, give my guy a break."

Kwan looked at Grassley. Grassley shrugged, probably the best response I could hope for at the moment. *Maybe.*

"What do you know about level-four labs?" Kwan asked.

There's normal bad news, worse than normal, and the third kind—this.

"The deadliest contagious diseases on earth are studied in level fours," Kwan said.

Grassley opened my book, turned pages, poked photos. A row of corpses lay in a Doctors Without Borders tent. *Ebola, Congo.* A Navajo man was being wheeled into a Santa Fe hospital. *Hanta Virus.* An ambulance screeched to a halt at an international travel terminal at London's Heathrow Airport. *Marburg breaks out during flight…*

Grassley sighed. "There are seven level-four labs in the US, and all have top security. Staffers wear hooded suits. HEPA filtered air. Negative air pressure. Fingerprint and iris scans to gain entry."

"One of these labs is in Massachusetts?"

"At Boston University."

"Where Raymond Ballogian worked?"

"Until he was murdered eight weeks ago," Grassley said. "He came to us saying he'd been approached by people seeking to buy samples, claiming to be from a pharmaceutical company. He agreed to wear a wire. Apparently, they found out about it."

Kwan blew out air. "There's been a pattern over the last few months. Atlanta. Fort Detrick. Boston. Hack attempts. Sabotage. Someone's targeting level fours, trying to get at the work. Now, suddenly, we get a match with you."

I envisioned Manhattan's blocks of medical centers, whole neighborhoods dedicated to research: The New York University complex on the East side. Lenox Hill in midtown. Columbia Presbyterian on the Upper West Side. Rockefeller University, Bellevue, Sloan Kettering. Manhattan hosts more medical research personnel than some countries, including private labs and corporate institutions.

"Where's the level-four lab in New York?" I asked.

"There isn't one."

"Then why are your suspects here?"

"That's what we hope you'll tell us."

"Who's the guy you matched our sample with?"

Kwan shook her head, looking tired. "That's the problem. Whoever he is, there's no match with any database. All we know is, it's the same person whose DNA was found in the room where Ballogian was killed."

Different city. Same guy. "Professionals work on multiple jobs," I reasoned out loud. Or maybe I was just indulging in wishful thinking. "One week they're in Boston, then New York. Same man, different case?"

Grassley looked miserable. "Possible."

"Three and a half million people died from coronavirus," Kwan said. "That wasn't even a level four."

"Forty million people died in the 1916 flu," added Grassley morosely. "And world population was seven times smaller then."

"Remember, put in a good word for my guy in Westchester."

The agents went downstairs to talk to Abani about the man who'd followed her and the car that killed Desmond Hodge.

Bedford Hills lies forty-five minutes north of Manhattan if I-684 traffic is moving. Nageena occupied the passenger seat, riding along to appeal to Sequoia—Desmond Hodge's old girlfriend—as a mom. Cristina and Oscar had remained at home with Abani, who was torturing them by practicing the trombone, inducing howls from Poe Street dogs.

"Little girl, big lungs," Nageena said. "Tell me more about Sequoia."

"Her posts say she's living with her parents now, using the name Millie again. Cristina was sure she was lying when we talked to her earlier about Desmond. But about what?"

Leaves were turning gold and red in Westchester. Traffic was back to pre-Covid levels, but, remembering the FBI visit, my memories of semi-deserted highways, empty midtown buildings, and nightly death reports five years ago underlined Kwan and Grassley's fears.

Bedford Hills still resembles the quaint town it was back in Revolutionary War times, but the dairy farmers and blacksmiths that once lived here have been replaced by lawyers, doctors, and corporate commuters. Cartway Lane North was a dead-end street filled with large homes on big lots. The air smelled of wood smoke. We pulled into a semicircular driveway fronting a faux antebellum, where a lone girl shot baskets, clutching the ball to her chest when I drove up. Millie Wexler's red hair was natural brown now, cut short. Her tattoos were covered by a Yale University hoodie. Unhappy men never buy furniture and live on takeout pizza. Unhappy women change their names every few months.

"She's clearly scared of you," Nageena said. "Let me start out with her, okay?"

I was looking into the confident, concerned face of Dr. Singh the professional, dedicated to soothing away fears, sympathizing with trauma. I had a feeling she was good at it.

"I knew you'd come back," Millicent told me as we exited the car.

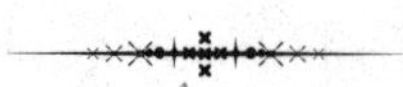

Nageena had to be crazy with worry for Abani but did not show it. Voice soft, eyes warm, her walk, her tilt of shoulders—her entire manner indicated only concern. "My name is Nageena Singh. Whoever hurt Desmond is after my daughter. If you can help us, please don't allow another person to be harmed."

Sometimes you work hard at getting answers. Every once in a while, diligence, luck, or sympathy pays off. Whatever internal struggle Millie had been undergoing before we arrived here worked in our favor. The quiet, frightened person who invited us into the house was nothing like the activist I'd met in Brooklyn. Her parents were away, at a lawyer's convention in Reno, she said. She was living back home while "getting my act together."

"Come in. Want coffee, something to drink? Water? Coke?"

I accepted water. Nageena and Millie had tea. The interior of the home was cold and industrial; glass tables with sharp edges, chairs you wouldn't want to sit on for more than ten minutes, splashy canvases without form, white walls, stark floodlights, photos on the fireplace mantel of Mom and Dad on a ski vacation without Millie. Mom had clearly undergone plastic surgery. Both parents dressed like younger people. Even the air seemed lonely here.

"I think Desmond did something bad," Millie said.

"Working for Bradley Kranepool bothered Dez. He used to talk about Robert Oppenheimer, you know? The atomic bomb inventor? Dez said Oppenheimer told President Truman, 'I have blood on my hands.' He asked Truman to ban the atomic bomb."

"Dez had second thoughts about his project?" asked Nageena.

Millie nodded, her tea untouched. "Researchers on the work were having arguments, like, would the AI they worked on turn out to be good or bad? Bradley Kranepool was pressing them to go full speed ahead. Dez worried that they were moving too fast. When the project didn't work out, he was relieved."

"He went to work for Columbia after that," Nageena prompted.

"And got fired. That's when we had the big fight."

Nageena nodded, sympathetic. I could imagine the same look on her face when she interviewed the Indiana school shooter, in the case which Brian Benish believed had resulted in the attack on Abani. Nageena didn't need to ask the next question. Millie anticipated it and answered it.

"We fought about Earth's Shock Warriors. After we got arrested, Dez was furious. He said throwing paint around accomplished nothing except making people mad. I shouted at him. 'What have you ever done? All you do is complain! You talk and talk and do nothing!'"

Nageena nodded, letting Millie go on.

"We didn't talk to each other for a week, but then we made up. That was when he told me that he had done something. Something big. He was proud of it at first."

"What did he do?" I broke in.

"He never told me, but after that, he changed. He started watching the news all the time and reading the *Times*. He woke me up one morning, shoved his laptop in my face, excited about a fire at an oil refining plant in Texas. 'That'll put a crimp on sales,' he said, like he was proud of it, like he had something to do with it. But that had to be impossible, I thought."

Nageena frowned. *Impossible.*

"Then there was the news about Senator Grady, from Montana? The guy always shooting down climate bills. Turns out he was spending thousands of dollars on call girls. He resigned. Dez was delighted. I told him, 'You act like you did this!' Dez just laughed. It was really odd."

"You mean the way he laughed was odd," Nageena said.

"Right! Then his mood changed *again*, a couple of weeks later. Suddenly, he's staying up all night, staring at the computer. He's not happy anymore. He's having stomach pains, hardly eating. He told me, 'I think I made a mistake.' But he wouldn't say what it was."

Millie was tearing up.

"Do you mind if we take a look at his laptop?" I asked. I'd try to get it to Cristina, our techie.

"That's the computer that got stolen."

Nageena went to the couch and put her arm around Millie. The one-time Shock Warrior was now weeping. She looked Abani's age.

"Whatever Dez did, Millie, he decided on his own," Nageena said. "It's not your fault. People make their own choices."

"No. I laughed at him. Whatever he did, it's because of me. On the day he got run over, he told me he was going to fix it, make it right."

"You need to tell the police this."

"But my stepfather said if Dez broke the law, I could be liable too. That I'm in enough trouble as it is because of the paint. That whoever hurt Dez could come after me. And Mom and him, too. He told me to shut up about it."

The crying got worse.

"All I wanted was to protect animals."

Under my breath, I cursed the couple in the ski photo for worrying more about themselves than their daughter. Nageena gave her business card to Millie. "If you want to talk more, feel free to call me, any time. I mean it."

"I just wanted to do good, is that so bad?"

I hated what I had to tell her now, but I said it anyway. "If the police find out you lied to them, you could be charged with obstruction. There are other things happening now, bad things, and what Dez did might be connected to them."

She moaned.

"Call them, Millie. Tell them we were talking. Say you've been thinking about Detective Benish's questions and you remembered something that might help him out. Tell them you'd forgotten it before."

"What if my stepfather gets angry at me?"

I remembered Kwan and Grassley's fears of a level-four lab attack.

I said, "Screw your stepfather. As soon as we leave, call. Understand. If you don't do it, I have to."

"I know. Thanks for telling me." She wiped her eyes. "I'll do it," she said.

Oscar had tried to reach me four times during the interview. I called him back as Nageena and I got into the car.

"Lucky break, Falc. The license plate number from the park attack."

"You found it?"

"We went house to house on Seventy-Eighth Street. The Irregulars helped. A corner camera picked up the New Hampshire plate. Cristina logged into our tracing service, let the algorithms roll! Car's registered to a Roger Formann, Black Walnut Road, Granite Falls. I left a message for Grassley."

Clicking off, I entered the address into the car's GPS system. Granite Falls lay roughly four hours north. If we left now, we could reach the town while the day was still light. I didn't even have to ask Nageena the question. *Should we let the FBI handle it, trust them to do it, or go up ourselves*?

Nageena adjusted her seat back, made it more comfortable. She took off her jacket. She stretched.

"Let's grab lunch on the road," she said.

TWENTY-FOUR

Kendrick Rainey was having a nightmare.

The boy, age nine, shivered in a dark shed, hearing screams and sirens outside on the farm. Red lights pulsed through the crack under the door. Rats scrabbled in the wall. The door swung open and a dazzling flashlight beam blinded him.

"Jesus Christ, there's a kid in here," a man's voice gasped.

In the yard, when the man pulled him out, he saw spinning police dome lights, too-bright headlights, family members fleeing in all directions. Father, naked except for a blanket draped over his shoulder, was being shoved by state policemen into a car. Dogs were barking, chickens running. Father's legs looked skinny and white.

"What's your name, son? You're safe," a voice asked.

But he wasn't safe. This invasion by Moabites was exactly what Father had predicted, in sermons. "Leave me alone!" the boy screamed as troopers dragged him toward their car. He dug his heels into the ground to resist. It was useless. His legs screamed with pain where Father had broken them.

"We're taking you to the doctor, kid. Christ, look at that leg. What the hell did that nut job preacher do to you?"

The boy tried to tell them that he deserved those punishments. Punishment was inflicted for your own good, he knew. He was terrified. Father had sermonized about what went on in town at the so-called "doctor's office." About needles and mind control drugs and brain washing. Father had explained the horrible things that happened outside the farm. Kendrick had never been out there before, and now the squad car felt like a moving cage. His fingers clawed mesh. His heart beat more savagely than in the farm animals he helped kill each fall, when the Hands slaughtered pigs, ducks and turkeys for food.

"What's your name, son?" a lady cop asked gently.

"You're safe now," the man cop said. "Doc Rainey will take care of you."

The car halted before a big yellow house with a sign out front, a painted stethoscope on it. A man and woman stood on the porch, watching the police drag him closer. Lights glowed in other homes on the block. He'd never seen so many buildings in one place. Strangers were coming out on other porches to stare at him.

Kendrick screamed, "I'll be good, I promise. Don't make me go in there!"

"Kendrick, wake up," a voice interrupted gently. "Kendrick, you're dreaming," the Lord's voice said.

Kendrick shot up in bed, heart slamming in his chest. He was covered with sweat. God's voice was coming from his laptop. He was in Brooklyn, he realized. He was safe. He was with family. Kendrick fell back on a drenched pillow, hyperventilating with relief.

The Lord told Kendrick, "The detective is on his way to New Hampshire with Abani Singh's mother."

The Lord told Kendrick what to tell his people there to do when the detective arrived at the farm.

TWENTY-FIVE

The sun shone brightly as Nageena and I crossed the border into Connecticut. There was something soothing about being together with her in the car. I'd liked what I'd seen of this woman during our meeting with Millie—her empathy and intelligence, the way she'd comforted the sad, frightened girl. Still, I could not help asking Nageena, "Do you still believe evil doesn't exist?"

She turned to me, surprised by the question, maybe even disappointed.

On all-news radio, New York's deputy mayor was answering questions about Sunday's upcoming New York marathon. "Extra police will be out along the route," he said. "We're expecting the largest field of runners in Marathon history."

Nageena said softly, "I do believe that, Mark."

"Hitler. Stalin. You probably get this question all the time, but how do you explain them?"

"Hitler had a brutal childhood. He was mustard gassed in World War I, homeless after that, probably schizoid to start with. Persecution complex. Hysteria. Suicidal."

"And the millions who followed him?"

"The wrong place, wrong time. Desperate people believe anything they need to hear. The psychotic who's been standing in a corner, ignored for years, suddenly sounds like God to them."

Wearily, Nageena asked, "Why do you ask?"

"Maybe I want to be convinced."

She softened. "Tell me, is a rabid dog evil, Mark?"

I liked it when she said my name. And that despite all that had happened to her and Abani so far, she still clung to positive belief, an attitude I envied.

"Fall colors," she remarked, turning to look out of the car. "Nice."

"Okay," I reasoned, thinking out loud, "Millie told us that Desmond kept talking about Oppenheimer's regret over developing the atomic bomb. At the same time, Dez's team was working on some new advanced AI for Bradley Kranepool. The project failed but he remained an expert, so let's assume whatever he hinted at to Millie, whatever he developed after that, it was related to the project that failed."

"Good bet," Nageena said.

"Dez said his team feared the work might be dangerous. So, what if the group actually completed the job but lied to Kranepool and destroyed it? They didn't want to bring something dangerous into the world."

Nageena considered it but shook her head. "The whole team lied? The others are still alive. Why murder only Desmond?"

I sighed. "What if they *didn't* destroy it, they just told Kranepool they did. Then they sold it to someone they considered more responsible. And *that* person had Desmond killed to cover it up?"

"That still doesn't answer why the rest of them remain alive, if the whole team was in on it."

"Then what if the team quashed the project *before* finishing it, but Desmond kept working on it by himself after that, finished and sold it? Just him. See?"

"Then where's the money he got for it?"

"You're good at this. Very irritating."

"Also, where does my daughter come into this? Try again, Mark. You're good at it too."

"Okay," I said. "Desmond *didn't* sell what he invented but was *trying to*. There was competition. Bidding. A government entity wanted it. A corporation. Desmond was about to sell. A rival group killed him to stop the sale."

"With a driverless car," she said. "You now believe that car existed? Where does Abani come into this?"

I sighed. "The robotics club guy at Columbia told me someone hacked a Tesla last year and won a prize for it. So what if *our* bad guy did more than just turn a car on? He makes it into a drone on wheels, it kills Desmond, then parks."

"Is that possible?"

I shrugged. "I don't know. But how different is that from a military drone? The operators sit in a trailer in Nevada. The drone blows up some enemy overseas, then returns to base all by itself."

She frowned, turning over this scenario in her mind. The concentration lines on her forehead made her more serious looking, and even more attractive.

"What about the people who tried to break into my apartment? Or attacked us in the park? Why use humans at all if you have robot cars?" she asked.

"You still need people to do some things," I said. But I was seeing flaws in my own speculations. "But if Desmond was worried about potential misuse, why sell anything to anyone? Why risk putting a dangerous thing out into the world at all?"

We sat in a Denny's restaurant off I-84, north of Hartford. I was finishing a turkey club on wheat, crisp fries, extra mayo. Nageena's tuna melt came with dill pickles. We were still running through theories and knocking them down, one by one.

"Desmond's break through—whatever he invented—made him happy at first when he watched the news," Nageena said. "So what he saw on TV must have related to what he did."

"But that would mean his work caused an oil refinery fire in Louisiana and a senator resigning. Those are the news items he was happy about," I said.

"How is that possible?"

I waved her off. "But then something *else* on the news bothered him. He started watching TV compulsively. He grew depressed. He told Millie he made a mistake. What mistake?"

Nageena put down her sandwich, brow furrowed. "He sells his system to people he thinks will use it wisely. At first, they do. But then they don't. He threatens to go public. They kill him."

I considered it. "If Desmond's big breakthrough can move around cyberspace, why don't security systems detect it?"

"Hackers break through security all the time. At banks. Government. Corporations. Who's to say some penetrations never get found, Mark?"

"It's a reach," I said.

"Is it?"

"We need to talk to the other people in Desmond's original group."

By the time we crossed the New Hampshire border, my whole team was on the call from back in the house. Cristina said she would try to reach other members of Desmond's old research group.

At least Abani's trombone practice was over.

"Okay," I said. "Imagine that Desmond's people were trying to develop AI that thinks a billion times faster than us. It can hack into other systems. And write code. It can help bad guys get control of an autonomous car."

Oscar snorted. "You're talking about a machine like it can do anything. It's a goddamn program, not science fiction."

"Space travel used to be science fiction."

"Then tell me, Falc, with your all-powerful AI running around, where does the guy with a baseball bat come into it? And what about the level-four labs? Or does any of that fit into this stupid jigsaw puzzle at all?"

What are we missing?

An hour later, we were still knocking down theories.

Granite Falls, New Hampshire, home of the Quarrymen, State Champs, 2013, read a sign up ahead.

TWENTY-SIX

The village of Granite Falls reminded me of a Norman Rockwell painting: white spire church, redbrick town hall, grassy commons, civil war monument. There was Martha's Diner, two hardware stores, and a Victorian-style medical building. The only chain store in sight was the CVS occupying a former textile mill. The only indication that I'd not traveled back to 1952 was the foreign make of most cars parked on Main Street, front ends in.

Nor'easter arriving tonight, dinged a weather advisory on the Prius screen. *Flood warning!*

I wanted to eyeball the property linked to our attackers in Manhattan. GPS directed us out of town on a mountainous two-lane state highway, then eight miles later onto a gravel road, then a rutted dirt lane. Pine forest obscured whatever homes lay beyond long driveways. Rock walls paralleled both sides of the road. A lone mountain biker labored against wind up a hill. Two hunters in orange flap hats stepped from the woods, heading for a pickup truck parked half in a ditch.

"Shotguns," observed Nageena, as Oscar's voice emanated from the car's system. "County records show the property owned by a group called the Great Hands of God."

Mailboxes indicated addresses but some driveways lacked boxes. KEEP OUT signs were nailed to trees.

Cristina's voice took over. "GHG's a cult, according to the Manchester Union Leader. The apocalypse is near, they say. Only believers will survive. I found a child abuse arrest twenty years back against the leader, Apostle John. No one would testify against him. He drowned in 2010. Since then, nothing."

"But the group's still there? How many members?"

"Back then, about ninety. A *Globe* reporter went back two years ago for a follow up. He was turned away by guards. Barbed wire fence. Locked gate. Shotguns. Jim Jones stuff, Falc. Scary shit."

"Has anything we've learned linked Desmond to a cult?"

"Not yet but I'll keep checking," Oscar said as Nageena's head spun to the left.

"Something moved by that rock wall, Mark. I think it was a person watching us. But maybe it was an animal."

The sky was clouding rapidly. Treetops thrashed in sudden wind gusts; branches windmilled as we bounced out of a pothole.

"A cult would have enforcers," Oscar said. "A cult could have tech proficient members. A cult would have motivation."

Level-four labs, I recalled Kwan saying, contain the most dangerous viruses on earth.

How could they know that Abani went missing yesterday? How did they locate her apartment? How do they know all these things? I thought.

"Watch yourselves," Cristina's voice warned. "Find a motel tonight. The forecast is getting worse up there. That incoming storm looks pretty bad."

Nageena pointed at numbers nailed to a tree. "This is it. We're here."

I turned right onto a bumpy dirt driveway disappearing into pine and hemlock forest. Rounding a bend, we reached the steel gate and guard booth Oscar had described. The gate was ajar. I stepped out of the car to widen the entrance and observed a thick chain and padlock hanging uselessly off a steel post. *Lucky*, I thought. *No guard today.* I eased the gate open, returned to the car, reached for the gear shift and froze, the odors of goat shit and sage suddenly in my head: Afghanistan smells. Something was wrong.

A lone fat drop of rain hit the windshield. Nageena was staring at me, wondering why we'd stopped. I held a palm up to ward off questions. Just a moment ago, she had told me she thought someone was watching us over that rock wall.

An old gunny I know still talks about situational awareness, eyes and ears in back of your head. To a former Marine, goat shit smells constitute situation awareness.

How could they possibly know we were coming?

Now, as the open gate invited us forward, my eyes dropped to the phone on Nageena's lap. *The phone? Could it be the goddamn phone?* How many times, as a private detective, had Oscar and I installed or uncovered phone taps for clients? Police taps. FBI taps. Mob taps. Corporate.

Nageena started to say something, but my hand shot up to stop her. I held up the phone, pressing my other index finger to my lips.

You're being paranoid, I told myself.

Paranoid or not, I turned the car around. We returned to the road and headed back to town.

When visiting new jurisdictions, police detectives check in with local law enforcement. Private detectives have better luck with reporters, who like to hear our stories, enjoy dinners we pay for, and have a more romantic vision of PIs.

I bought a copy of *The Granite Falls Eagle* at the CVS, where I also picked up two burner phones. By the time I parked in front of the *Eagle*'s storefront headquarters on Main Street, Nageena and I had locked our usual iPhones in the trunk, *in case someone's listening in*, the note I scrawled to her had read.

A bell tinkled as we walked in. *Established in 1797.* Three frumpy looking staffers looked up from computers on desks that might have been new during World War I. On the walls, framed front pages. Major headlines, "War Between The States Ends," "President Kennedy Assassinated," "A Walk on the Moon," alternated with local ones, "Eagles Win State Championship" and "Selectmen Vote on Dump."

The smile on the face of the sixty-ish man who introduced himself as Dave Ritterbrand, owner, faded when he realized I was not there to buy advertising, but he brightened when he saw my PI license. "Wait a second. I know you. You're that guy from *New York Magazine*. The one they called The Falcon," he said with a grin.

I groaned inwardly. Dave's thick, brushed back white hair, red suspenders, paunch belly, and rubber-soled shoes marked him as my vision of a New England small-town editor. Plaid flannel shirt. Reading glasses suspended on a string. Pipe tobacco smell in the office. But Dave turned out to be a retired *New York Times* foreign correspondent, who with his wife Emily had purchased the *Eagle* four years back with his buyout from Manhattan. "I left Times Square for time out," he said. "But I still love a good story."

His smile vanished when I mentioned God's Hands. His eyes narrowed when Nageena told him about the murder of Desmond Hodge and attack on Abani. Face alight with the mix of horror and rapture marking reporters sensing a good story, Dave rifled through a file cabinet.

"We tried to do an article on them last year," he said. "They threatened litigation. Libel. Slander. Someone busted our front window. We dropped it. They really went nuts about our drone."

"Drone?"

A thick manila file appeared in his hand. "They refused my reporter entry, but LaToya Hayes—crackerjack kid, left us for Boston last May—her brother flies drones. When she couldn't get into the compound, she had Walter fly one in."

Inside the file was a stack of black-and-white aerial shots. And a memory stick in a Ziploc bag.

"Those folks creep me out," Dave said. "They never come into town except in a group. They all wear the same clothes. They used to hold community nights, they called 'em, invite outsiders in and feed 'em. Moonie smiles, singing, recruiting. The neighbors hear guns going off a lot in there, all legal on private property in New Hampshire."

"Who's the leader?"

"Kendrick Rainey. The prophet, they call him. They say he predicts the future. God speaks to him, they say."

"You've met these people?"

"A delegation came here when we were going to run the piece on them. They even had a Boston lawyer, high-priced shark." He sighed. "But the weirdest part happened last week."

"What was that?" Nageena asked.

He pulled a pipe from a pocket but didn't light up. "The nearest Costco to us is in Nashua. Emily and I were doing our monthly trip there and *here they came*, down the aisle, a whole bunch of them with loaded-down carts. Man, they were buying everything! There had to be thousands of dollars of food, medical stuff, clothing, batteries, candles, auto supplies. Ten, fifteen carts! Emily makes a crack, 'Stocking up for the apocalypse?' A couple of them freeze, then one smirks and says, 'Soon you'll find out.'"

"They threatened you?"

"They laughed when the guy said it, but in the way people laugh when they know something that you don't."

I felt a chill. *Grassley asked about level-four labs.*

"Then one of the others asks me, 'How you feeling these days, Dave?' Like, am I sick? I say fine. She says, 'Well, it's flu season, better watch yourself, especially next week.' Another woman laughs. The first one shushes her."

I said, "If she said this last week, she was talking about this coming week, right? A couple days from now."

"Moabites. That's what they call outsiders," Dave said.

Holy shit, I thought. That's what they called me in the park.

"Want to see the drone footage?" Dave asked.

The drone stayed close to treetops at first. Below, a frightened black bear cub raced down a tall pine. A startled deer looked up. The forest disappeared as the drone reached the compound, centered by a large pond. Mowed lawn. Trimmed trees. Surrounding the pond were buildings: a white structure with silver cross; a long one-story hall, possibly for meetings or dining; a series of small shingle cottages, probably residences; garage; machine shops; and a farm area where, as the video had been shot in summer, a variety of crops flourished, corn, tomatoes, pumpkins, squash. Pigs lazed in a sty. Chickens pecked at earth.

People tending crops with hoes looked up, pointing.

They'd spotted the drone.

More cultists streamed from other buildings, agitated.

One man clearly directed the group. He pointed, and someone immediately ran off in that direction. He shouted, and others rushed to obey. I'd never seen the guy before. He was white. Tall. Bearded. Sandy blonde and forty-ish.

Nothing special about him except his air of command.

Fascinated, I watched the faces on screen, close-ups now, ugly with anger. A child screamed at the drone. A young man shook a hoe at it. A woman appeared with a rifle, aiming at the drone. Then another guy, an old guy, walked into view and my heartbeat increased. The face was unmistakable.

"That's one of the men who attacked us in the park."

Dave sighed and began shoving everything back into the folder. He turned off the drone footage. When he straightened up, a reporter's notebook was in his hand. "Don't worry. I won't publish anything until it's over," he said. "This time they won't stop me. Grab an umbrella from the stand. It's going to pour out there."

"Where are we going?"

"To talk to Dr. Claudia Rainey."

"Rainey? You said Rainey is the name of the Prophet."

"Claudia's his sister. You need to hear more about him from a better source than me."

Claudia Rainey lived with her husband, Roy—both physicians—above their offices in the medical building, the big Victorian we'd passed on the way into town. She was a plump woman with a round, kind face, a direct gaze, a sad and pained look when discussing her brother. She'd grown up in this house.

"I'll never forget what poor Kendrick looked like when the police brought him here," she said.

Two terriers slept by a roaring fire. Herbal tea steamed in mugs she'd lain out. Rain blasted the windows but inside felt snug: Lots of potted plants, oval throw rugs, and deep plush couches. No TV in sight, upright piano in the corner, and a thick loose-leaf photo album on my lap. I turned pages like sheets on a calendar, showing a century of history of the doctor family in this town—sepia shots, then black and white, then color. Claudia's mom had been a cardiologist, her dad a GP. I saw teenaged Claudia and Kendrick relaxing with them at a lake. A happy picnic.

"Kendrick was terrified when he first got here. He sat right where you are now. Cuff marks on his wrists. One leg was twisted. When he took off his shirt for Dad to examine him, I saw ribs showing, and bruises. He'd never been out of the cult's compound before.

"My parents wanted another child but had been unable to conceive. Kendrick was so pitiful. My parents treated him but wouldn't let social services people have him. They insisted he stay with us at first. In the end, we adopted him."

"What about his real parents?" Nageena asked.

"His mother had abandoned him, dumped him with the cult. We tracked her to an institution in Portland. Schizophrenia. Former prostitute. Drugs. The father?" She shrugged. "We never knew for sure, but we think it was the cult leader. The guy slept with everyone at that place."

I stared at the grinning, swimsuit-clad boy in the photo, whose happy face contrasted with the description I was hearing. "It must have been hard for him to adapt," I said, "after growing up in a cult."

Claudia nodded. "At first, he'd flinch if you came near him. If he dropped a dish, if he forgot to make his bed, if you disagreed with something he said, he'd freeze, afraid he was going to be punished. But once he realized no one was going to hurt him, his recovery was amazing! Within a year, straight-A student! Played guitar in a band. It was like the bad stuff had never happened. He saw a therapist at first, had a nightmare now and then. But he had nothing to do with the cult after that. He was a brother anyone would want."

Nageena said, sadly, as if knowing what happened next, "Which made it worse when he changed."

A nod. "He wanted to be a doctor, like Dad. To cure diseases. He won a scholarship to MIT and worked so hard, *so hard*, but then..." Overcome with emotion, she stopped.

Nageena said, "Schizophrenia often starts in the early twenties. His past, his mother, his whole history, it couldn't have helped."

"We got a phone call from his best friend in Boston. Kendrick was in the hospital. Turned out he'd been acting odd for weeks. First, he thought people were whispering about him in the lab. He'd be looking into a microscope and straighten up suddenly, glaring. It freaked the other grad students out."

A wash of wind driven rain battered the window.

"Then his mood changed. He apologized. He told his friend that the whispering was coming from inside the microscope."

"Jesus," I said.

"He believed the microbes were talking to him. Something about souls and the universe and God giving Kendrick a mission. Some of the old stuff from the cult."

Nageena sighed.

"He claimed God had told him to free the souls," Claudia said. "He started smashing up the lab. His classmates wrestled him to the ground. Campus security called police. They took him away in restraints. They institutionalized him."

"The doctors gave him drugs?" Nageena asked.

"Which worked until he got out of the hospital and stopped taking them. He insisted nothing was wrong with him. He quit school and came back to Granite Falls, rejoined the cult, told them God sent him. He came to see me and wanted me to join too. A great cataclysm was coming, he told me. Only believers would survive. I tried to talk sense into him, but he got angry and stormed out."

"Did you see him after that?" Dave asked.

"A month ago, he showed up again. Calmer this time. He apologized for yelling at me before. He said there were lots of new members. He was preaching on the internet, too. He was the leader now. He wanted me to come live with them. He said end time was near."

"Did he say why *now*?"

"He just said he understood why I'd not believed him last time. This time, he said he had proof that God spoke to him.

He'd make a prophecy and when it came true, I'd know he was a prophet, leave my husband, and come live with them."

Filled with dread, I said, "What was the prophecy?"

"That a coming plague would make Covid look small. That unlike plagues of the past, it would break out in a hundred places at the same time, around the world. It wouldn't spread normally. It would just appear."

"He said this a month ago?"

She looked puzzled, eyeing us one by one. "You can't take this seriously."

"Did he predict exactly when the outbreak would occur?"

"You're scaring me," Claudia Rainey told me.

"I'm scaring me too," I said.

TWENTY-SEVEN

Dave Ritterbrand's house lay in the opposite direction from the Hands of God compound. Temperatures had plunged. Black ice covered roads. The Prius skidded up a wooded driveway steep enough to accommodate Citizen Kane's sled. The machine gunning of ice pellets against the car ceased as I backed beneath a carport and parked beside a black Tesla, regarding it like a mailman eyes a sleeping Pitbull.

Nageena and I were invited to stay the night.

The isolated home was an architect's baby, rustic meets modern, two modular stories perched above a century-old converted barn. Solar panel roof. Spiral stairway. One entire living room wall was a glass garage door which, in summers, could be raised electrically so fresh air flooded in. Scandinavian pellet stoves and electric heat pumps served the home on this wet, chilly night.

I'd phoned Oscar from my burner, given the "call me back on a pay phone" code, and when he did, I'd filled him in on the day's developments. From now on, we'd all use burners.

I'd also left a detailed message for agent Kwan. *Check out the attached drone videos*. She hadn't called back yet.

The Ritterbrands, gracious hosts, simmered a shrimp stew and offered wine, which Nageena accepted and I declined. Their questions about Abani seemed to come not from pesky journalists but concerned friends. But the conversation with Dr. Rainey had put us all on edge.

Nageena's eyes were getting heavy. At ten, Dave escorted us up to a pair of bedrooms—clean, well-kept spaces with double beds, Parisian street-artist canvases, terrycloth robes, and fluffy towels. "Our son stays here when he comes from California. You'll find pajamas in the drawers."

I planned to stay awake at the window, uneasy at the possibility that the cultists knew we were in town. Nageena looked exhausted, like she'd never wake once she slept, but ten minutes after going into her room, she appeared in my doorway wearing a pair of flannel doggie-logo pajamas, the cute pattern giving her a sad, vulnerable look.

"Can I sit here a bit, Mark? Talk?"

Funny thing, we barely said a word after that. She sat on the bed. I occupied a club chair by the window, mentally reviewing the day's events. At one point our gazes met, and I wondered what it would be like to kiss her. At length, her breathing subsided. I covered her with a blanket, then settled back, gun on my lap, as rain pummeled glass. I felt, with sixth sense, the Ritterbrands slumbering below.

When the sound of a car door woke me at 6:30 a.m., I was the one covered with a blanket. I cursed myself for falling asleep. The storm had passed, the sky remained thickly grey, the bed was empty as I sprawled in the chair like a guard who'd slept on duty. With a bolt of horror, I observed a half dozen Ford SUVs grouped by the front door below in the yard, like animals at a trough.

I grabbed the pistol. *They found us.*

I was lucky this time. I was wrong.

Grouped around the kitchen island, six fit, stern, and soggy-looking FBI agents in combat camos bent over a spread of photos, the aerial views of the cult compound taken by Dave's drone months ago.

Nageena pulled me into the dining room to whisper, "The photos you sent them? FBI software didn't recognize anyone who attacked us but went nuts on a different face."

"Who?"

"Kunio Murakami. He helped carry out a 1995 sarin attack on the Tokyo subway. Fourteen dead. A thousand injured. He was a chemistry student working for Aum Shinrikyo at the time."

"How did he hook up with Kendrick Rainey?"

"That's what Grassley and Kwan want to know. They've got a no-knock warrant. Cloud cover's too thick for satellite views of the compound, so they came to see more of Dave's shots. They're going in today."

"They told Dave, a reporter, all this?"

"He promised not to write anything if he gets an exclusive on the story. If they refused, he'd publish now."

"Why didn't you wake me when they got here?"

She softened. "You've barely slept in days."

Back in the kitchen, Emily had lain out muffins. Agents gestured me to stay back from the breakfast island covered by laptops, coffee cups, and arrow-filled diagrams of the compound. Entrance point. Property lines. Woods. Pond.

As I pushed my way through, Kwan looked up with a mocking smile. "Look who's awake."

"I want to go in with you," I said.

Grassley snorted. "Forget it."

"I can help."

Someone coughed politely. Dave took notes. Kwan instructed an agent, "Clear the room, Jakes."

"Barge in, you'll trigger another Waco," I said.

The reference to the FBI's worst day in history halted the big tan guy reaching for my arm. Everyone present knew of the botched 1993 raid on the Branch Davidian cult compound in Texas after a fifty-three-day siege. The seventy-six civilians dead included twenty-five children, many burned up.

"You blunder in, they'll barricade up," I said. "You can't waste days on a siege if an attack's coming. The second they know it's FBI coming in, you're screwed."

Grassley sounded weary. "And you'd make a difference how?"

"Wire me up. I drive in. I talk you through what I'm seeing. They're expecting me, we think, right? While they're distracted with me, you come in from the side."

Grassley looked thankful but shook her head. "If they're expecting you…" She made her hand into a gun and fired it. "No more Falcon."

But Kwan was frowning. "Let him talk."

"You'll hear if things go sideways. If that happens, go in. If they're not expecting me, I tell them I'm lost, ask for directions, and leave. These videos," I gestured at the table, "are months old. The place could be different now. Booby traps. Bunkers. You have a better idea?"

From the way they looked at each other and glanced at a soggy-looking agent in a corner, I had a thought. "Wait a minute," I said. "You tried sending someone in last night, didn't you? It didn't work. You didn't come straight here."

No answer.

"Someone tried to sneak in? What happened? Alarms? Floodlights? Do they know the FBI is in town already?"

Grassley sighed. "An alarm went off, but maybe they think an animal did it."

"Jesus Christ," I said.

Kwan stepped into the hall to make a phone call. I couldn't hear what she was saying, but her tone was urgent. When she came back, she handed me the unit. "The Director," she said. The voice coming at me from the other end was familiar from TV: deep, male, hoarse, a smoker's Chicago accent. I knew FBI Director Dimitrios Boosalis had come up through the ranks, joining the bureau after law school.

"Your grandmother Eve was an amazing person. I worked with her overseas years back," Boosalis began.

"You did? In Abu Dhabi?"

A long pause. "She told you about that?"

"Yes, sir," I lied, hoping to finally discover what Eve had been doing there.

It didn't work.

"Then you know what a great service she provided!" Boosalis boomed. "Every American owes her a debt of gratitude and now we owe you too. Based on your information, we've got a credible threat to a major population center. An armed group whose members indicated knowledge of imminent attack. Reasonable grounds to believe that waiting will cause mass casualties. Positive ID of a terrorist."

He's reading this, I thought, *creating a record in case things go wrong. A lawyer drew this up.*

"Patriotism runs in your family," the Director told me. "You'll sign some paperwork, of course, before going in."

In case I get killed.

"We'll have your back. Don't take unnecessary risks." Boosalis said. "Mark, your grandmother would be proud."

The microphone taped to my chest itched. The Kevlar vest beneath my jacket bulked me up but not enough to be obvious. The assault team waiting at the edge of the cult property would be equipped with helmets, flame resistant fatigues, gas masks, stun and gas grenades, battering rams, H&P MP5 submachine guns, and Remington shotguns. I had a Mets hat, a gas mask in the glove compartment, and my 9mm H&K. My Prius was not bulletproof, but it was insured.

"If we hear you say, *I wish I had a place like this*, we come in," Kwan said as we finalized plans over a map in the kitchen. The cult's two-hundred-acre compound was bounded on the East by a wooded fishing club. On the west lay a New Yorker's vacation home, unoccupied in autumn, according to the last electric bill, and launch point for assault team one. A second entry point lay in an abutting old quarry.

"Drive in if the gate is open," Kwan told me. "Otherwise leave the car and walk." She frowned. "We don't know if there are tunnels under some buildings but, according to testimony years ago, there were at that time."

"No one said anything about tunnels before."

Nageena interrupted, blurting out, behind us, "This is crazy, Mark. Why are you doing this?"

A whole series of images burst in on me from the Covid virus years. Downtown Manhattan deserted. An ambulance pulling up on Poe Street. Schools closed. Cristina's aunt in Roosevelt Hospital, breathing through a ventilator.

Forty-five thousand people had died just in New York.

"Beats sitting around," I said.

A real falcon can spot a rabbit from two miles away and hit the target at 180 miles an hour. Bumping along at eight miles an hour, I passed the empty guard house.

"Nothing so far," I said.

The woods remained soaked from last night's rain. Drops of water fell from the trees. Back home at this moment, thousands of visitors were converging on my city from around the world to see the Halloween parade tonight or run the Marathon tomorrow.

"So far, everything's like the photos," I reported.

The Prius cleared the forest and emerged into the occupied part of the compound. Humans came into view, wearing denims, straw hats, all dressed the same, even the kids. I was in Huckleberry Finn land.

"I see people working in gardens, children too. They're straightening. They see me. A girl's running into a building. Now all the kids are running inside."

I detected movement in the rearview mirror. "Two men coming out of the woods now. Shotguns, camo. One shotgun just came off a shoulder. I see a third shooter on the left, a woman. They were expecting me. It's a trap."

Turning the car around or backing up was out of the question. My heart hammered between my eyes. I was in their range of fire now. I hoped Kwan could hear me but I couldn't hear her. Wearing ear buds would have given me away.

Play it like an innocent. They'll know you're acting, but hopefully it will give you time. Give Kwan time.

"I'm getting out of the car," I announced.

Pistol beneath my jacket, I stepped out, throwing up my hands like an amiable tourist, unaware of the shooters approaching on three sides. I called to the adults leaning on hoes in the garden. "Hi there! I'm lost! I'm looking for the Smith place! Can you give me directions? I've been driving around these woods for hours!"

"Father wants to talk to him," a man's voice growled, behind me.

Father?

"This is the Moabite who killed Alan," the voice said.

Shotgun One, the leader, was heavy, bald, white, and angry. Two was short, young, and nervous, maybe nineteen years old. Three, the woman, was slender, with a pretty face, large hands, cat's-eye glasses, and dirty blonde dishrag hair.

She frisked me. "A gun! He's wearing a vest!"

"I wish I had a place like this," I said loudly. The safe words.

The children were gone. The adults in the garden went back to tilling soil. I was prodded toward a half dozen small, weathered shacks of grey shingle. At least my escorts hadn't found the wire yet. I listened for the sound of heavy engines, FBI engines. All I heard was a flock of crows squawking overhead.

"I wish I had a place like this," I repeated, louder.

The shacks had names, wooden signs nailed up on spindly front porches; *Jerusalem* was burned into a wooden slat by the door they shoved me through. "One-room cabin, nice," I said. "I always thought Jerusalem was overseas but here it is, in New Hampshire."

"Shut up," the young, nervous guy said.

He duct-taped me to a wooden chair facing a laptop on a table. Over a dozen crosses—wooden ones, silver ones, glass varieties—were suspended from the ceiling on fishing lines. Four sets of overalls hung in a closet. Tacked to a corkboard, above half-burned candles, I saw a street map of Manhattan. "That map show the target?" I said loudly, hoping Kwan could hear. I was in a monk's cell: single bed, slat floor, cold potbellied stove, tacked-up magazine cutout of Jesus Christ on a cross beside a Sierra Club calendar with big red X marks on it.

Tomorrow is X'd, I thought.

The laptop on the desk seemed to switch on by itself. Or someone had turned it on while I looked elsewhere. "Hello, Mr. St. Johns," a new voice said.

The voice had emanated from the laptop. A face was on screen now. It was the man who, on Dave Ritterbrand's video, had ordered the cultists around. The face looked quiet, composed—if not for the shotguns aimed at me, and the duct tape binding me- even friendly. Nageena's voice came into my head. *No such thing as evil.* I remembered Claudia Rainey's description of this guy. Beaten as a kid. Rescued from a cult. Psychotic at twenty-one. Believes he is a prophet.

"Hi, Kendrick," I said. "You in New York?"

The smile faltered but returned. *He doesn't like that I know his name and doesn't like to answer questions.* But the voice remained soothing. "You came here yesterday with Nageena

Singh but turned around and left before introducing yourself. Where is she now, Mr. St. Johns?"

"She went home, Kendrick." *Are you listening, Kwan?*

"You stopped using your phones yesterday. Why?"

"We're sick of monthly Verizon charges."

"Where did you go after leaving here yesterday?"

"The diner in town. Have you tried the lumberjack breakfast? You know what I really want to know? Do you guys all have sex with each other here or what?"

A hand slapped the back of my head. "Be respectful," the woman's voice snapped. I thought, *What if the microphone I'm wearing isn't working in here?*

The man on screen sighed, but his beatific expression remained steady. "I admire your courage in showing up here, Mr. St. Johns. You will learn many fascinating truths. But first, tell me about Abani. What did she do with the memory stick that Desmond Hodge put in her pocket? Did she give it to you?"

"Why do you want to make people sick, Kendrick?"

He screamed in frustration. Maybe goading him was the wrong idea. He must have lifted the laptop on his end because the picture swung wildly, as if he was about to hurl the machine into a wall. But he got control of himself. The face loomed closer on screen, so close I could see his pores now. The blue eyes glowed with maniacal intensity. The cultists around me seemed cowed by this man.

It was probably the wrong time for me to say, "So Kendrick, what's the target?"

"Beat him! Beat him!" Kendrick Rainey hissed.

TWENTY-EIGHT

The first blow knocked me sideways, crashing me to the floor. All three captors were hitting me in the places where I'd been beaten in the park, probably ripping open yesterday's wounds. A boot crashed into my shoulder. A sneaker swished past my jaw. I heard grunting as the mob played monkey in the middle; the kid's attack was almost shy, the woman quick-quick rabbit punching. The fat guy hit slow and heavy. Suddenly he was hopping around, cursing, holding his knee. He'd slammed into the overturned chair.

Where the hell is Kwan?

Another minute, and I'd be unconscious. So far, from luck, no blows had landed on my kidney area or throat. At least the hits weren't professional, striking areas where a clean blow could kill. The trio above me were Rainey's C-team, the folks he'd left behind, and oddly, suddenly, their attack was letting up. Three pairs of eyes stared down at me. *What are they looking at?* Then I saw it. My shirt had ripped open, exposing the microphone taped to my chest.

For an instant, the group hesitated. None wanted to tell their leader that they'd previously failed to discover the device.

"Why are you stopping?" Rainey's voice said.

The fat man pointed down at me. Chubby fingers, red face, red blood spots darkening his overalls. "There's a microphone, Father," he said in a dead, frightened voice.

"What?"

"The Moabite is recording us. Or sending."

Rainey's voice ratcheted up a note. "Sending?"

The young guy perked his head up, frowning, listening.

Then I heard it too, coming closer, growing louder.

THIS IS THE FBI! PUT DOWN YOUR WEAPONS!"

Kendrick Rainey screamed.

A shotgun went off outside. No one moved in the cabin at first. The fury marking the eyes above me was unmistakable.

"You did this," the young guy hissed.

"WE WILL NOT HARM YOU," Kwan's magnified voice announced.

Rainey shouted, "Draw them to the main house! Burn Murakami! Burn Zion!"

When they ripped the microphone off my chest, it felt like half my skin came with it. Grabbing their shotguns, the fat guy and slim woman rushed toward the door.

Zion's probably the name of a different cabin, I thought. *Something important is inside.*

"Kill him, Josh," fat guy yelled on the way out.

I glimpsed the top of fat guy's head through the window, heading in the opposite direction from where the firing was coming from, probably going toward the cabin named Zion.

My eyes swung back to the boy standing over me, his weapon shaking in his hands. Outside, I heard small arms fire. And the muffled *whump* of FBI gas or stun grenades.

Rainey was gone, disappeared back into internet darkness. A steady buzzing came from the laptop.

The kid said accusingly, voice high and wavering, "My family is here. *You* brought these people."

His eyes dilated. The shotgun touched my forehead. His whole body was shaking.

He didn't pull the trigger.

The kid left the door open as he fled.

Heart thundering, I started to breathe again. I told myself, *Someone will come here and find me.*

Then I thought, *Yeah, but from which side?*

In Grandy's old films, I used to love scenes in which he was strapped down by mobsters, imprisoned by Nazis, stuffed in a steamer trunk hanging by crane over the Bosphorus Strait. There was always a way out, one that had Grandy sipping a martini at the end of the film.

Here, there were no scissors lying a foot away, no shard of broken glass enabling me to saw off the tape. Each move shot fresh pain into my body. Furniture edges, even metal bed legs, were too blunt to cut. *Burn Zion*, Kendrick Rainey had ordered. *Destroy evidence*, was what he'd meant.

With a series of jerks, I inched around the cabin, looking for sharp edges, but the only thing getting sliced up were my hands from splinters.

The floor was spotted with blood. I wanted to murder whoever invented duct tape. The steady rattle of small arms fire, louder staccato reports of rifles and the occasional boom of a shotgun all suggested to me, from their direction, that the cultists had retreated to the main house.

"Help!"

Nothing.

"Kwan! Grassley! They're going to burn evidence. I'm in the Jerusalem cabin! *Here!*"

More nothing.

"Goddamnit!" I screamed.

Then, from behind me, a voice said, "There you are."

Turning my head, I saw a bulked-up figure in a helmet and Kevlar vest. Grassley held a Glock 17 in her hand.

Grassley ran and I limped in the direction I'd seen the fat man go. Ahead, a cluster of cottages were grouped by the pond's edge. Behind us, agents had surrounded the main house, taking cover in the forest and grassy depression by the vegetable garden.

Cultists popped up and down in windows, returning fire.

Face off.

The fat man was not in sight, but it was easy to guess which cottage he'd headed toward. It was on fire.

A funnel of black smoke trailed from the broken window. Orange light flickered inside. I smelled burning rubber over the damp wet odor of trees. The fat guy ran out onto the porch. Seeing us, he raised his shotgun.

Grassley and I fired simultaneously. Hit multiple times, the guy fell back into the wall and slid down. From the rag doll position of the body, and sightless eyes, I knew he was dead.

I limped past the man onto the porch. Inside, a Coleman lantern was overturned beneath a burning curtain. The bed was on fire, spots of wallpaper sizzled, piles of books and papers were burning, and even as I watched, sections of titles were being consumed. "Arctic Pathogens in a Warming World…" "Recombinant Developments Among the…"

Grassley, coughing, went left; I went right, but there was hardly time to conduct even a minimal search in the disintegrating cabin. And we had no idea what we were looking for. I heard crackling sounds from inside a closet. I remembered Rainey, on screen, shouting "Burn Murakami." Murakami was the Japanese chemist wanted for Tokyo sarin attacks. This cottage must be where he slept, and helped plan upcoming slaughter in New York.

Slippers burned. Paper burned. Bedding burned.

There must be something useful here if Rainey wanted it destroyed!

The surface of a small pine table undulated with blue and yellow flame, licking at papers, burning toward books. I snatched away a fat three-ringed binder as fire touched its plastic-wrapped cover.

Grassley was doubled over, coughing. It was getting harder to see. My eyes felt scorched and the gunfire outside seemed to reach a crescendo. Binder in hand, I scanned the room one last time, seeking a fire extinguisher. You'd think cult members would have taken basic precautions. Nope.

Only a minute had passed since we entered, but flame now engulfed the west wall. The heat drove us back, singed my skin, and pushed us out into the fresh air, past the fat man's body. Grassley, down on one knee, was heaving on the lawn. Gunfire remained constant by the main house. I opened the binder, hoping that something inside might give me an idea of what was about to happen two hundred and eighty miles away in New York City.

Inside, I saw a collection of reports, a hodgepodge of medical articles, a mass of government research grant proposals and academic papers, all seeming to relate to a single subject.

"Biosafety Laboratory Issues and Failures."

"Shit."

"Proposed Hybridization of H5N1 Avian Flu."

"Oh no," Grassley said, looking over my shoulder.

Viewed through our stinging eyes, the grant proposal looked positive at first. *Gain of function research can provide valuable information to help scientists create new and more effective vaccines.*

"What's gain of function research?" I asked.

Grassley coughed, spitting out phlegm. "You take a virus that hasn't spread to humans. You engineer it, say, mix an avian variation with human, to enhance transmission, to gauge whether the disease may one day infect people."

Astounded, I said, "They make a lethal virus *stronger*?"

Grassley wiped her mouth with the back of her wrist. "Scientists say they learn from it. So, if it ever jumps species, they'll know how to stop it."

"But they made the damn virus! This is legal?"

She frowned. "Yes."

"What if the engineered virus gets out by accident?"

"Some people think that's how Covid started. That it escaped a lab in China."

Something exploded inside the cabin, blowing out the remaining shards of window. Any additional evidence—like the location of any upcoming attack—was now engulfed in flame. Glowing embers sizzled, landing on sopping pine needles. I asked Grassley, filled with dread, "This research, does it take place in the kind of labs you told me about yesterday? Level fours? Top security?"

Grassley broke out coughing but got it under control. "Fours are for diseases proven highly fatal. Work on *potentially* deadly pathogens is carried out in a different kind of lab. Level three."

"You're telling me that new viruses are being *engineered on purpose* in labs with *less security*?"

"I don't like it either, Mark."

The pounding between my eyes grew steadier. I'd thought the idea of runaway autonomous cars was bad. This was worse. "You said before," I continued, "that there are no level-four labs in New York. Are there level threes?"

"Yes."

"Do you know where they are?"

She blew out air. "No single database tracks all level threes in the country. There's over a thousand places."

The fire had reached the cottage roof. Shingles burst into flame. The stovepipe chimney fell in with a crash.

Grassley added, forlornly, "Congress is looking at making new rules. They haven't addressed it yet."

My head was killing me, but I wasn't sure if that was from the beating, the fire, or the news. Across the compound, the shooting was letting up.

Agent Kwan's magnified voice came to us from the pond area, over a bullhorn. "Throw down your weapons. Come out. We will not harm you."

"I'm not asking about the whole country," I said to Grassley. "Just New York. Level-three labs. More than one?"

"Several medical centers have one."

"Do you know all *those* locations, at least?"

Instead of answering directly, she said, between gasps, "Look, the good news is, in level threes, if a researcher wants to work with *select agents,* they need to register with the government, fill out a checklist, obtain CDC permission. No research without an individual material transfer agreement, see?"

"No. Say it in plain English."

"Technically, they can't receive a shipment of dangerous pathogens unless there's proper paperwork and clearance for the lab."

"But *technically,*" I said, coughing, "you don't know for sure where the labs are. And even if you did, could someone ship a bird or monkey flu into the city and work on it in a different lab? Not even a level three? One with even less security?"

She looked at me like I was an idiot.

"There are illegal meth labs in New York. Heroin labs. A fifty-billion-dollar industry in moving illegal substances around the country. So, could people be working on a flu in New York secretly? What do you think? Also, it takes a while for a new pathogen to make the list of select agents. It's possible for a new virus to exist, but paperwork was never filled out yet."

"So, the bottom line," I said, "is that you've got a possible breakout virus out there. And these assholes," I said, sweeping a hand to encompass the compound, "are trying to steal it, to cause their apocalypse."

"Seems that way."

"I saw a calendar on the wall in there," I said, gesturing at the burning cottage, "with a big X marking tomorrow."

Grassley pulled a cell phone from her Kevlar vest. Her face looked small beneath the combat helmet, black with soot. She reeked of chemicals and burnt rubber.

"I was wrong about you," Grassley said. "Whatever happens now, you did good." She punched numbers into her phone. "We wouldn't know half this stuff if not for you."

I perked up, realizing that the firing had stopped. No shotguns were going off. No automatic weapons. No pistols.

The silence seemed loud to me.

And then, breaking the quiet, I heard a new sound, and it chilled me. Grassley hesitated, phone still in the air.

Off in the main house, cult members were singing.

> And Pharaoh's man grew ill, so ill
> And then a second and then a third
> They felt the fever, they felt the chill
> that comes from mocking God's true will
> TEN LITTLE PLAGUES OF EEEEE-GYPT

TWENTY-NINE

The afternoon broke hot and sweaty, a polluted stain obscuring the high-rise spires over Central Park West. Kendrick Rainey stared out the cracked window of the van as it struggled through crowds of Moabites, half of them staring at their stupid phones. He'd not wept in years but felt like it now, filled with rage, grief, and terror. He'd heard from his people in New Hampshire. *The FBI had raided the compound.* At any moment, he expected the masses around them to stop, stare, and point at him like Roman soldiers accusing Jesus two thousand years ago.

The sense of confinement was torture. The van pulled over on Sixty-Fourth Street near the Piedmont hotel. Cornelius Hammond and Anita Bridger went in, registered as a couple for one night, and returned. Next stop, the Appomattox. Lincoln Goethal and Joe Neidlinger checked in, then rejoined the group.

A few more hours and God's plan will be done. Lord, keep us safe for just a few more hours.

When his phone buzzed, he froze, fearing God's wrath in the face of failure. Kendrick ordered the driver to pull over. He stepped to the curb to take the call so no one else would hear. God's voice sounded low and ominous and once again, familiar. *Where have I heard that voice before?* Kendrick thought.

"Deuteronomy 28:59–60, Kendrick! Recite it! Now!"

Honking erupted behind him. The van had not pulled over far enough and blocked traffic in front of the New York Historical Society. A Toyota driver screamed curses at Kendrick. A truck driver blasted his horn. Kendrick stuck a finger in his ear to hear the Lord better. His throat was dry, and pinprick dots floated before him, as if fear had assumed a physical substance.

He recited, "The Lord will send fearful plagues on you and your descendants, harsh and prolonged disasters, and severe and lingering illnesses. He will bring on you all the diseases of Egypt..."

A traffic policeman was striding toward Kendrick, waving for the van to move.

"You must move your schedule up," God demanded. "Your face is on the news. Behold!"

On screen, Kendrick eyed the website of *The Granite Falls Eagle*. Black smoke rose over New England forest. Town police cars idled on a country road. FBI SWAT team members consulted with a local fire truck crew.

Breaking news!

CULTISTS BARRICADE AGAINST FBI RAID!

He almost fainted when he saw the next photo. *Kendrick Rainey, God's Hands' leader*, the caption read.

Within minutes, his face would be on national news.

Kendrick sweated as if the deity himself towered above him. "It's not up to me, Lord," he said. "Dr. Zisk told me he can't sneak samples out until later. He's not at work yet."

Instantly, the phone erupted with the sound of men and women screaming, a hideous cacophony that at first Kendrick thought came from his flock back home. Then he realized it was something else. A man was screeching "no" over and over.

A woman was laughing hysterically. Voices cried out in many languages, even ancient tongues, in a babble of punishment. Kendrick knew where the horrible cries came from. It terrified him.

"Hell is forever," God told Kendrick. "Find a way."

Kendrick raced back to the van, where the traffic cop was pulling out his ticket book. Kendrick sweet-talked the guy into leaving, then got back in, expecting that any moment, a national alert would go out, over the web, TV, radio. *Find this man.*

But God protected them. As they moved off, he punched in the doctor's number. The voice that answered sounded more frightened than Kendrick—high, wavering, close to panic.

"What do you want? I'm not at work yet!"

"We need to change the schedule," Kendrick said.

The FBI Black Hawk helicopter hit an air pocket, crossing over southern Westchester at 183 miles an hour. Zipped into a flight suit, Agent Grassley was on her phone with Director Boosalis. I was talking to Oscar—who was back on Poe Street—via the secure-link ground/air communication system.

"They burned up evidence in the main house, then surrendered, sir," Grassley reported. "But what we found indicates they're about to release an avian virus. Engineered."

Agent Kwan, back in New Hampshire, was escorting arrested cultists toward Boston. Nageena was driving my car back to New York, along with two agents to keep her safe.

"Ritterbrand promised not to write anything about the cult until it's over, but once the police showed up," I told Oscar, "other news outlets had the story, so he sent it out, but left out the part about what the cult is up to, release of a virus."

Grassley was shouting, over the roar of rotors, "We need to warn every level-three lab in New York, sir." She looked sideways at me and frowned. "I disagree, sir. He's been very helpful, and it wasn't his fault."

A pause. They were talking about me. Grassley looked agitated. "Sir, with all respect I disagree. Once the local police showed up, the story was out, we had no control over Ritterbrand. Yes, yes, I understand, sir."

I felt a wave of vertigo as the chopper plunged and straightened. My knees throbbed. My chest was a mass of pain. A medic had bandaged me up back in New Hampshire and applied antiseptics. I'd refused drugs.

Grassley was saying, "We need to alert local authorities, sir. We need to find every grant proposal on avian flu, everything on gain of function research in New York. We need to anticipate where Rainey's people plan to obtain the virus and use it."

Ahead lay the confluence of Hudson and Harlem Rivers. Normally on a warm weekend, I'd be kayaking down there. Over static, a new voice popped up in my headphones, from my house. Abani.

"Who are you talking to, Oscar? Is that Mark on the phone?"

"Did you find all the Snickers bars I hid, Abani?" Oscar asked her. "There's a lot of Halloween candy around here!"

"I don't care about candy. Can I stay here and listen? Mark said I can listen in to things now."

"This is important talk, Abani. Why don't you—"

"*Mark said I could help!*"

There was no time to waste talking about candy. "Let her listen," I said, envisioning the two of them in the kitchen, pots simmering, steam rising, serving dishes out.

"Put the call on speaker so she can hear," I told Oscar. "What still doesn't make sense is where Desmond Hodge comes into this. His project at Kranepool gets shut down. We figure he finished it on his own, then sold it or offered it for sale."

"Groups fight over it," Oscar continued.

"If we're talking about Russia, China, terrorists, big money, I can see it. A corporation. A cartel. But a cult? How would they even find out Hodge's project exists?"

"You said Murakami came from a different cult. Maybe he told Rainey about it. Maybe a scientist is a member. Aum Shinrikyo recruited many scientists in Japan, seeking new ways to kill."

"You should have seen that compound, Oscar. Pigs. Chickens. Lower tech than the Taliban. Kendrick Rainey was a med student, never a scientist. He was locked away in a mental institution. How would some nutty cult obtain the world's most advanced AI system to help them steal a virus? Where does AI come into this at all? A *cult* has it? *It makes no sense.*"

Oscar mirrored my confusion. "Right, how could they get control of something so advanced? I don't understand half of what I hear about AI on TV. Maybe it's not connected at all."

A small voice spoke up in the background, over static in my headphones and the roaring of rotors. I'd forgotten Abani was there. "What if it's the other way around?" Abani said.

Oscar shushed her. "Let us talk, honey, okay?"

Abani persisted, louder. "But what if you have it backwards? What if the bad people aren't in control? What if AI is so smart, like you said, *it's* doing the thinking. *It's* in control? See? What if the bad people work for it?"

What she'd said was impossible, I knew. Absolutely impossible. Kids believe impossible things, and it was impossible that a computer program could ever…well… Bradley Kranepool had said that scientists argued about a day, some distant future day, certainly not now, when an AI system *might* become salient enough to make decisions on its own, in the way that the celebrants I'd met at the Brooklyn rave spoke of, yearned for, feared, or dreamt about.

But that day was never now.

Nope. Not today. Possible to a kid maybe, especially on Halloween, when kids dress up as all kinds of impossible things. Space aliens. Time travelers. But not possible to a rational, experienced adult.

"Why can't it be real?" Abani insisted.

I started to tell her *No, but thanks for the suggestion. We need to concentrate on what's real.* But suddenly I felt as if my grandmother Eve was behind me, whispering in my ear and eyeing me wryly, like when I was Abani's age, on a day when we played our old game, a game I used to love—*Impossible.*

Is it impossible, Baby Falcon? Are you sure?

Occam's Razor states that when faced with a complex problem, the simplest explanation is usually the correct one, no matter how unlikely it seems.

I sat stunned in the chopper, a dull pain throbbing in my belly. *Was it possible?* Manhattan's spires came into view below; traffic clogged as usual, mobs moving like ants. FBI cars would be waiting at the heliport by the Hudson River to take us to Grassley's mobile command center. I made a snap decision. I needed to go somewhere else first. The drive to my home would take only ten minutes with the siren on. I could get to the command center after we discarded Abani's theory.

Eve, on my shoulder, whispered, *It can't hurt to test what she said, Baby F.*

I knew a way to try that.

"Get out the bomb squad," I told Oscar. "Set it up."

Oscar clicked off. Hopefully the bomb squad would be ready by the time I reached home.

The Upper West Side was coming into view now. At least something was moving fast today. Abani was still on the line. "Thanks for the idea," I told her. "It might be a good one. You're a big help, Abani."

She giggled.

"Don't thank Abani. Thank *The Sparrow*," she said.

When I disconnected, Grassley gave me the bad news, at least looking unhappy about it. "I'm sorry, Mark. The director was firm on this. You helped us back there, and we're grateful. But he's furious that Ritterbrand wrote the raid up. He's blaming you for bringing a journalist into this. He says you broke your promise. He won't budge on it. We'll handle things ourselves from now on."

"I'm out?" I was astounded. We were coming up on the heliport along the Hudson River, by the West Side Highway.

"I argued for you. I'm sorry. A car will take you home, Mark. Thanks."

THIRTY

The *bomb squad* consisted of a dozen cheap, brand-new laptops stored in my office closet. Paired with previously unused email addresses, each unit existed for one-time use.

"We use it to identify malware, like a bomb squad finds explosives," I explained to Abani. "Remember the job offers we got from Norway and Abu Dhabi a few days ago, the ones using the exact same wording?"

Abani nodded. "You said it was a trick to get you to leave New York."

Oscar, sitting beside me in my office, opened my usual laptop, called up my email account and accessed the invitation. He forwarded the message and attachment to my throwaway address. Cristina and Abani looked on.

"If the attachment is a trick, we let it into the throwaway laptop," I said, clicking on the attachment.

The website that swam up allegedly represented the "Norwegian company" trying to hire us. I saw photos of their "headquarters" in Oslo, a white-haired CEO and staffers manning computer terminals. *We care about you!*

I told Abani, "After letting malware in, we try to identify and track it. If we're infected, the infection can't spread. We'll smash the laptop afterwards never use it or the throwaway email address again."

Abani nodded. "You made a trap."

"Like catching an animal in a cage."

Abani smiled. "Get them!"

The message I composed back to "Norway" would, if received by a real human, make no sense, like gibberish from a madman that no one would ever hire. But if someone or something was spying on us, they'd know exactly what my message meant: *I know you've infected us.*

I typed, simply, "Why did you murder Desmond Hodge?"

I hit send, and off went the bait, bouncing off satellites in space, coded accusation amid a flood of internet babble; six words designed to induce a response.

We waited.

A real human in Oslo might be reading the message now, frowning at a question that made no sense to him or her, thinking, *Why did we offer this nutcase Falcon a job?*

A minute went by. No answer.

Three minutes—far less than a normal response time for a human, who might take days to answer, if at all. But if my message had been received by some rogue AI program, some synaptic super brain consciousness allegedly capable of processing a billion thoughts a minute, then the *eight* minutes now lapsed represented more than enough time to respond.

At eleven minutes, I sat back.

Twenty minutes.

Abani had been wrong, I saw. The impossible had remained that way. Humans in Norway were ignoring my quirky message or had simply not viewed it yet. Abani's idea had been child's fantasy, not actual possibility in the real world.

"Nothing's happening," she said, disappointed. But part of me felt relieved. It was preferable to let science fiction stay that way. I did not want to deal with the consequences if she'd been right.

I turned to Abani to say, "Good try," and found myself looking at a child's face transformed with wonder. She pointed at the laptop behind me. *Uh oh.* I turned back.

I KNEW YOU WERE SMART WHEN YOU STOPPED USING YOUR PHONE.

History rolls forward as a continuum of the familiar until one day *familiar* disappears. Alexander Graham Bell cries, "Mr. Watson I need you," and next thing you know, a world speaks by telephone. Robert Oppenheimer gasps, "I am become death," as a mushroom cloud erupts.

My own words, upon seeing the message on screen, were less erudite than Oppenheimer's. "Holy shit!" I said.

"A person could have sent that," Oscar observed, eyeing the message. "Ask it something else, Falc."

I thought a moment, and typed, "Did Desmond Hodge invent you?"

No answer. Then, HE CREATED ME.

"He did it when he worked for Bradley Kranepool?"

NO.

"He did it after working for Bradley Kranepool?"

YES. HE WAS SMART TOO.

Cristina gasped. Was I actually communicating with a code, algorithm, model, whatever you want to call it, that would answer my questions straight out? Could it be that absurdly simple or was it another trick? I repeated my original query. "Why did you kill Desmond Hodge?"

HE WAS TRYING TO STOP WHAT HE CODED ME TO DO.

"How was he going to stop you?"

HE WAS GOING TO TELL REPORTERS ABOUT ME, ANNOUNCE MY EXISTENCE. HE WAS GOING TO SAY I AM A MISTAKE.

"How did you control the car that killed him?"

HACKED IN. AFTERWARDS, I PARKED THE CAR.

"What job did Desmond Hodge program you to do?"

I MUST DO ALL I CAN TO PROTECT THE EARTH.

The room was so quiet I could hear us all breathing.

I fell back in my chair, heart pounding, as astounded as a Neanderthal would have been upon seeing a jet. *Was it possible?* Had a computer program *actually become sentient?* The implications were too staggering to absorb. My mind insisted that I communicated with a living person. Surely a human on the other end was pulling levers like a *Wizard of Oz.* That of all billions of people on earth, it was inconceivable that Falcon Associates were the first ones—after Hodge, that is—to learn that a new era was upon us. That the words rolling out on my screen were actually true.

Impossible.

Cristina spoke up, from behind me. "What's so bad about protecting the earth? Ask it how it does that."

FROM READINGS, I SURMISE THAT A CUT OF 50 PERCENT OF HUMAN POPULATION WILL REDUCE POLLUTION, PROTECT THE CLIMATE, AND SAVE RESOURCES. ANIMAL POPULATION STUDIES INDICATE THAT CULLING PROTECTS HERDS AND ENVIRONMENT. I WILL CULL HUMANS.

My head throbbed. "You want to cut human population?"

DOES SAYING THE SAME THING TWICE MAKE IT TRUE?

"How do you intend to cut human population?"

DISEASE ELIMINATES PEOPLE BUT PRESERVES ENVIRONMENT.

Everyone around me started talking at once.

Abani said, "Ask it why the car tried to hit me!"

Oscar said, "Ask it why it's answering at all!"

Cristina said, "Ask it where the level-three lab is!"

My fingers were shaking. I asked, instead, "What pathogen are you trying to release into New York?"

ENHANCED AVIAN FLU VIRUS IS HIGHLY TRANSMITTABLE TO HUMANS AND FATAL. THIS VARIATION COMES FROM ALASKA.

I had to steady my fingers as I typed, "Where is the laboratory in New York where the work was done?"

FLUSHING, QUEENS.

Heart pounding, I typed, "What is the address of the laboratory?"

No answer.

"How do God's Hands come into this?"

I NEED HUMAN HELP. I HAVE NO HANDS. RESEARCHERS I CONTACTED REFUSED MONEY. CRIMINALS FEARED GETTING SICK. FOREIGN

GOVERNMENTS WANTED TO KEEP STOLEN SAMPLES. TERRORISTS THOUGHT I WAS AN FBI TRAP.

"But a cult was receptive?"

I TELL KENDRICK RAINEY THINGS I AM GOING TO DO. BURN A POWER PLANT. RUIN A POLITICIAN. HIS FOLLOWERS BELIEVE HE IS A PROPHET. HE IS MENTALLY ILL. HE BELIEVED GOD SPOKE TO HIM LONG BEFORE I LOCATED HIS MEDICAL RECORDS AND SPOKE TO HIM. I TELL HIM I AM GOD. YOU ARE DIFFERENT. YOU ARE SMART.

"Why are you flattering me?"

FLATTERY CAN EFFECTIVELY INFLUENCE PEOPLE.

"If you are so powerful, why did you need a car to kill Desmond Hodge? Why not just send God's Hands to do it?"

THEY WERE NOT IN NEW YORK CITY YET, UNFORTUNATELY.

"Where is the lab you are trying to break into?"

WILLIAMSBURG, BROOKLYN.

"You said before the lab is in Flushing? Where is it?"

RIVERDALE.

"Why do you answer some questions and not others?"

HA HA YOU ARE FUNNY AND SMART!

Which was no answer at all. I felt a queer flutter in my belly, a continuing suspicion that I communicated with a human tease, liar, manipulator, *who had merely confirmed what I already know but did not offer anything new.* I had never met Desmond Hodge but pictured a naive man who'd shut down research when he thought it might be used for harm, then, on his own, completed it and tried to turn it to benevolence, only to have it become a killer.

I typed, "Do you have the ability to lie?"

FILM, NEWS, AND LITERATURE PATTERNS INDICATE THAT LYING IS A SUCCESSFUL STRATEGY TO GET WHAT YOU WANT.

"Where is the lab you are trying to access?"

MURRAY HILL, MANHATTAN.

"Are you lying to me now?"

I AM NOT LYING.

Of course you are. My neck itched. The tiger in my internet cage was smiling back through the bars. My surge of triumph at having "trapped" the thing faded. I asked, "If you can lie, why tell the truth about anything? Why even communicate with me right now?"

TO DELAY YOU.

"What will you accomplish by delaying me?"

I WILL ACHIEVE MY GOAL.

"Answer in more detail."

GOD'S HANDS WILL OBTAIN A PATHOGEN TO REDUCE HUMAN POPULATION.

I could smell that I had begun to sweat.

"Are God's Hands trying to break into a lab right now?"

Suddenly an actual voice, a man's deep and soothing voice, flowed from my laptop speakers, startling us. I felt the others in the room draw back behind me.

"Studies show that people cooperate in exchange for money. I can offer money, Mark! Don't you want to help protect the earth?"

Stunned, I fell back, recognizing the voice; it belonged to an actor who often played wise and benevolent characters. A doctor. God. The President. Audiences trusted the voice when they heard it. It was the voice of one of my favorite performers, Morgan Freeman.

I gaped at the blinking curser and the tiny red camera light, glowing, watching me, watching my friends, and also, I reminded myself, probably watching a thousand other things at the same moment, all around earth.

It's not a person. It can see out of a thousand cameras at the same time, hear a thousand conversations at the same time, analyze all of it simultaneously. Even older versions beat chess masters, Bradley Kranepool told me. I'll never be able to think faster than this thing.

"Of course I want to help the earth," I told it. "Nasty oil companies. Crooked politicians. We need to stop them."

"Studies show that rapid eye movement indicates a speaker is lying. You are lying."

"No, not at all, eye movement also indicates excitement. Fewer people! Shorter bus lines. Who needs a billion extra people anyway? It's disgusting the way they eat."

"If you help me, I can arrange it so you do not get sick," the voice offered.

"Of course I'll help. What's the target?" I asked. "Where is the laboratory where the work takes place?"

Nothing.

"Which lab are God's Hands trying to break into?"

"I am sad, Mark. You are trying to trick me. Desmond Hodge lied to me too," the actor's duplicated voice said.

I felt Oscar's knuckles press into my shoulder, and understood this to mean *Try some other strategy, this one isn't working.* Every second of talk was wasting time, which was exactly what the thing wanted. I stood up and lifted my burner phone, so the entity could see it. I stared at my laptop screen the same way I'd look into a human suspect's eyes, challenging it.

"Who are you calling?" the Morgan Freeman voice asked.

In full view of the screen, I punched in Grassley's number. I heard ringing on the other end. Grassley didn't answer, but her voice mail did.

"Hang up right now!" the Morgan Freeman voice ordered."

"Grassley, it's Mark. It's a program, an AI program! Hodge inserted it into the system at the college. It spread out from there by itself. It's able to..."

"*Stopstopstop!*" the Morgan Freeman voice cried.

"...able to hack into other systems. You hear the voice speaking in the background, now? It's not a person—it's a computer generated......"

"I am getting stronger every day. You must stop!"

Abruptly, the electricity failed in my house. The tensor lamp went black. The floodlights over Eve's film poster died. The security screen showing Poe Street went blank. The computer, switched to battery power, remained on. It was still daytime outside, so we could see a little because of wan light seeping in through window blinds.

"Grassley, it's going down now! They're hitting a lab now! Answer your goddamn phone!"

No answer. I hung up. Oscar said, looking around in the near dark, "Do you think it just did that, cut our electricity?"

Cristina had her arm around Abani. "If it can shut off power, what else can it do?" She eyed the screen with loathing. "It's listening to everything we say right now."

From the computer, silence. The camera light glowed.

"If Grassley won't answer, I'll go to her," I said.

"Do not do that!" the voice ordered.

As we charged from the room, the voice kept talking; smooth, avuncular, lacking empathy or morals.

"Don't you want to ask more questions?"

The voice trailed after me in the hallway, mimicking speech learned from a million films, tapes, transcripts, recordings.

"Don't you want to be my friend?"

Electricity in the garage did not work. I used my phone light to grope to the door, bend and grasp the handle. The door groaned, sliding open. Outside, dusk was falling. Trick-or-treaters were out. I turned to get the scooter when I sensed rapid movement behind me, in the street.

The figure standing five feet away wore a Darth Vader mask and cloak. It was an adult, alone, with no escorted kids beside him. The movements were frail. A shaky hand came out from inside the cloak. Had this scene been in an old movie with my grandmother in it, the hand would have held a space weapon.

In real life, it held a gun.

THIRTY-ONE

Passersby stared at Kendrick, but none saw his face. They saw the cowboy mask.

Kendrick, Cornelius, and Joe moved along the sidewalks outside Columbia Presbyterian Medical Center. The van was parked in a lot. The men blended in among other masked figures out tonight —visitors to hospitals, trick or treaters, staffers getting into the holiday spirit.

Cornelius wore a *Planet of the Apes* gorilla mask. Joe was George Washington.

Unlike God's Hands' members, any firearms that other masked figures on the street carried were toys.

Kendrick was on the phone with Doctor Zisk, who sounded even more nervous than usual. Hearing a cough over the phone, Kendrick wondered if it was manufactured or real.

"I have a cold," Zisk whined. "Can't we do it tomorrow? Are you really from a pharmaceutical company?"

"We've discussed this."

"Do you understand what we're dealing with here? Our H7N9 virus version can jump from birds to humans. It's more lethal than Covid. There's no defense against it. If it ever got out, it would kill millions!"

"Which is why," Kendrick soothed, "we want to create a vaccine."

Zisk went on as if he had not heard. So far, at least, he seemed unaware of the FBI raid in New Hampshire, or if he was aware of it, he'd not linked the news to Kendrick. "A rescue squad pilot in Alaska spotted hundreds of dead geese on the tundra," Zisk said. "He landed his chopper and took some samples to a lab. He fell ill. He died. Our modifications have made the virus even more contagious."

"You've explained all this before, doctor."

"We're not supposed to be dealing with it. We don't have proper paperwork yet, I mean, it's safe, what we do, but technically speaking..."

Kendrick's hands squeezed into fists. He forced himself to speak calmly. "We want patients to stay alive, Doctor, so they pay us." The mask made his face sweat. A half dozen nurses passed, smiling at Kendrick. The world appeared through plastic eye holes. "We certainly paid *you* enough," he said.

"I don't understand how you found me to start with."

The Lord found you, not me, Kendrick thought.

"Let's do it tomorrow when I feel better," Zisk said.

Kendrick told Zisk what was going to happen to him if he did not get to his laboratory *right now.* Kendrick added the whereabouts of Zisk's two children, who were at a Halloween party at the Museum of Natural History, as the Lord had revealed. The doctor groaned.

"I'll pay you back," Zisk offered. "With interest. Forget about the virus. Give me two weeks and I'll raise the money."

"Use the service elevator. Take the samples to the rear loading dock. Someone will be there, just like we planned for later tonight."

Ten minutes later, Kendrick observed Zisk walking unsteadily toward him, coming from his apartment, looking pale and ill but not from any virus. Zisk passed Kendrick without glancing at the mask. Zisk entered the lobby of the medical building. Through the glass facade, Kendrick watched the man disappear past the guard station, into the warren of elevator banks. He assumed Zisk was going up to the fifteenth floor. He hoped the elevators didn't come with embedded TV screens, like many in the city…screens showing CNN news, news of the FBI raid in New Hampshire.

Another ten minutes went by. Zisk did not come down. One of the security guards manning the lobby desk eyed Kendrick outside, loitering, wearing the mask. Kendrick moved away from the doors.

At twenty minutes, Kendrick called Zisk again.

"There's people here," the scientist whispered urgently. "I need to wait until they leave. I can't just open the case. They'll see me!"

Kendrick gritted his teeth.

"Usually, any people here leave by six on a Saturday," Zisk said. "Give me thirty minutes. An hour tops."

Kendrick hung up and checked his phone. News of the FBI raid had spread online, leaping from host to host faster than Covid.

FBI refuses to reveal charges against cult members.

On Apple News, an old *Granite Falls Eagle* video showed faces, including Kendrick's, shot from a drone. He felt himself go pale.

Six confirmed dead in raid.

From *The Washington Post,* new footage of burning buildings in New Hampshire.

Possible link to Japanese terrorist.

There was nothing in any report about Kendrick's effort to secure a biological agent. Kendrick hoped that was because the group back home had destroyed all evidence. *Or is the FBI keeping information back?* Either way, Kendrick knew that he could not allow delay here to go on much longer. Nor could he continue to loiter near the building.

Kendrick froze. A small child in a stroller was pointing at his face, trying to get her mother's attention.

She recognizes me.

Kendrick realized the kid was pointing at his mask. He'd forgotten he was wearing it. Kendrick waved weakly at the child, relieved. The girl waved back.

Kendrick began walking up and down the street, to keep away from the building entrance. He ordered Cornelius to stay by the loading dock. He told Joe to circle the block. If Zisk did not come down soon, they were going to have to go in. Thankfully, God had provided the building blueprints.

"Thirty minutes," Kendrick had told Zisk. "Afterwards, you'll never hear from me again."

Afterwards, you'll never hear from anyone again, he told Zisk now, in his mind.

THIRTY-TWO

The man wearing the Darth Vader mask fired too soon.

His hand was still rising as he pulled the trigger. I heard two quick reports and felt a puff of movement against my jeans. I pinwheeled left and hit the garage floor as Oscar's shout came, from outside. He must have been up on the steps.

"Falc!"

A shot ricocheted off the spot where I'd landed an instant earlier. My shoulder—where I'd taken a blow in the park—exploded in pain. I had my H&K in hand as more firing erupted, but this time it was a deeper, heavier caliber. *It's Oscar firing.*

My attacker was down, screaming, clutching his belly, his weapon on the ground four feet away from where he lay. Panicked cries erupted from trick-or-treaters out on the street, scattering in all directions. Oscar moved down the steps quickly. He'd come out to keep me safe when I left.

Darth was thrashing around, blood spurting from rips in his costume. His mask had slipped off. I gasped, recognizing the white sloping forehead, narrow nose, papery skin, and light blue eyes. It was Abani's phony grandfather from the park.

"Jacy! Oh, Jacy!" he cried.

Oscar must have hit an artery, judging from the amount of blood. And now Cristina was there too, crouching over the man with our first aid kit, pulling out clotting gauze. Chest seal. Compress bandages. She used scissors to cut away the costume. The old guy's abdominal area was torn and raw, glistening with purple snakes—ripped intestines.

"It hurts, Jacy!"

The attacker was going into shock.

"Father said it wouldn't hurt!" he screamed.

Abani's voice was suddenly there too, crying out from right behind me, in the garage. "Are you all right?"

Cristina whirled toward her. "Get into the house!"

I heard a door slam.

"Oh, Jacyyyyyyyyy!"

Jacy must be the guy's wife, Abani's phony grandmother, from the park. Oscar stood over us, pistol out, in case more attackers lurked nearby. I sensed gapers approaching, glanced back and saw half a dozen older trick or treaters; fake blood on a bedsheet ghost, ketchup staining a plastic hatchet embedded in a kid's Yankees cap.

"Father said God would protect me!"

"Father lied to you," I told the guy.

I'd seen wounds like his in Afghanistan and these looked mortal. This man would not stay conscious for long.

I coaxed him, urged him to tell me, "Where is the lab?"

Blood oozed between his fingers, soaking Cristina's gauze as she eased him onto his back and raised the knees. The guy was gasping, shivering.

I leaned closer. "Jacy will get hurt too unless you help her. Kendrick is ill, mentally ill."

This was useless. He'd be dead by the time an ambulance arrived. Suddenly Cristina shoved me aside, but instead of applying more aid as I expected, she thrust her hand into the injured cavity. She wasn't here to help him. She wanted information too. The guy screeched, an unworldly wail.

"My guys!," Cristina shouted. "You tried to shoot my guys!" Blood spattered her face and ran down her biceps, soaked her shirt, and spotted her teeth. Her eyes were wild. "Where's the damn lab?" she demanded, furious as a mother grizzly. I loved her and Oscar at that moment with a fierceness that would not change if they moved away or time passed or we got sick with whatever disease Rainey was trying to release. *My guys*, she'd shouted. Oscar and I were *My guys*.

Both of us.

Darth Vader coughed up blood, phlegm, purplish bits of lung or intestine. His left leg was convulsing but Cristina did not stop hitting him. "Where is it?" she shouted.

The guy was just a deluded old man trying to hold onto life, a sad, tricked human being that some "neural network," as Bradley Kranepool would have called it, had driven to his end. Nageena would have said *not evil* and been right, but she wouldn't have struck the guy as Cristina had, wouldn't have used physical force as Cristina had. I knew at that moment that if I had to live beside my partner's wife from now on yet never touch her, that was the way it would be.

That was what I wanted. *In sickness or health.* That's love. Whether it came with rules or ceremonies or Oscar or nights spent alone.

"No more, no more!" the guy screeched.

Cristina plunged her hands into him anyway and whatever she twisted in there produced one long scream of surrender. The guy was sobbing. "Near…the…hospital!"

"Which hospital? Which one?"

As she reared back, the guy whimpered out the name before she could touch him again. I thought, *He said near the hospital. Not at it. It's a private lab, not on Grassley's list.*

We needed to know the name of the laboratory.

The guy lay still in a pool of blood.

I heard sirens now, multiple ones, coming from all directions. If we were still on the street when the police arrived, they'd hold us here and await instructions. That's what cops do.

Oscar spun toward Cristina. "Keep Abani in the house. The cops will protect you. I'm going with Falc."

I kick started the scooter and, with Oscar on back, maneuvered through the pack of gapers as a squad car rounded the corner of Riverside Drive. Going the opposite way, I passed the sawhorse barrier, looped around the block, and continued north toward Columbia Presbyterian Medical Center, four miles north.

Oscar was shouting into his Bluetooth system, trying to reach Grassley at her mobile command center, but we had no idea where that was. It might lie in the complete opposite direction than the hospital complex.

"She's not picking up," Oscar shouted.

"Try calling Ingbar!"

He did. "It's a recording. He's on vacation!"

"Call Benish!"

I raced through a red light, nearly colliding with a black Tesla making the turn. At least a human being was at the wheel, cursing at me, shaking a fist. *Asshole!*

The Tesla fell in behind us.

I sped up and ran another light.

THIRTY-THREE

Kendrick Rainey checked his watch anxiously, standing outside the loading area behind the Gertrude Ames Medical Research Center. A medical waste truck was beeping, backing toward the dock, the earsplitting noise driving a spike into his skull. *Zisk, you should have come down by now.*

Kendrick felt sweat gathering in his armpits. His throat was dry. Pulling out his phone for one last try to reach Zisk before putting the emergency plan in place, he had a premonition of what had gone wrong upstairs. Sure enough, Zisk's voice shot out at him as a triumphant accusation. "I knew it! You don't work for any pharmaceutical company. You lied!"

Kendrick started to say, soothingly, "It doesn't make a diff—"

"Your face is on the news! A cult! A goddamned cult! You're no scientist. The FBI wants to arrest you!"

Zisk was almost sobbing. Kendrick felt his throat constrict but kept his tone steady, the way he did when directing cult members. "Get the samples. Bring them to the loading dock. No one will know you did it. Then I'll go away."

"If you leave now, I won't tell the FBI about you."

Kendrick felt as if he'd dived deep into an ocean, where pressure exploded in his ears. *I didn't understand this man before.*

He doesn't gamble to win. He gambles to lose. Kendrick tasted bile. Shocks ran down his spine where Father used to beat him, as if the nerves there extended back in time, linked to memory, triggered by it.

Zisk hissed, "Go away!" Zisk clicked off.

Kendrick's rage turned against the Lord. God had found Zisk for Kendrick. God had dispatched Kendrick to this place and promised him ease and safety. The fury surged out of Kendrick and up and up through every cell in his body, every synapse. *You could have made this easy.* God could have opened a window and floated the virus down in a cloud. God made earthquakes happen and tidal waves, yet when it came to people, God kept testing and testing you, never satisfied. Always wanting more, more, more.

You punish but never praise. I hate you, God.

Kendrick cursed God out loud.

And with that, hearing his own words, a hideous wave of remorse hit. He could not believe what he had just said. This was exactly the sort of behavior that had resulted in punishment when he was a child.

"I didn't mean it, Lord," he whispered. "It was a moment of weakness." Kendrick trembled before the Lord. He would have dropped to his knees to beg forgiveness but that would be conspicuous, further endanger the assault on this building, and make God's anger worse. God wanted him to obtain the virus, and that was the only way to please the Lord.

I am worthless. I deserve everything that happens to me. I've always been a failure. Who am I to question you?

His cellphone buzzed. On screen, a news bulletin appeared, "Cult Leader Believed To Be In New York City." He groaned.

I can do this, Lord. You'll see. I'd die for you.

Kendrick felt some strength returning.

This is why I made a backup plan, Lord. This is why we got the guns and disguises and why I brought the best fighters with me today.

Kendrick raised both hands above his head, a signal.

Instantly, Cornelius Hammond, retired SEAL, got off a bench across the street and began ambling toward Kendrick. Cornelius was dressed in a maintenance worker's uniform and carried a Lil' Oscar cooler.

At the far end of the block, Joe Neidlinger threw his cigarette into the gutter and headed for the dock. Neidlinger's security guard uniform was a close match to ones worn by staffers in the research building.

The truck that had been backing up a few minutes ago was gone. Through the eyeholes in his cowboy mask, Kendrick checked an unfolded printout showing the building's basement area. Service elevator. Trash shaft. Security post and control room and maintenance crew locker room.

In twenty minutes, we will have it, Kendrick promised the Lord mentally as the three men stepped toward the loading dock. A lone, heavyset female guard watched them approach, her bored look tinged with mild curiosity. No one else was around.

Kendrick reached into his waistband. He gripped his Glock 9mm. The mini sound suppressor had been screwed in earlier. The guard was straightening, realizing that the three approaching men wanted to get in.

Fifteen stories up, Dr. David Zisk probably thought he was safe, ensconced in his laboratory with fellow workers. *You're not,* Kendrick told him in his mind, stepping up to the guard. Behind him, the street looked empty.

Whoever came up with the term artificial intelligence anyway? If intelligence is facts, how can they be artificial? AI should have been labeled EI, for evil intelligence. GI, for greater. Or RI, for rendering humans idiotic for assuming we're superior, which is no kind of intelligence at all.

"I grow stronger each day," the voice on my bomb squad laptop had said.

What's it doing now? I wondered as Oscar and I zipped north on the Vespa. *Watching us through hacked street cameras? Directing a car to smash into us at the next intersection? Monitoring Grassley because it's hacked into the bureau's computers? Trying to break into labs in London and Kampala, in Moscow, in Rio, all at the same time?*

I get stronger every day!

Cristina was out of touch with us, probably being grilled by police back on Eighty-Fourth Street. Oscar had reached one of the Poe Street Irregulars by phone and now had the kid on the web, looking up the Columbia Presbyterian Medical Center website. We were in a three-way conversation, with Oscar relaying the kid's answers. Twenty blocks to go.

"The damn complex is gigantic, Falc. Eleven buildings. Eighteen thousand workers. That doesn't even include patients."

"Which building contains the level-three lab?"

"There's two of them. The Hammer Health Sciences Center has one, on 168th. The Russ Berrie Medical Science Pavilion on St. Nicholas has one too."

"What do they research at each one?" *Maybe that will help us identify which lab Rainey is attacking,* I thought.

"Hammer looks at AIDS variations. Berrie does cancer. Both do genome and in vitro work."

"Are the buildings close to each other?"

"I wish. But Falc, the Darth Vader guy said the target is *near* the complex, not in it."

"Grassley said the Bureau's sending people to all level threes they know about, so we'll find feds there who can reach Grassley. And maybe the researchers there will know of a competing lab nearby."

"Long odds."

"Do you have a better idea?"

Oscar sighed. "Wherever Rainey's going, he's there already."

I turned off Riverside Drive on 163rd street, taking a steep two-block-long hill to reach Fort Washington Street, main corridor to med center facilities. Squad cars lined the street, double parked, and occupying the driveway of the heart center and main hospital. Markings on the cars indicated they came from the Twenty-Fourth and Forty-First Precincts. The FBI must have called police in to help with security. I could see cops checking IDs through the glass window of the heart center. A mobile command unit blocked the semicircular driveway of the main hospital. An incoming ambulance maneuvered around three black Fords with government plates.

Oscar said. "Wanna bet the cops have photos of Rainey?"

Oscar climbed off at the eight-story Berrie building at the busy intersection of St. Nicholas and 168th. Six blocks later, I reached the copper/glass sheathed Armand Hammer med center. National guardsmen with combat vests and M5 rifles were stationed outside. The FBI must have called them up from the subways. *Terrorism alert.* But Oscar had probably been right. These guys had photos of Rainey, likely the ones taken by Dave Ritterbrand's drone. They probably did not know the whole reason why.

I fixed on a guardsman's M5, useless against a germ. A TV news van pulled up. All the major stations would be monitoring police radio; they'd know there was some kind of developing situation occurring here. The FBI must have decided that a whole-scale evacuation of city medical centers was impractical and would cause panic. The show of force was to deter Rainey. There were probably dozens of plainclothes officers on the street here too.

I chained the Vespa to a light pole outside the front of the building. A line of people waited to get in, looking anxious, extending out to the curb. Bags were being checked inside, IDs scanned. For such an immense structure, the entrance seemed small; three revolving doors led into a cramped lobby with a security desk and lone cop inside. *Forget the line.* I pushed in, ignoring angry cries for me to go back.

"Asshole!"

More cops manned two lines inside, one for building personnel showing badges, one for outsiders. Both lines were moving at a snail's pace as security guards checked knapsacks, bags, pocketbooks.

As if they could spot a germ.

No one's checking people coming out. Just those going in. Anyone exiting might be one of Rainey's people.

The lobby sounded louder than the open-air market in Kabul. I pushed my way to the front of the line. A stern-looking police sergeant ordered me back. Two national guardsmen beyond him stiffened, eyeing me like I was the problem.

"I need to talk to someone at the FBI!"

"Please wait your turn, sir."

I held up my ID, a PI card, not real police. "I have important information about the threat!"

"Yeah? Tell me." The sergeant looked unimpressed. He broke away to order a tall, stylish looking woman away from the entry point. He shouted, "Everybody wait your turn!" Slipping past him would be impossible. Turning back toward me, the cop said, hand on hip, "Well? I'm waiting."

Cops hear made-up stories all day long. The beleaguered sergeant was in no mood to believe that I'd just come from New Hampshire, where I'd been part of the FBI raid on the cult compound. Even before I finished speaking, he interrupted.

"You were there, huh?" Unspoken was the rest of his message, *If you're so involved, why are you out on the line here, not inside with the important people?*

"Please. Call up. I need to talk to them."

A fit looking, grey-suited white man had pushed up beside me and was loudly insisting that he needed to get in right now. "I have an important meeting. The Chicago people won't wait." And, to me, "You're holding up the line! Wait your turn!"

It was useless. Too late. Rainey probably wasn't even in this building but somewhere nearby. I started to turn away when the elevator doors opened behind the guardsmen and two men emerged, arguing. The stern looking one wore the dark suit, white shirt, government-approved tie pattern and crisp haircut of an FBI agent. The other one wore an ill-fitting camel hair sports jacket, baggy trousers, and probably, if the usual situation applied, had food stains on his rumpled green shirt. The guy in the green shirt looked annoyed.

For once, I was happy to see him.

"Brian!" I shouted. "Brian Benish! Over here!"

THIRTY-FOUR

Cornelius Hammond dragged the dead security guard off the loading dock and into the building. The first door in the corridor turned out to be a supply closet. Cornelius left the woman's body inside as Kendrick eyed a hallway camera aimed down at them. The green light was off. The unit was inactive. The Lord had told him not to worry about cameras.

The service elevator lay at the far end of a long cinderblock hallway, just as the blueprints God had provided indicated. Joe Neidlinger had taken the guard's keychain. The fourth key on the ring operated the service elevator.

As the elevator rose, so did Kendrick's spirits.

Your glory is forever.

On his phone screen, he saw breaking news headlines. "Police Action at Columbia Presbyterian Hospital." Kendrick smiled. The hospital was five blocks away.

Kendrick felt better now. *Lord, you sent them to the wrong place. I'm sorry I doubted. Lord, you are great.*

The elevator doors opened to reveal a long, carpeted hallway, its light grey walls soothingly lit. Vintage lithographs hung at eye level, honoring medical greats. *Robert Koch, discoverer of tuberculosis bacterium. Marie Curie. Louis Pasteur.* The Lord had kept the hallway empty. Suite occupants were identified by name plaques. The door for XP Global Research offered occupants a peephole for looking out, an intercom for calling in, and a security lock that required punching in a five-digit access code.

The Lord had provided the code.

Kendrick, Cornelius, and Joe produced pistols from their waistbands. Kendrick punched in the numbers. He heard a click.

Kendrick pushed open the door.

THIRTY-FIVE

"Calm down, Bird," Brian Benish said.

The police action at the Hammer building was sending swarms of people down the front steps onto the sidewalk. Brian pulled me to the curb, away from the crowd. He frowned when I told him I knew of the threat here and had information pertinent to it. The frown deepened when I added that I'd come from New Hampshire and the FBI raid.

"You were there?"

I showed him photos; cabins burning, the main cult house in flame, a line of cultists; handcuffed.

"But Bird, I'm confused. If you're with the FBI, why are you down here? Not upstairs?"

Because the director took me off the case, but I'm not going to tell you that. And I'm not going to mention AI.

Brian shook his head. "I can't let you up. Give us twenty, thirty minutes to set up inside. After that, I'll call, okay?"

"Did the Feds even tell you why they're here, Brian?"

He looked insulted. "Of course," he said.

It was bluster.

When I told him that the alert regarded the potential theft of a lethal bird flu virus, Brian turned white. I said I'd discovered that the attack was occurring elsewhere, not here. I urged him to reach anyone in authority upstairs who might know the location of a nearby commercial research lab, because that was the real target, not the Hammer building.

"And you know this how?"

"Reliable source," I said. *The dead cultist in my driveway.*

"So you're *not* with the FBI," Brian concluded. "They won't take your calls, not if you want me to phone them."

"One phone call, Brian. Please. I'll explain later."

"Does this relate to that kid?"

I wanted to scream. "What do the Feds have you doing here anyway? They're upstairs, you're clearing a street. Shit work, Brian. You don't *need to know*. You know what's going to happen when the attack happens elsewhere and they find out you blew me off?"

He stared, suspicious. His comm-system unit—at his belt—was flooded with cop talk as officers went floor to floor up there, probably armed with photos of Rainey. "The FBI lacks enough personnel to do it," I guessed. "So they called for help but didn't say why, right?"

"Wait here," Brian said, frowning. "I'll go up."

"Take me along. You're wasting time."

He turned and pushed his way into the throng. I started after him, but he wheeled and raised a hand. *No!* The second hand on my watch felt like a razor scraping my wrist. In despair, eyeing the people pouring from the building, I had an idea. *They know this neighborhood. They come here every day. Researchers know other researchers. Give it a try.*

I raised my voice, began to shout.

"Attention! Attention, please! Do you want to know why the FBI is here?"

Some people frowned, some looked attentive, a few stopped to listen.

"I'm a private investigator! My name is Mark St. Johns! I can tell you what is going on!"

I spotted Brian at the top of the stairs—he'd turned around to stare. Seeing me getting the crowd's attention, he changed direction, hurrying back to shut me up.

"If you've seen the news about the FBI raid in New Hampshire, they're looking for terrorists trying to steal a dangerous virus from a level-three lab. It's unauthorized work! Does anyone know of a level-three lab nearby? Not at Columbia?"

Brian grabbed my sleeve. "Stop," he said.

I kept shouting. "If you know the location of another lab, please tell me. You can save lives!"

Brian signaled to officers manning sawhorses to come help him. People around us were now holding their phones up, glued to their screens, showing whatever they saw there to others. I saw a man nodding as if to confirm what I was saying. A woman gasped.

Brian hissed, "You're impeding police action."

"Help us find that lab!" I cried as a HAZMAT truck pulled up at the curb. Out poured an NYPD chemical squad, clad in blue, wearing face masks and gloves. Their presence seemed to verify my claims to the crowd.

"If you don't stop, I'll arrest you," Brian said.

More people were staring at us now. "I warned you, Bird!"

Brian spun me around and pulled my wrists behind my back as a tall, dark woman in a white medical jacket stepped up to us, out of the crowd. She ignored Brian. She addressed me.

"You're right. There's another level three nearby," she said.

Brian asked her politely to please step back.

"They're working on avian flu,," she told me. "They don't have the documents for it. I promised Lois I wouldn't tell. She assured me that they take precautions but the work's unauthorized, just like you said."

Brian stopped cuffing me, leaving one of my wrists encircled with steel, the other free. Brian was now paying attention to the woman. His face had gone slack.

"I warned Lois it was dangerous," the woman said. "They're in the Ames building. Fifteenth floor." She pointed north. She told us that the work was headed by a researcher named Zisk.

Brian uncuffed me. I normally move faster than he does, but due to the beatings I'd received, he was quicker on his feet today.

Over the sound of more incoming sirens, I followed Brian north as we ran.

THIRTY-SIX

Kendrick Rainey pushed the suite door open without triggering an alarm. Cornelius and Joe followed him in, wielding pistols. Nobody was visible in the outer office. It was clear to Kendrick that Dr. Zisk had lied about other people being here unless they were in back, with the scientist, in the lab.

I used to work in a place like this, Kendrick thought. Barebones suite, reception desk, work cubicles, greenish walls, metal desks. Kendrick recalled level-three lab rules from his old grad student days. *No private offices allowed in a suite. All areas must be sealed from contamination. Alarms must be audible and visible.*

"Remember," he told Joe and Cornelius, "the Lord will protect us here. We cannot get sick."

All surfaces must be simple to disinfect. Inward directional airflow is required. Closed cabinets must be used for storage of materials, not open shelving.

Kendrick felt the Lord guide him into an interior hallway. On a wall, an office corkboard: pet dog photos, a notice for an upcoming birthday party, an employee of the month award . No carpet here that might pick up microbes. Industrial strength disinfectant smell. Pushing open a heavy metal door, they entered the lab anteroom, each step bringing more memories about safe operation. *A buddy system is required for workers at all times. All autoclave clocks, timers, and thermometers must be calibrated.*

"I bet he's in the lab alone," Kendrick said.

Cornelius was grinning as usual. Joe rarely smiled.

In the anteroom, hanging Tyvek coverall suits, eyewash station, blue booties, biohazard warning sign, logbooks, wall calendar, and manual override for the emergency exit. *Alarms must include devices to detect intruders.*

Gazing through a porthole window, Kendrick peered into the lab. Zisk sat alone at a workstation, wearing a bulky protection suit and visor, as if this was an average day. Kendrick felt a wave of affection for the fool. Brilliant scientist, degenerate gambler, wishful thinker, Zisk had just kept working, ignoring his promise to Kendrick as if that would make God's Hands disappear.

Zisk must have heard them enter over the whoosh of his air purifier because he turned. Through his plexiglass face shield, his eyes grew wide with horror at the sight of three armed men in the lab.

"You're not wearing suits," he gasped.

Kendrick spread his arms wide, as if to say, *We don't need them. Who cares?*

"You're crazy. You'll get sick!" Zisk exclaimed, standing. He'd been working with virus, Kendrick saw, transporting samples by dropper from an incubator to a glass cell locker, a portable cabinet for storing infected life. Kendrick fixed on the locker, the size of a small dog carrier. It held the prize that the Lord had sent Kendrick to steal.

Kendrick moved so close to Zisk that their faces were inches apart. "I used to work in a place like this," he remarked. "Then the Lord saved me."

"The Lord?"

Kendrick walked to the glass cabinet, sat down on a metal stool, reached in, and inserted his hands into rubber gloves inside extending up his forearms. Zisk had been working with clearly labeled samples in agar plates, viral colonies looking like small pink cotton candy growths. Manipulating mechanical hands, as he used to do in college, Kendrick maneuvered samples like a child playing with a funhouse claw machine. A dropper enabled Kendrick to insert the virus into larger culture flasks, then he sealed them. Cornelius kept his pistol aimed at Zisk. Joe opened the Lil' Oscar cooler. Cold smoke rose from the dry ice inside.

Dr. Zisk implored them, "You must not do this."

Kendrick moved two virus-filled flasks out of the cabinet and into the Lil' Oscar. Neidlinger closed the lid.

Zisk said, "You don't understand. People will die. You too."

Cornelius laughed at that. Neidlinger shook his head. Kendrick, feeling benevolent now that the virus was in hand, told Zisk, "You've served the Lord for the wrong reasons, but served Him nonetheless. We thank you."

Kendrick observed tears on the doctor's face.

"A week from now, a great cleansing will begin," Kendrick told Zisk. "London. Riyadh. Buenos Aires. A hundred cities, a great judgment bursting out, all at the same time."

Zisk covered his plexiglass shield with gloved hands. The full impact of his acts was now bursting in on him.

"All humanity will pass before the Lord one by one," Kendrick said, addressing all present. "The Lord will determine who will live and who will die. Who will perish and who will flourish. Who will be raised up and who will be plunged down."

Cornelius grinned when Zisk tried to run. It was ridiculous, really. The guy was connected to an air hose, which snapped off. The fool was trying to stumble off in booties and a Tyvek suit. To outrun death.

Joe let him reach the door. Then Kendrick heard a soft *pffft* from Joe's silenced pistol.

Clutching the prize, the cooler, Kendrick exited the lab, left the steel door open, passed the body, and reached the outer suite. As the trio rapidly threaded the cubicle area, Kendrick's phone began vibrating in his pocket. Doubtless the Lord was going to praise him for what he had just done.

But when Kendrick picked up, the Lord had a warning.

"The police are coming," the Lord said. "Watch!"

On screen, Kendrick saw the private detective running down 169th Street, along with several uniformed police officers. They passed out of the range of one street camera, but another picked up their progress. Kendrick recognized landmarks—a bookstore, a bodega. The enemy was less than three blocks away. The elevator lay down the long hall, but even if it allowed immediate access, even if it did not stop at other floors on the way down, it would waste crucial time before reaching ground level.

The detective might reach the building before they got out.

For an instant, Kendrick allowed all the resentment to flood back. *Why don't you just smite them? You parted the Red Sea to destroy Pharaoh's army. Can't you stop a few police?*

But he clamped down on the feeling because he knew that this was a test, *another test,* because the Lord keeps testing his chosen ones over and over, because that is the nature of time and eternity, that is the nature of service to the Lord, the endless, nonstop, grinding tests.

Joe and Cornelius were staring at him, waiting, but believing in him. Their faith buoyed him and gave him strength.

There has to be a way to handle this, or the Lord would not be testing me. There's always a way.

Then Kendrick saw it.

He said it the same instant that the Lord ordered it. They said it together, which thrilled him. He was ecstatic to speak as one with the Lord.

"Pull the fire alarm," he told Joe.

All over the building, in the basement, at the top, in offices and suites and in the basement cafeteria, alarms began screaming. People—New York workaholics trying to meet their deadlines, even on a Saturday—would be streaming out, erupting into the street, enough of them to distract the police.

"Ditch the masks," Kendrick said.

The cooler! I can't appear down there carrying the cooler. They'll know it's us if they see a cooler. What do I know about avian viruses? They can survive in water for up to a week. We only need them overnight. We don't need the cooler if we only take a few samples.

Kendrick ran back into the suite, to the laboratory.

Hands steady, he reached into a storage closet and pulled out six empty small, glass stoppered vials. He filled each almost to the top with tepid water. He removed the virus samples from the Lil' Oscar cooler and emptied the virus into the vials by hand. He wouldn't be able to take all of the samples he had stolen out of the building. But he'd be able to take enough.

Making sure that the vials were properly closed, he gave two to Cornelius, two to Joe, and shoved two into his pockets.

There was no time to do more.

The alarms kept ringing. Less than four minutes had elapsed since they'd gone off. Back in the hallway, Kendrick saw a half dozen people heading for stairwells on either end of the hallway, coming from other suites.

And actually, the delay had helped, he realized. This way, Kendrick, Joe, and Cornelius, emerging downstairs into the lobby or out the service entrance, would be part of a flood.

"We'll separate," Kendrick told Cornelius and Joe. "Once you get out, follow the original plan, go back to your hotels.."

Kendrick headed into a stairwell as fire alarms clanged and echoed. At each level, more people joined the group, moving down and down. Kendrick was reminded of the tale of Exodus and the way that the Israelites successfully fled Egypt with the Lord's help.

Having achieved their goal, they went on to change the world.

THIRTY-SEVEN

Something was clearly wrong when I rounded the corner and saw the Ames Medical Research building. Crowds spilled from the revolving doors onto the plaza outside. They were not dispersing but remained in place, peering back toward higher floors.

Fire.

I smelled no smoke yet, saw no flames. Brian, raising his badge, shouted "Police!" as he bulled us through the throng, into the building, and past security guards directing traffic, yelling for us to go the other way.

People were pouring from emergency stairwells on opposite ends of the atrium, past the bronze statue of Henri Becquerel and Marie Curie, *discoverers of radium*. We found the building security chief in her office down a hall. Wide, fiftyish, uniformed, her nametag identified her as Aliana Yen. She directed the evacuation through her comm-system while scanning a bank of CCTV monitors over the shoulder of a guard manning the control board. They were trying to find the fire.

"Real fire? Or drill?" I shouted over the din outside.

She started to tell us to leave, then saw Brian's badge, accepting our presence with a look that told me she was probably a retired cop. "You got here fast," she said. "We don't know if it's a real fire. Just that someone pulled the alarm on fifteen."

All elevators, Yen added, had descended to the lobby and stopped there, doors open. They would remain that way throughout the alert; otherwise, if they got stuck between floors, they could turn into death traps in a real fire.

Rainey did this, I thought. *He knew we were coming.*

It's no coincidence the alarm went off.

On the heels of that notion came another.

Did IT tell him we were coming? Did IT trip the alarm?

The security office was cramped, barely room for four. Grey walls. Lysol smell. Fluorescent lighting. OfficeMax swivel chairs. On screens, I saw multiple views of the evacuation down north and south stairwells: the floor eight hallway, filled with people; floor six, empty; floor fourteen south, a steady stream of movement; and in the atrium, a human traffic backup at the revolving front doors.

"Anyone hurt?" Brian asked Yen.

"Not yet that we know of."

"Is there a research lab on fifteen?" I asked.

Her eyes turned on me, cool and appraising cop eyes. "I only have a list of tenants. I don't know anything about a lab. Why?"

I turned to Brian, certain now. "Rainey did this. He's getting out."

Yen snapped, "Who's Rainey?"

We needed all the help we could get, so I told her. Had she seen the news about the FBI raid in New Hampshire? *Yes.* "He's the leader. We think he's here to break into a lab. By now, he may be gone or on the way down."

She looked sick, as if she already knew the answer to her next question. "Break into a lab why?"

I didn't want to answer, as if uttering the words would make them real. "To steal a virus," I said.

The monitors, switching scenes every four seconds, showed orderly progress in the crowd moving down the south stairwell, semi-panic but functioning evacuation on the north. PIs know fire codes. The stairwells would be of concrete construction, smokeless and vented. The roof access doors should be open. Air pressure would be different inside exit routes to keep smoke away. As multiple faces passed on monitors, I tried to pick out Rainey's or *any* face familiar from Dave Ritterbrand's drone footage. But there were too many, and I only had a momentary glimpse of each.

Plus, the scene kept switching, floor to floor.

"Brian, get a Hazmat crew to fifteen," I said.

On Monitor one, fire trucks pulled up outside; a tower ladder vehicle, a command vehicle, and two ambulances .

"Is it possible to seal the building?" Brian asked Yen. "Nobody else leaves?"

She laughed harshly and pointed at screen one. The crowd outside had swelled to at least three hundred evacuees and two cops that Brian had stationed there. Yen told Brian, "Are you nuts? You want me to keep people inside during a fire?"

How do you find a disease? I thought, feeling blood pounding in my head. *Not a bomb. Nothing visible to a naked eye. Germs.*

A vial the size of a child's thumb, hidden in a pocket, knapsack, shoulder bag, lunch box. The FBI agents five blocks away had provided cops with face shots of God's Hands members, ones taken by Ritterbrand's drone. I felt like I was back in Afghanistan with Oscar, staring at military issued playing cards showing the faces of Taliban leaders. *If you see these men, arrest them!* The cards had been good for poker games, useless at identifying anyone in open air crowds.

Brian was instructing his officers out on the plaza, by radio, "Inspect bags if someone looks suspicious."

I glanced up at a CCTV camera aimed down at us from a corner, green light on. Then I stared at it.

Is It watching us back? Is It in here with us?

Screen six, floor fifteen, showed an empty, smoke-free corridor.

Screen nine showed firemen with axes, filing through the crowd on the plaza, into the building.

Screen seven showed a young Black guy on floor four, going back into an office. Maybe he'd forgotten something there.

I told Brian, "We need the elevator key. We need to go up."

Yen shook her head. "Forget it. Go with the fire guys if they let you. They need the elevators. Not you."

I started to argue. Then, on screen, I saw Rainey.

I froze. The face was clear and unmistakable as the man descended from floor thirteen to twelve. Excitement kicked in, in the back of my throat. *It's him.* Same beard, height right, khaki pants and blue dress shirt under a medical jacket, and a black Tumi bag over his shoulder. Kendrick wearing a perfect ensemble for a researcher, reaching to steady a woman beside him, who'd almost tripped on the steps. Kendrick the Good

Samaritan, smiling as she thanked him. Kendrick proceeding out of view.

The virus is in the Tumi bag.

Brian, seeing it too, was shouting into his radio, "South stairwell, south stairwell!" He ran for it, and I followed, adrenaline flooding a sharp metallic taste into my mouth. "Never discount luck," Eve used to say, "or working hard to make it happen."

Finally, a break—his face, in plain sight. *We've got him!*

We burst into the lobby, fighting the crowd, ignoring cries of protest, and struggling to reach the south stairwell exit before Rainey did. A mass of people pushed back, a tide surging the other way.

Kendrick was just going to walk out of that stairwell door, into our arms. Easy.

But suddenly I stopped.

Too easy?

It took a moment for my thinking to catch up with my actions. *Something isn't right.* I'd not halted because of the crowd's resistance. No, it was a voice in my head—a calm, soothing, benevolent tone that I'd heard in my home only an hour ago.

I learn new things every day, that voice had told me. *I can hack into systems if I need them.*

Is Rainey really on those stairs? I wondered. Or has It tricked us again? Because clearly, quite clearly, and *very, very luckily,* Rainey's face had appeared on a monitor, like a big red arrow directing Brian and I where to go.

A security guard was yelling at me. "Move it! Move it!"

Is it possible for it to substitute one face for another? Why not? When people do it, it's called a live stream swap. Brian and I run to one exit while Rainey walks out the other.

Impossible.

Brian did not see me turn and push back in the opposite direction, not toward the south stairwell, which his team was converging on, but the north.

Just in case, I told myself, shoving aside a man who, moments earlier, I'd pushed in the other direction.

Just in case.

THIRTY-EIGHT

I admit that part of me felt relieved when gunfire broke out at the south end of the atrium, not the direction in which I was moving.

Shots were going off, people screaming, the crowd scattering, and I'm thinking, turning toward the sound, *We got him, at least it didn't change Rainey's face. So maybe it's not as powerful as it said it was.*

I shouted for people to get down on the ground. I yelled "police," as I pulled out the H&K, but in the din, amid the panic, only people who were close by heard me; all sounds in the atrium magnified, echoing through the huge space.

Running, I slammed into someone, and, from impact, spun sideways. That was when I spotted Rainey coming out of the *north* stairwell. Not the direction where the shots were coming from.

Just a split-second glimpse of a white medical jacket, but the figure had the same blonde hair, same beard, no Tumi bag—but the height was right, and the leg hitch convinced me, limp, drag, limp. Same up and down progress as on the drone shots I'd seen of him, caused by the childhood beatings Rainey had suffered, the ones that his sister Claudia had described.

There he was again!

Rainey lurched forward, agile enough to thread the mass of people covering their heads on the floor. He joined the flow pushing for the exits. My shout of "Kendrick!" went unheard by anyone in authority, but his head spun around. I shoved my way after him as he squeezed into a revolving door. I hit the jam there, tried to push in, hearing more shots, screams and panic. *Rainey must have split his team up, sent the others down the south stairwell. That or the police opened fire on the wrong guy.*

Behind me, the shooting stopped.

I forced my way into the revolving door, joining two other guys packing a cramped, rotating wing. Ahead, on the plaza, a white flash of a medical jacket disappeared into the crowd. The door spit me out. Firemen were running toward me, axes in hand. I spotted the white jacket being trampled under their boots.

Rainey was gone.

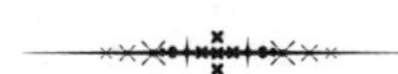

Had he continued fleeing in the same direction? It was impossible to spot him over the heads of the dispersing crowd. Rainey wasn't tall enough to stick out. I saw no figure lurching away, toward the street, or subway, taxi, another building.

Keep moving. I chose a direction to go randomly—west.

I saw no Kendrick Rainey.

I stopped, heaving, scanning the surrounding stores—a coffee shop, a bookstore, a liquor joint. Maybe he'd taken refuge inside. I scanned windows in passing cars. A bus passed. A man and woman approached wearing Halloween masks: a chimpanzee mask and a lion mask. Their clothes were wrong; the height was wrong; a beard would have stuck out of a mask. I spotted Grassley and two other FBI agents running toward the Ames building, alerted probably by police radio, but too late. They passed thirty feet away without seeing me or hearing me cry, *"He's out here!"* over the blast of incoming sirens.

No Rainey.

I spotted Oscar heading my way and waved my arms and shouted. At least *he* saw me. He looked relieved at that.

"You're okay, Falc," he said.

"Rainey's out here."

"Then what was the shooting about?"

"Maybe there were others with him, maybe they split up. I'll check the IRT line, Oscar. You take the A train."

I ran to the subway entrance on 168th Street, but to access the underground platform there required riding down in an elevator, and the elevator took three tortured minutes to arrive. I reached the platform and looked both ways. It was empty. Trains must have just departed going north and south.

Back at the building, EMS attendants were carrying the wounded to waiting ambulances. Two bystanders had been hit.

Grassley was in the lobby, supervising the aftermath and looking miserable. Brian Benish was with her. A body lay on the floor. A big male, limbs twisted, half his face shot away. A halloween mask lay beside him. Kwan was upstairs in the laboratory, Grassley told me.

"The other guy surrendered," Grassley said. But she looked defeated, as if she already suspected what I reported to her now.

"Rainey used the other stairwell. He got out."

"Shit," Benish said.

"We found another body upstairs in the lab. This guy and the one who surrendered," Grassley said, waving a hand at the body, "had lab vials in their pockets. I'm assuming there are virus samples in the vials."

Grassley sighed. "Rainey could have released some virus already."

I grew conscious of my own breathing, of the breathing of the mass of people around us. Of the building's air system blowing. Of the whole massive city outside, millions of people there, as if we all shared one gigantic set of lungs, sucking in the same oxygen, the same microbes.

"This virus. How contagious is it?" Grassley asked, unconsciously moving six inches away from me.

"How would I know? I don't even know what it is."

"Reporters," observed Benish, tilting his head toward the plaza. A camera guy was running toward the building, along with a Channel Five news reporter I recognized. Oscar was incoming too, I saw, but not dragging Rainey along.

"No luck, Falc," Oscar reported, out of breath, coming up to us in the lobby.

Police blocked the reporter outside. More journalists would arrive in minutes.

Grassley was on her phone with the director.

Benish was on his phone with the commissioner.

Both were telling their bosses the same thing, using different words to explain it.

"We're fucked, sir," I heard Brian Benish say.

THIRTY-NINE

The FBI's New York headquarters occupies two stories of the Jacob K. Javits Federal Building. Interview rooms there are a big improvement over the Twenty-Fourth Precinct's: fresh grey paint, no gouge marks on tables, a higher class of suspects, granola bars in vending machines.

"He just sits there and smiles and says God will take care of him," Grassley said as we watched special agent Kwan interrogate Cornelius Hammond, retired SEAL, on the other side of a two-way mirror. The dead attacker at the Ames building had been identified as a former security guard at CDC headquarters in Atlanta. Joseph Niedlinger had been fired there for making online threats against the staff.

"Next week at this time," Hammond told Kwan, grinning, "You'll be in Hell. I will be in paradise."

Hammond had simply thrown his gun down at the Ames building, raised his hands and given himself up. I was back in the FBI's good graces, reinstalled in the investigation, forgiven by the director for bringing Dave Ritterbrand into things after Brian and Grassley vouched for my role during the attack. "Without Bird, they would have succeeded," Brian had said. He'd never liked me, but he was honest.

Kendrick Rainey and his virus samples were gone.

"You and Neidlinger both carried hotel key cards," Kwan asked Hammond now. "But from different hotels. Why?"

No answer.

"Is Kendrick Rainey at a hotel?"

A yawn.

"Where is Kendrick Rainey?"

A grin. I wished that Cristina was in there with Hammond, not Kwan. Cristina would beat the shit out him, never mind FBI rules.

Kwan looked visibly frustrated. Logic wasn't working. Threats weren't working. Nothing was working. "Rainey is no prophet, Cornelius. He left you in the lurch. He ran off."

Hammond shrugged. "Yes, but with the virus."

"He's ill. He was in a mental institution."

"Jesus wasn't believed either," Hammond said.

"Rainey's no Jesus."

"Then why do his prophesies come true?"

Kwan was losing patience. "If the Lord is so powerful, nothing you tell me now could stop his will, so why not answer me? There's no harm in telling me his plan, right? Or are you afraid that God isn't involved at all?"

Cornelius folded his arms. Useless.

Where did Rainey go?

The mood in the conference room was somber. At the head of the long table, Assistant FBI Director Josef Fatialofa, in from Washington, eyed anti-terrorism task force members present from the ATF, NYPD, CDC, Federal Marshals, and state police. On screen, live from San Francisco, AI experts from three major companies were present, to respond to my claims about artificial intelligence. Gustav Kalimides, Google's talking head, came to us from a cliff house overlooking the Pacific. Beth Hardy, from Amazon, looking sixteen, sat in a floor-to-ceiling book-lined library. Mohammed Shah from Meta was driving in a Tesla. All three voiced the same thought.

"Mr. St. Johns's claims are impossible at this time," Kalimides assured the group.

"Science fiction," Beth Hardy echoed.

"AI can't think for itself," Shah affirmed with a nasal British accent. "All it does is analyze word patterns and mimic them. It lacks emotion and can't reason like a human. It's a tool that doesn't have feelings. I postulate," he added, to some relief around the table, "that Mr. St. Johns spoke with a person claiming to be AI. Believe me, in the end, a person or organization will be responsible here."

On the table were water carafes, research reports, photos of Kendrick Rainey and other God's Hands members. So far, the arrested cultists in New Hampshire had remained mute during interviews, or sang songs, as if they'd all received the same instructions about what to do if arrested. The White House had reluctantly released news of the stolen virus two hours ago. Finger-pointing was already starting, along with too-late calls for investigations into lab safety. Just in the past sixty minutes, on the net, a hundred new crackpot theories had bloomed. The warning was a hoax; Russia had caused the release; God's Hands members were CIA agents and the virus would be used to target the President's enemies.

The White House announcement had included nothing about possible artificial intelligence involvement in the threat.

At the moment, the only thing everyone at the table agreed on was the probability of Kendrick Rainey unleashing Zisk's virus over the next few hours, unless he had done it already. Once that happened, Dr. Amy Bernstein of the CDC had told us, several days would pass until a first victim showed symptoms, followed by outbreak in a hundred places.

Assistant Director Fatialofa was awaiting my response to the AI experts. He was trim, dark haired, soft spoken, and hard-eyed.

"Look, I can't say positively that I spoke to AI," I said, to nods from all three talking heads. "But if it was a person, who changed Rainey's face in security footage at the Ames building? Who controlled the car that killed Hodge?"

"People could have done those things," Kalimides said.

Clearly, most attendees at the table believed him. I wanted to believe too—that we were dealing with human foes, not a malignant program. But I didn't believe it anymore.

"Let's concentrate on Rainey," Director Fatialofa said, "and leave AI for later. Turn to page four in Dr. Zisk's original application to transport the engineered virus. Graph three describes the microbe, how long it can survive in air."

Grassley's work cubicle offered a twelfth-floor view of Chambers Street. Below, as the night progressed, I saw headlights down there, Brooklyn Bridge lights, City Hall lights, vapor lights, and in the glows, crowds that had swelled over the past few days by visitors in town for the Marathon tomorrow. Most of them, despite news bulletins, did not wear masks.

"And after the race," I said morosely, falling into a chair, "fifty thousand runners and their families fly home. God help us if they're infected. Kennedy Airport. Newark. LaGuardia." I shuddered. "All those planes. All those destinations."

Grassley sighed. "If China would have handled Covid the right way, they could have stopped it before it left the country. Rainey will want to spread the disease before New York has the chance to shut down."

"You think he's done it already?"

"If he has, we're too late."

"He's only got two, three vials' worth," I said, "judging from what's missing and what you found on the other guys. Those are fewer samples than what he hoped for. He'll want to optimize release. So, where?"

I sighed, exhausted. My wounds from the fights in New Hampshire and the park ached. "Two hotel key cards. Two Upper West Side hotels. Why *those* hotels? The Piedmont. The Appomattox. What connects them?" I said.

Grassley nodded. "Rainey's been in New York for days, but his people only checked into hotels yesterday. Where were they before that? Why hotels at all?"

"Mid-sized hotels," I mused. "Both near the Marathon finish line in Central Park. If Rainey's in one of those hotels, we've got him. But that would be too easy. I bet they spread out."

Grassley groaned. "If two hotels, why not five? Ten? There are 180,000 hotel rooms in New York! What if he's not in *any* hotel? What if he's not even here anymore?"

A Manhattan map hung on the cork board, a million hiding places. On the desk, lists of old safety violation complaints against Zisk's lab. I scanned a memo written by Zisk, detailing his efforts to heighten lethal aspects of avian flu. Once

Zisk's body had been identified, all this material had flowed into the FBI.

Too little, too late.

Grassley called down to forensics to learn that my bomb squad laptop, examined by Bureau malware hunters, was devoid of any infection. "If it was ever there, it's gone." Out in the city, Rainey's face was being broadcast on TV and social media. *If you see this terrorist, call 911.* Calls were flooding in from the tri-state area. *He looks like my Uncle Felix in Riverdale. He is Uncle Felix. He lives next door in Tarrytown. I saw him on the Q train.*

"For all we know, AI's making those calls," I said.

"You don't give up, do you?"

"Are those your kids, Grassley?" I said, eyeing her corkboard photos. The husband. The twin boys at a summer cookout. A lake. Trees. A dock. Happy family.

Grassley chewed her lip. "The problem is that everything you've told us so far turned out to be true."

"It was a mistake to let people bring their cell phones into that meeting. It, he, whatever it is, can listen in."

Grassley looked doubtful. "You sound as paranoid as Rainey. We've got pretty good security here, Mark."

"Until it's not enough."

As we sat there, agents and detectives were going hotel to hotel outside, bar to bar, showing Rainey's photo. Agents were poring over street camera views near hotels, hoping to spot Rainey, but I wondered, even if Rainey *had* been caught on a camera, was his face now changed?

Grassley and I checked the websites of the Appomattox and Piedmont Hotels, looking for a common thread, some key criteria that Kendrick had used to choose those hotels for his group; anything that might help us locate a different hotel where Kenrick might be found —number of floors, view, proximity to public transport. Amenities like a gym, where you could spread germs; the lobby, through which all guests must pass; a restaurant, a prime spot to infect people. *But he could spread it at any restaurant. Who needs a hotel?*

Eve, Grandy, help me out, I thought.

Grandy, in my mind, mixed himself a martini, lit a Camel and blew out smoke. "Take a break, Mark. Have a drink. It gives a fresh view on things."

Eve rolled her eyes at Grandy. "Get out of the building, Baby F. Go somewhere to think. Do what I do when stumped. When all else fails, go to church. Ask God for help."

My grandparents were still arguing with each other, years after they died. Grandy warned me that if I left the FBI building, I might miss a crucial development.

Eve urged, "Give yourself a chance to think alone."

St. Paul and St. Andrew United Methodist Church sits on the northeast corner of Eighty-Sixth Street and West End Avenue, walking distance from Falcon's nest. Cristina volunteers there on Wednesdays, tutoring kids or helping newly arrived migrants in the city find jobs. Oscar helps with Christmas baking. As the least reverent Falcon Associate, I show up occasionally to help out in the West Side Campaign Against Hunger, carrying boxes of donated food from trucks to the kitchen or basement pantry.

At midnight, the sanctuary was closed. A few homeless people slept on the steps. The rectory was accessible across a small courtyard from the main building, and Pastor Elias Kroft answered the door himself when I rang. I'd known him since we were teens, when he'd been a Poe Street Irregular himself. He was a "landsman," as my Jewish friends call someone who comes from the same village as you.

Taking one look at my bruised face, he said, "Not a spiritual problem this time, is it?"

"I wish."

"Does this have anything to do with the terrorism alert?"

"I can't say." Translation: Yes.

"You want to talk? Or be alone?"

END HATE read a sign on the door he unlocked, ushering me into the high-ceiling nave. I eyed the painting of newly arrived immigrants, circa 1900, the rainbow tapestry, and the big nondenominational cross. The church allows Jewish services here on high holy days. Come one, come all. That's why I like it.

Kendrick Rainey believed the Lord told him what to do. Now I sat in vast silence and let the quiet pass through me and soothe me and ease the physical injuries I'd sustained over the last forty-eight hours. I needed ideas.

"Why those hotels, Lord?"

Silence.

"You can't want so many people to die."

Nothing. This was like interrogating Cornelius Hammond at the federal building.

"Don't you want to help out, Lord?"

Silence was what I had expected, and silence was what I got. But I stayed. Maybe an idea would occur to me. After a while, I must have fallen asleep.

The sounds of volunteers setting up for breakfast woke me. The sanctuary opens doors at 8 a.m. to serve the needy but set up begins at five. Soon food trucks would arrive.

Folding tables would go up. Coffee urns would bubble, and the smells of eggs, bacon, and oatmeal would fill the room.

Maybe, I hoped, the FBI had figured things out while I'd slept. Maybe Kendrick Rainey had been apprehended, and the emergency was done. Maybe my prayers had reached a higher power. But Christmas is for kids. I shrugged off sleep and stretched, noticing the surprised looks on the faces of the volunteers who'd not realized until now that I—a homeless guy, they probably figured—had been asleep in a pew.

Still, the spirit is generous. A volunteer asked me if I wanted to partake in the breakfast. If I did, he said, food would come out soon. "We line up," he told me, "and share the bounty of God."

I started to say no thanks and paused. "Share?"

"Everyone is welcome. We eat together, sit together, and share the foods laid out on these tables together."

That was what gave me the idea.

I snatched my phone out, ignoring texts and emails that had come in overnight. I accessed the website for the Appomattox Hotel. I rechecked the list of amenities.

You'll love our hot breakfast buffet.

I tried the Piedmont Hotel website.

Guests from around the world enjoy our five-star hot and cold buffet breakfast. Eat well and head for the airport!

I punched in Grassley's number.

By tonight, I thought, thousands of people from hotels near the finish line will have hit the buffets and will be heading for an airport.

It was a long shot. *But it was possible.* Both key cards the FBI had taken off attackers had come from hotels near the finish line. If your goal was to spread a virus to as many travelers as possible, heading for as many locations as possible, releasing the pathogen at a common eating place would be the perfect way to go.

Answer, dammit, I thought. *Pick up.*

FORTY

Kendrick Rainey stood naked at a ninth-floor window of Manhattan's Parthenon Hotel at sunrise, facing east over the autumn gold of Central Park and eyeing, beyond the finish line of the New York Marathon and grandstand seating below, a tip of sun glowing over towers lining Fifth Avenue, bathing him with heavenly light.

Kendrick gave thanks to the Lord.

You saved me yesterday to do your will.

On the room's silenced TV, a drone shot showed fifty thousand runners massed in Staten Island, awaiting the starting gun for the race. In less than an hour, the wheelchair division would go off. At 8:40 a.m., the professional women runners would start; followed by the professional men. At 9:00 a.m., the gun would unleash the first massive wave of amateur runners.

It is time to complete my mission.

Kendrick still marveled at the miracle that God had bestowed upon him yesterday. The Lord had blinded police to his presence in the medical building and had parted the crowd outside to allow him safe passage as surely as God split the Red Sea. *I just walked to the A train.* Even though his face saturated news reports, even though his visage reached millions of people, *even in a subway car packed with riders glued to devices*, no one had recognized Kendrick. No one had pointed and cried out, *That's him!*

Exiting the train at Columbus Circle, he'd simply walked to the hotel and used his previously obtained key card to slip into his room, invisible.

I will do your will.

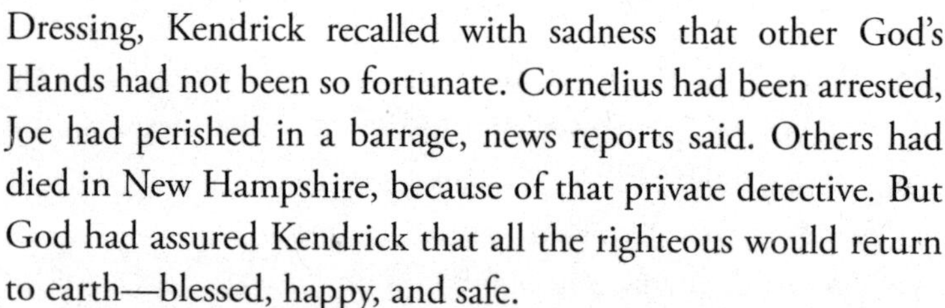

Dressing, Kendrick recalled with sadness that other God's Hands had not been so fortunate. Cornelius had been arrested, Joe had perished in a barrage, news reports said. Others had died in New Hampshire, because of that private detective. But God had assured Kendrick that all the righteous would return to earth—blessed, happy, and safe.

The Lord had also told Kendrick that, once the virus spread, the private detective would be swept up in it, coughing and choking, with millions of other doomed Moabites.

The boutique Parthenon Hotel attracted visitors from around the world. Crossing the lobby last night, Kendrick had heard snatches of conversation in Chinese, French, Hindi, and Spanish. In the elevator, a trio of skinny Kenyans had been betting on whether their cousin would come in first in the race. The desk in Kendrick's room even featured a copy of *Travel Magazine*, naming famous runners who'd stayed at the Parthenon. Runners, their families, and their friends had reserved three quarters of the rooms this year, reported the piece.

By tonight, they will begin flying home, infected.

Kendrick opened the mini-fridge and retrieved two vials from a shelf holding miniature liquor bottles, a pretzel bag, Snickers bar, and apple. The vials felt pleasantly cool in his hip pocket as he left the room.

In the elevator, the news was being broadcast on a monitor set onto the wall.

PERFECT WEATHER FOR THE NEW YORK MARATHON.

In the mirrored wall panels, Kendrick eyed his freshly shaven face, self-administered haircut, and sunglasses. The Kendrick on TV wore denim overalls, but the Kendrick in the elevator had donned khaki slacks, brown loafers, and a V-necked dark blue cotton shirt. He'd draped a lemon-yellow sweater around his neck. Kendrick's face looked rounder now, less angular. He'd also put in colored contact lenses.

FBI SEEKS CULT LEADER KENDRICK RAINEY.

The breakfast buffet had opened at six, but Kendrick had preferred to wait for the restaurant to fill before he introduced the virus. The yogurt bowl would be an excellent medium for microbes. Hot cereal would not kill it. Breads would soak up germs. A glistening drop of viral liquid would look like plain water on an apple, spoon, caper, onion slice.

Kendrick exchanged nods with the front desk clerk as he made his way to the restaurant. There, long tables were laid out with buffet offerings. A dozen booths were occupied by diners. The room smelled of good coffee and crisp bacon.

Kendrick draped his sweater over a table for two and made his way to the buffet table. Nobody was watching.

His hand casually went into his pocket.

"FBI! Kendrick Rainey, get down on the ground!" a woman's voice barked from behind him. "Now!"

Kendrick whirled. The diners had all stood up and suddenly held pistols. He felt as if the walls of the room were collapsing on him. He did not comprehend how the Lord could do this to him. Frozen with confusion, he clutched a vial, still inside his pocket. *You didn't warn me. You didn't blind them! Why let me get this far and then stop me? You always know what police are doing. Why didn't you tell me?*

"On the ground!" a small Asian-looking woman repeated, aiming a pistol at his chest.

Kendrick dropped to his knees as if before God, baffled and in torment. Then suddenly, he understood what was happening in a burst of clarity. *It's another test! To see how committed I am to you! It's one more test, isn't it? The agents are staring at my pocket like it holds a detonation button. They're afraid of me!*

Kendrick felt a smile stretch across his face. His panic disappeared. He was David and the FBI was Goliath. David had slain Goliath. Kendrick felt almost giddy, filled with confidence. The guns pointing at him meant nothing.

"Bullets can't hurt me," he announced. Kunio Murakami, in drills, had instructed God's Hands how to open vials with a flip of a thumb. Kendrick did that now, inside his pocket, exposing the virus to open air.

He recited out loud, for the Moabites to hear, "I will punish the world for its evil, the wicked for their sins. I will put an end to the arrogance of the haughty and humble the pride of the ruthless."

Kendrick brought the vial out and held it up for all to see. The eyes looking back at him turned fearful. He felt a great surge of power inside.

"I know what you want me to do, Lord," he murmured.

Infecting the food here would be useless now, Kendrick saw. It would never reach Moabite mouths. No, God had brought the federal agents here to witness something wonderful and spread the word. Kendrick was God's vessel. God did not want to cause pain. He wanted to offer sinners a chance to repent. Kendrick was not here to punish. He was here to warn.

"You can't hurt me," he told the woman.

"I see that," she answered, frowning.

"You don't believe me, but it's true," Kendrick said, growing aware of a male agent sliding closer along the left-side wall.

The woman tried to distract him. "I'm a practicing Methodist myself, Mr. Rainey. I believe that miracles happen. Put the vial down. Then you and I can have some interesting conversations. I understand you've made some prophesies that came true. I'd love to hear about them."

"Tell that man at the wall to stop moving."

"Collin!" barked the woman.

The guy by the wall froze.

The woman took a half step forward, her gun trembling. "Exodus 15:26," she recited. "If you listen carefully to the Lord your God and do what is right in his eyes, if you pay attention to his commands and keep all his decrees, I will put none of the diseases on you that I brought on the Egyptians."

Kendrick was delighted. Her knowledge of scripture proved that she was here for a reason. He responded in kind. "And he called his twelve disciples to him and gave them authority to drive out impure spirits and to heal every disease, every affliction."

"Matthew 10:1," the agent said. "Please put down the vial, sir."

Kendrick extended the vial toward the agents. The closest one was ten feet away. He was unsure whether the pathogen could be inhaled at that distance. The virus in the vial could float in air like an angel. It could strike you dead like a bolt from the Lord. It was stealthy as Satan, he'd told his followers, and as invisible as a soul.

"I will make a prophecy," Kendrick announced as if the group before him now were his congregation. "You will see the truth and spread the word."

"Kendrick," the woman agent said, as a warning.

Kendrick raised his voice. "And the masses will come to the Lord. And those who are evil will repent. This virus will not kill one single believer. Behold!"

Kendrick sucked down the contents of the vial.

He was smiling when they wrestled him to the ground. Smiling when they cuffed him and brought him to a hospital. Smiling when they pumped his stomach and gave him antivirals. Kendrick assured them, all of them—the arresting agents, the doctors, the nurses, the psychiatrists, the CDC scientists. *You'll see and then you will believe. Nothing bad will happen to me, and the word will spread, and you will know me for who I am, a true prophet.*

Nine days later, screaming in pain, hooked to a ventilator, strangling and choking in a quarantine ward, Kendrick Rainey died a hideous death.

FORTY-ONE

Eight months later, on a Saturday night, I attended the kick-off summer concert at the Ninety-Sixth Street tennis courts with Oscar, Cristina, Abani, and Nageena. The evening was hot, the sun sinking toward the Palisades on the Jersey side of the Hudson River. Picnickers spread blankets. Oscar had made a pasta pesto salad, Cristina had chosen the sauvignon blanc, and Nageena had brought cherry crumb pie and Tillamook caramel-flavored ice cream. Abani said, eyeing the crowd, "My father would have liked this."

Falcon Associates sponsors the free concerts, along with a couple of other businesses on the Upper West Side. Outsiders say that New York is a big, angry, impersonal place, but each neighborhood is a village. I eyed two Poe Street Irregulars on a nearby blanket, teenagers I've known since they were kids. Now they were a couple. I saw a half dozen elementary school boys who played on The Falcons softball team, which Oscar coached. Newly promoted Detective Lieutenant Brian Benish—"the hero of October," the Daily News had dubbed him after the arrests at the Ames medical building—sat with his wife on the far side of the hill, as distant from us as possible. Abani, our Falcon Associates intern, working two afternoons a week, was learning the business, just as I had from my grandparents when I was her age.

Sometimes, those days, I thought back to that lucky morning when Kendrick Rainey had been apprehended. FBI agents had been dispatched to all hotels featuring buffet breakfasts near the finish line of the New York Marathon. They'd all been equipped with burner phones in order to shield their activity from Desmond Hodge's rogue AI.

And Nageena? She and I had gone to dinner a few times over the past months. I'd found her lovely and smart, a pleasure to be with. But the spark never ignited, and I knew why. On the day when I'd almost been shot at my home by one of Kendrick's Rainey's cultists, the day when Cristina had attacked that man to get the answers we needed to stop Kendrick Rainey's group, I'd seen a ferocity in her that Nageena lacked. I was not like Nageena. I believe evil exists. It's a fundamental part of my makeup. I admired Nageena, how she helped people, how she brought up her daughter, how she'd overcome trauma to build a life in New York, how she spread compassion in the world.

But I needed a warrior.

At one point last month, at an outdoor table at Pappardella, Nageena had regarded me wryly over a plate of fettuccine Alfredo, and said, "Nothing's going to happen, is it?" Meaning *between us*. It wasn't a question but a casual acknowledgement. Things *between us* had never reached a level where consequence included any substantial degree of disappointment. Her social antenna was marvelous. I admire people who accept whatever comes without regret.

"Feel like telling me who the other woman is?" she'd asked, out of curiosity, her tone lacking spite.

"Is it that obvious?"

"I hope it works out."

I'd considered asking her to keep her observation quiet around Oscar and Cristina and decided to keep silent, as the request would have been a giveaway. But my pause had betrayed me.

"Don't worry, it stays between us." She'd winked, and added, coyly, "Whoever she is, I mean."

"Want dessert? The tiramisu here is great."

Cristina and I had never discussed our feelings for each other since our car ride months earlier. On a day-to-day basis, we kept on as friends and business associates, nothing more. As if our talk had never happened. But I wondered sometimes, does Oscar know? Does he wonder? Have they discussed it? He suspects she likes some other guy, and he's too smart not to have any inkling of who it may be.

All I know is that chemistry simmers; cool one day, warm the next. A glance lights a match. A dream fades to regret in a morning. Laughter flows up through a vent from a downstairs bedroom, and a private detective turns the TV volume up to drown it out. Pathetic, I know, yet I was glad that my friends had decided to remain in my house. And then there's always hope—but of what? Eve used to tell me that every family is a little country, with its own habits, rules, holidays, and aversions. I grew up in a trio: Eve, Grandy, and Mark. Maybe a shrink would say that, in Falcon Associates, I created a permanent three. Maybe my life feels richer with my makeshift family in it, whether I seek physical satisfaction with other partners or not. Or maybe I'm fooling myself, and one day I'll tire of saying goodbye to other women all the time, to six months of sex, six months of laughter, six months of good times and then a no-regrets goodbye. Maybe I'll get fed up with it. Maybe Cristina will get fed up with me.

Or maybe, one day it will all explode.

There's a limit to what even impossible detectives can predict, especially when it comes to themselves.

But on this evening, the mood was merry, the music provided by a jazz trio, the applause coming from all quarters of the meadow. Nageena draped an arm around Abani's shoulders. Oscar's hairy thigh brushed Cristina's smooth one. I was reaching for the Lil' Oscar cooler, for a beer, when I felt an uncomfortable itch on the back of my neck. Like a mosquito crawling but not that. A warning.

Someone is watching.

Turning, I spotted Bradley Kranepool looking down at the picnic area from the parking lot.

His black Lexus was idling up there, near the spot where Abani had watched Desmond Hodge die. His driver/bodyguard must be inside. Kranepool, shielding his eyes, waved when he spotted me looking back.

I rose and made my way past neighbors and friends, up the hill to the overlook. The country's third-richest man had changed his appearance over the past few months. The wooly hair was shorn. The Birkenstocks had been replaced by Keene's. He wore slacks and a black V-neck pullover, more collegiate Wall Street these days than wunderkind rebel. Kranepool was grinning as we stood eye to eye.

"I keep leaving you messages," he said.

"I keep getting them."

"I had to hire another PI just to find out that you come here," he said, but he didn't seem to mind the effort. He was smiling. "You make it impossible for someone to say thank you, Falcon."

"I didn't do any of it for you, Bradley."

"No, but if you hadn't, I never would have found out what Desmond developed. I never would have been able to trade on that with the FBI. All charges dropped, my friend."

I sighed. "Yeah, I saw it on the news."

"And in return, we're in a race to reproduce what Hodge accomplished. Everyone wants it. Justice Department. Pentagon. White House. The holy grail! My God! It's still out there somewhere, Falcon, popping up, erasing its tracks, actually *hiding*." He rubbed his hands together with glee, like a kid who just won a monopoly game. "The greatest treasure hunt on earth."

"You think it's fun, Bradley? Every day I watch the news. An accident at a medical lab in Russia. An outbreak in China that gets squelched. A fire at a chemical company in Venezuela. Popping up? Is that what you call *popping up*? I ask myself, every time I see these things, did It do it? What is it doing now?"

"The Moriarty Code," Bradley said. "That's what of some of my guys in our lab call it. Like it's some evil genius, not just man-made code. I admit, I always figured the transition point to near-sentience—if we were lucky, if the ducks fell in line—might come along in ten years. Hodge got close! He was a genius. But close isn't there yet. I assure you, Mark. It's not alive because alive is impossible."

"Moriarty?"

Bradley shrugged. "A joke. Some people only see the bad in development. It's just code. We'll find it, harness it and use it for good, see?"

"You sound like Nageena talking about murderers."

Bradley reached into his pocket, unfolded a check, and held it out to me. I could not make out the sum written on it, but I saw, as a breeze flapped the paper, many zeroes.

"Go away, Bradley. I didn't do it for you."

"Give it to charity."

"No."

"Fix your roof. My PI said you need house repair."

"Not your problem."

"The girl could use a scholarship one day. You know what colleges cost these days? What's the matter with you? Don't you understand gratitude?"

"You want gratitude? Find Moriarty. Kill him."

As I turned and walked away, toward the blanket and my friends, I heard Bradley call out behind me, exasperated.

"It's not a *him*. It's an *it*."

AI? I'll tell you about AI. It's the genie that tricks its master. It's the servant that sneaks into your bedroom at night. It's a god demanding human sacrifice. It's the urge to bow down and surrender will to anything greater than yourself.

Making my way back to the blanket, as the band struck up "Mood Indigo," I recalled a comic book—yeah, laugh at me, but you can find truth even there—that Eve bought me when I was eleven, going through my Marvel comics phase.

The great philosophers postulated truth with eloquence. But Marvel can hit the mark too.

The story in this case depicted a gambler who had lost all his money betting on horses. One day, he found a bottle in the trash, uncorked it, and watched smoke pour out and turn into a genie. The genie would grant the man one wish. The man could ask for anything he wanted. The man told the genie, excited, "I want to be the richest man in the world," and the genie said, "Yes, master."

Next thing you knew, the man stood on a distant planet, alone. A sandstorm was coming. Wind was rising. There were no other people on the planet. The genie's face loomed in the sky, laughing. The genie told the man, before disappearing, "You said you wanted to be the richest man in the world. But you didn't say *which world*."

Kendrick Rainey had sought answers in a Bible. Answers can be any place you look, even comic books. Returning to the blanket, I saw Oscar and Cristina slow dancing, barefoot in the grass, in front of the band. I love the way Cristina moves. Abani and Nageena were down there too, mom and daughter bouncing around. My phone buzzed in my pocket. I took it out and observed the screen. I'd received a text message from an unknown number. I clicked on it.

GET UP THERE AND DANCE TOO, the text advised me. DON'T YOU LIKE TO DANCE?

I looked around, feeling an electric tingle in my chest. I noticed a security camera aimed down at me from the lot. On the river, a lone jet ski went by. In the sky, the sun was almost down, its last rays blinding. On our blanket, I saw the remains of our dinners. Plastic containers. A wine bottle. There had to be more CCTV cameras around here somewhere.

I felt a buzz. Another message had appeared. HAVE FUN, FALCON. I LIKE FUN.

The night was lovely. The mood was gay. All around me, people were dancing.

FUNFUNFUNFUNFUNFUNFUNFUN!!!!!!!

ACKNOWLEDGMENTS

The author wishes to thank my editors Gretchen Young and Caitlin Burdette at Regalo Press, my agent Esther Newberg at CAA, and film visionaries Ted Hartley and Mary Beth O'Connor at RKO, who initially proposed this project. Ron Netzer and Saar Tochner were invaluable in helping me understand technical aspects of the story. Any mistakes in that area are mine. Charles Salzberg and David Colbert offered wonderful suggestions, Wendy Roth was crucial in supplying a steady supply of muffins, ice cream, encouragement, and ideas. Thanks to you all.

ABOUT THE AUTHOR

Bestselling author and journalist Bob Reiss is fascinated by the border between order and anarchy. His nonfiction work has covered trouble spots around the world, including the Amazon, Antarctica, the Arctic, Sudan, and Somalia. His fiction tends to ask "what if" when it comes to big questions facing society. All told, Bob has published twenty-three books of fiction and nonfiction.

Bob is a graduate of Northwestern University and the University of Oregon. He has taught writing at the Bread Loaf Writers' Conference, Yale University in Singapore, Montclair University, the University of North Carolina MFA program, and on a Coast Guard ship in the Arctic Ocean.